Stained Sand

By Benni Chisholm

Copyright © 2011 by Benni Chisholm
First Edition – November 2011

ISBN
978-1-77067-659-6 (Hardcover)
978-1-77067-660-2 (Paperback)
978-1-77067-661-9 (eBook)

All rights reserved.

No part of this publication may be reproduced in any form, or by any means, electronic or mechanical, including photocopying, recording, or any information browsing, storage, or retrieval system, without permission in writing from the publisher.

Published by:

FriesenPress
Suite 300 – 852 Fort Street
Victoria, BC, Canada V8W 1H8

www.friesenpress.com

Distributed to the trade by The Ingram Book Company

Acknowledgements

Thanks to Renée and the staff at FriesenPress who provided incredible help, Mary Jane and Warren who read the manuscript, Haley who modeled for the cover, and of course Merritt who after all these years can still make me laugh.

Stained Sand

Bill + Christine
Best Wishes
Benni Chisholm

CHAPTER 1

As scheduled, the airplane landed at the Kahului airport at nine p.m. Brent's prematurely white hair and broad shoulders appeared in the arrival area and I hurried toward him. We met on the run and enveloped each other.

"You've just turned Paradise from partially perfect to perfectly perfect," I said.

Laughter rumbled from the depth of his being. It contrasted with his first words, making them sound superficial and shallow: "Will perfectly perfect last nine days?"

"Of course," I replied, and my voice rang with the authority of a seer. Then, because perfection of any kind is a rare and fleeting thing, I felt a twinge of fear. Would my confident guarantee tempt fate?

Suppressing the notion I took hold of his hand and led him toward the carousel. Our bodies absorbed the cheery ambience of the airport and our eyes watched people of all ages embrace and kiss and laugh. The jolly season had infected everyone, including us. Brent retrieved his bag and we danced our way amidst the happy throng to the open doorway then blithely crossed the street to the parking lot.

"Warm weather," he said, "on Christmas Eve."

"What better place for two denizens of the Great White North to impart peace and goodwill?"

"None better."

Our hands swung in yoyo fashion and our feet skipped past parked cars. My free hand took the remote from my shorts' pocket and gave it a click; the lights of my sapphire blue rental car came alive and the doors unlocked. I tossed the keys to him and eased into the passenger seat. He, in alpha male fashion, climbed behind the steering wheel, turned on the ignition, and under my tutelage drove the car from the parking lot to the highway.

During the drive to my sister's condominium we chatted about our week apart. He explained the project that had delayed his arrival and I told him about the beach, the condo, and the unnerving appearances of a weird couple.

"Forget them, Philomela. Enjoy the holiday."

Next morning I awoke to the feel of warm air caressing my skin and the sounds of surf and birdsong brushing my eardrums. Brent was here and life was good.

With eyes closed, I rolled over and stretched my hands along the bottom sheet. I opened my eyes, sat up and scanned the four corners of the room. I jumped out of bed and went into the bathroom. The reflected sight of green eyes and unruly red hair made me freeze, and then in the living room I melted at the sight of Brent standing outside on the lanai.

He reminded me of Apollo, the Greek god of light and truth. He gazed at the world from our Mount Olympian lanai, and his posture was so relaxed and his reverie so peaceful I hated to disturb him. He was still on Calgary time, three hours ahead of Maui, and he had risen before dawn spread her rosy fingers in the eastern sky.

Moving toward him with airy footsteps, I glanced at my wristwatch: six-thirty.

He heard me and turned around. "Bad news," he said.

"What's wrong?" Surely fate hadn't been tempted.

"No sign of Santa."

I giggled. "Santa delivered our gifts...airfares to and from Maui...a week and a half ago."

Snuggling against each other, we watched wave after wave rise in the shallows, crash against the shore, and ebb under the incoming wave. He voiced my innermost thought, "Paradise." A few minutes later I twisted from the warmth of his body then returned carrying two glasses of pineapple juice.

"Fresh from the fridge" I said.

We moved to the green plastic table, sat down on two of the four matching chairs and sipped our beverages. Sporadically touching each other, we confirmed the reality of being together again.

"Guess what," he said. "I bought you a present."

"You never buy presents." I gazed at him with a hint of suspicion. "Are you trying to compensate for some wrongdoing?"

He shook his head, stood up and marched from the lanai. On his return he dropped the gift on the table.

"Oh Brent, what a splendid surprise. Bidulka's latest mystery novel."

"It was in the airport bookstore. For my own relaxation I bought two adventure novels."

A short while later we showered, donned shorts and T-shirts and flip-flops, and went outside. To avoid waking neighbours, we spoke softly and tread lightly on the outside corridor and down the two flights of stairs. We hurried through a dim passageway, crossed a lawn, and entered a path between two sand dunes the height of my eyebrows. We exited to a wonder-world of sand, sea and sky.

On damp sand we walked side by side and carried our flip-flops. Brent chuckled every time a large wave splashed over his ankles. I sang angelically but a bit off key: "God rest you merry gentlemen, let nothing you dismay...."

Suddenly my voice stopped singing and my feet stopped moving. My eyes stared down at a reddish-brown splotch the size of a luncheon plate. What was it?

"Brent," I said, "see that strange stain on the sand."

He stopped walking, ignored my observation and zeroed in on my syntax: "Bad alliteration." He grinned at me.

"Seriously, Brent, look at that stain."

"I see it."

"What do you think it is?"

"I don't know. But I do know the first high tide will wash it away." He resumed walking.

His attitude annoyed me, but his words made sense. Why should I worry about a stain on the sand that concerned me not one whit? I ran and caught up with him, took hold of his forearm and several steps later forced him to stop. I pointed to a series of black rocks jutting out to sea.

"That's where Motor-Mouth counted his wad of money. He was so creepy." I shuddered involuntarily.

"Philomela, you'll probably never see the dude again. On a cheerier subject...have you snorkelled yet?"

My train of thought quickly followed his. "No, I waited for you. There's a dive shop in a nearby mall that sells and rents equipment."

"After breakfast we'll go there."

"It won't be open."

His thick brows furrowed and then cleared. "Of course. Christmas."

We resumed our promenade and greeted other walkers with a friendly "Aloha" or a cheery "Merry Christmas." Reaching a straight stretch of beach I again grabbed his arm and pulled him to a stop.

"This is where the girl hit me. She looked dreadful. Paradise didn't agree with her."

"Who but the devil could find Paradise disagreeable?"

"Who indeed?"

At the end of the bay we turned around and started to retrace our steps. Passing the straight stretch of sand and the black rock promontory, I looked toward Haleakula, the sleeping volcano, and tried to eradicate thoughts of the weird couple. At the reddish stain, my abdominal muscles contracted and I stopped walking. Brent, unhindered by either a gut-feeling or a mild curiosity, strolled leisurely on.

I squatted on my heels, scrutinized the splotch and concluded it was too red to be spilled coffee. I dabbed it with my fingertips and felt a slight crustiness. Was it dried blood? Could it have been caused by an injury?

Rising to a standing position, I noticed something my eyes had missed earlier—a trail of reddish blobs. The blobs led me to the base of a high sand dune covered with green groundcover. I studied several damaged leaves and then my innate curiosity took over. I slipped into my flip-flops and slogged up the sandy slope.

Feeling like Hera on top of Mount Olympus, I surveyed my realm. The green carpet, the size of a small lawn, was decorated with an irregular pink and turquoise flowerbed. I moved toward it.

And then I screamed.

CHAPTER 2

My scream erupted like a newly awakened volcano. The sound surprised me because I had no idea my vocal chords could be so loud. The noise disrupted the balmy air but the body in front of me remained silent and motionless. My surprise turned to fear then to shock then to a state of near paralysis. I moved with the mobility of a petrified tree stump.

After an hour long minute, my head finally turned from the grim spectacle and my supreme willpower dragged my lower appendages across the groundcover. I stopped before tumbling over the edge of the dune.

I peered down to the beach and saw Brent. His lack of interest in my pursuit of reddish blobs had allowed him to walk a fair distance on the sand. However, he must have heard my piercing scream for his legs stood motionlessly on one spot while his head swivelled from right to front to left then returned to front and right. Obviously searching for the source of the scream, he turned his body one-hundred-and-eighty degrees and looked out to sea, exactly the wrong direction.

"Brent," I yelled and wildly waved both arms above my head.

He swung around from viewing the sea and turned toward me. I thanked the gods when he looked up and acknowledged my flailing arms by waving one of his own. With the speed of Pegasus, the mythical winged horse, he ran toward the base of the dune.

The sight of him racing across the sand prompted my throat to swallow a potential second scream. My heart thumped against my ribcage and my microscopic cells overflowed with relief. With renewed courage I glanced behind me. The body, clad in turquoise and pink flowers, remained silent and motionless on the carpet of green groundcover.

The sight reminded me of a disturbing event that had occurred a week earlier at the Calgary airport. In the most unlikely of places, a ladies' lavatory, I had experienced a strange feeling of murder and mayhem. That event, though imaginative, had been disturbing. This one, being real, was far worse.

The two incidents were related by the person involved. Going back in time, my mind's eye returned to the airport.

* * *

The spray of water ceased automatically. I gazed in awe from my clean hands to the magical tap and paid silent homage to the creators of modern miracles. I thanked the gods for my good fortune at living in the here and now where everything was feasible and nothing was impossible.

Water gushed in the sink adjacent to mine. Startled, I raised my eyes and stared at the mirror image of a drop-dead gorgeous girl.

Her face was a perfect oval, her skin was peaches and cream, her almond shaped eyes were wide apart but not far enough to appear cow-eyed. Her brunette hair shimmered with auburn highlights and flowed in gentle waves from the crown of her head to the curve of her shoulders. Her irises, a vivid shade of violet, were surrounded by seas of white. Her dark lashes swept toward her cheeks. I was entranced.

Then my sight dimmed as if filmed by cataracts. The reflection flashed to the young girl on a beach inundated with feelings of mayhem and murder.

Reality returned and I stared at the girl in the mirror. Apparently sensing my scrutiny, she looked directly into my reflected eyes.

Unnerved by the foreboding flash yet at the same time embarrassed at being caught staring so rudely, I grinned like an idiot and turned away. A paper-towel dispenser hanging on the wall became an object of interest. Feeling her eyes on me, I walked sedately over to the dispenser and searched for a button to push or a handle to crank. My fingertips fumbled and found no indentations or protrusions. My sedateness disintegrated.

I peripherally glimpsed her eyes still watching me. My right hand moved near the bottom of the machine and a paper towel magically eased out. I dried both hands, stuffed the towel in the waste bin and surreptitiously glanced back at the young girl.

Her interest had shifted from me to her hands. She vigorously soaped them and let a spray of water wash the suds down the drain. With rapt care and attention she repeated the entire procedure a second time.

When she began a third soaping, I worried that her skin would crack and her epidermis be destroyed. What bothered me most, however, was how her hand-washing went beyond cleanliness and godliness and bordered on obsession. I was no psychology major, but her actions certainly indicated a problem.

Her obsessive behaviour was disconcerting. I recalled the feeling of mayhem and murder I had just experienced and the hair on the back of my neck stood to attention. Would we meet again?

Good grief, I rather hoped not.

The girl rinsed away the third set of suds. I watched her soap her hands a fourth time and an unseen burden fell on my shoulders. My lungs felt congested, my breathing grew laboured, and my happy holiday mood dropped into a hidey-hole of depression.

The emotion was a puzzle. My life was great—health good; money needs nil; marriage with Brent happy; and my anticipated holiday promised relaxation and fun. There was absolutely no reason to feel depressed.

Trying to will the dark cloud away, I thrust back my shoulders, raised my chin, turned from the girl and walked to the doorway. I glanced back and saw her obsessively rinse the fourth set of suds from her hands. I blinked and strode out of the room to the concourse.

With a forced smile on my lips, I walked to the correct gate in the departure lounge, stopped at a row of cookie-cutter chairs and settled into an empty one. The utilitarian piece of furniture was uncomfortable, probably designed for the sole purpose of keeping travellers like me awake, enabling us to hear flight announcements. I pulled a paperback mystery from my purse and opened it.

Peripherally, I caught sight of the gorgeous girl walking in my direction. I craned my neck to see if her hands were red and irritated, but they disappeared from view as she turned to the other side of the aisle. Her every movement was graceful and her slim figure, like her hair and facial features, needed no improvement. Her form-fitting outfit, tight black pants and snug black leather jacket, accentuated every curve of her picture perfect body.

I glanced around and noted that most eyes, male and female, were on her. No wonder, for she gave meaning to the terms eye-candy and tasty-treat. Few humans are blessed with so many attributes, and her apparent unawareness of them added to her charm. She moved to the end of a row and sat down beside a man wearing a long-sleeved blue shirt.

The sight of her loveliness should have cheered my soul. Instead, it heightened my feeling of depression. I knew the feeling originated from something deeper and more worrisome than superficial envy.

I tried to alleviate this depressed state by losing myself in fictional detection. Two pages later, I accepted the failure of losing myself, not because the mystery was weak but because a voice over the intercom announced my flight number.

Boarding started with invalids and children and their guardians; business passengers next, and the rest of us lined up according to row numbers. My seat in row eight ensured me of being one of the last to board.

I made my way through the business section of the plane and once again noticed the attractive girl. She sat in a large, comfortable-looking chair beside the man wearing a long-sleeved blue shirt. His longish brown hair, parted on his left side, was white at the temples and he seemed the epitome of a successful businessman taking a well-deserved vacation. He looked up and our eyes met. Something about him made me quickly avert mine. I wondered about the young girl: Was she his daughter, his trophy wife, his secretary, his mistress, or a combination?

I entered economy and at row eight squeezed past a young man and woman. My narrow window seat was a model of comfort compared to the one I had vacated in the departure lounge. I tucked my purse under the seat in front, buckled my seatbelt, and leaned back in anticipation of a pleasant flight.

Then a god-like voice boomed from the heights: "This is your Captain speaking. A passenger who previously checked in has not appeared. We must find his bag and remove it from the plane. Sorry for the delay."

I sat upright and my anticipation dropped. The disturbing announcement revived memories of two crashing planes and three collapsing towers in New York City. Comprehension of those events still evaded me and a glance at my neck-craning fellow passengers indicated they, too, had similar problems. Was paranoia the dark side of our miraculous, modern world? Could any of us prevent this plane from exploding?

After a brief flurry of dismay, I leaned back in my seat, closed my eyes and let the fickle finger of fate run its course.

Since my arrival at the airport, security had been tight. My shoes, jacket and purse had been swallowed by a surveillance monster and my body had been checked under an arch bearing no resemblance to the yellow arches of the world famous fast-food outlet. Thankfully, I had triggered no bells or alarms.

Once, during the serious security procedures, humour erupted. A U.S. customs officer, young enough to be my daughter, checked my passport and boarding pass while I bragged about my cleverness at obtaining the latter on my home computer. My pride crashed when she noted I had neglected to obtain a destination tag.

Looking me straight in the eye she added, "You remind me of my mother...who is a very smart woman."

I beamed at the implication.

She leaned forward and whispered, "There are two things in the modern world my mother refuses to do—learn the computer and floss her teeth."

After I stopped laughing, she pointed toward a young lady at another desk. "She'll give you a destination tag."

Now, securely belted in my seat, I waited to be blown to bits by a terrorist's indiscriminate bomb. If I had heeded Brent's suggestion and booked a business class seat, it would have made no difference. I'd still end up in fragments.

"Unlike you," I had told him, "I don't need lots of leg room. Economy will be fine."

"Philomela, it's your choice."

Provided I survived the pending explosion, he would join me in six days. Together we would soak up sunshine, stroll on sand, snorkel in surf, and swim without sharks.

My thoughts splintered as the captain's voice again boomed from the heights: "The unclaimed bag has been located and removed. We'll be on our way."

A moment later the huge metal bird taxied to a main runway. Its engines revved to a roar; its tires tore over the tarmac, and its wings flew to the sky. I looked out the window at powder puff clouds above the line where land and sky meet. The view was as lovely as any ever witnessed by the gods on Mount Olympus.

Fortunately, those immortals would greet no one from this airplane, at least not immediately. Passengers in both economy and business would live to see another day.

CHAPTER 3

I leaned over and saw Brent prepare to climb the sandy slope. I watched his feet gain toeholds in the groundcover and his body move slowly upward. Then I nervously glanced behind me.

The body lay in peaceful repose, yet I suspected death had not resulted from natural causes. After all, the corpse lay in perfect alignment: legs straight, feet together, arms neatly placed at each side. In my mind two people must have been required to position the body so perfectly.

Upset by the scenario I felt my own body stiffen into a state of partial paralyses. Notwithstanding the warm weather, goose-bumps rose on the skin of my arms and shivers made my teeth chatter. My eyes moistened, my muscles melted, my stomach felt nauseous, and my spinal column weakened. Even in a state of shock I wondered how the innocuous turquoise and pink flowers could appear so ominous. Would a spectre rise up and float toward me?

I longed to be somewhere else, anywhere else. Turning my gaze from the body to the edge of the dune, I experienced an impulse to throw myself over the side. The impulse dissipated quickly: crashing three metres below would be painful, maybe even life threatening. A better way to increase the distance between me and the motionless body would be to climb down the dune and flee. Paradise was lost so the Great White North with its blowing snow and freezing cold would be a more desirable destination.

Brent's head and shoulders appeared over the rim of the dune. He clambered up on top and his final exertion brought forth a loud groan and a bout of heavy breathing. He straightened his knees, put his hands on his back and stood tall.

Watching him, I swallowed my squeamishness and stiffened my spine. "Are you okay?" I asked. Awareness of my physical and mental states shifted to his.

He replied with a nod of the head and started to walk toward me. Suddenly his eyes widened and his face paled. His breathing grew audible and shallow, his footwork became problematic, and his mouth opened but no words came out. I forgot the horror on the groundcover and contemplated a worse one: what if Brent suffered a stroke or a heart attack? A feeling of tremendous relief washed over me when he cleared his throat and spoke.

"Gawd." He stared at the motionless figure then looked over at me and whispered, "Alive?"

"I don't think so." His question quelled my feeling of negativity and replaced it with a positive spark of hope. "I'll check."

Brent's breathing returned to normal, which was good, so I walked to the prostrate figure, squatted down on my heels and studied the motionless form. Without so much as a shudder, I picked up a limp arm and my fingers moved around the inner wrist, searching desperately for the beat of a pulse. My fingers felt only skin and bones. Nothing indicated blood coursing through the arteries and veins. Completing my search for a flicker of life, I let the arm fall to the ground.

"There's no pulse and the skin feels like ice." I gazed up at Brent.

His expression registered both disbelief and horror, but he stepped close to the body and squatted down beside me. He studied the immobile face and after a few seconds said, "Look at the sores on the lower lip and cheeks."

"I see them."

From his squatting position he rose and slowly shifted from one foot to the other, as if seeking no special purpose except physical action, any kind of action. His horror-stricken expression gradually grew contemplative and he nodded his head.

"We need help," he said. "We have to find someone with a cellphone to call the police."

Neither of us carried a cellphone. We purposely had left them at home, thinking our vacation together would be more peaceful without them. That, it seemed, had been a mistake. But even if we had packed them, would either of us have carried one on our early morning promenade? The phones likely would have stayed in my sister's condominium.

Unsure of what to do next, I stood up beside him. Brent started to walk toward the rim of the dune so I followed. The body, of course, remained behind us, motionless and alone. We stopped at the edge of the dune and gazed down at a white haired couple walking on the sand near the water. They shuffled closer to us and Brent called to them.

"Hello, you two on the beach. Hello." Their response was no response. He yelled louder, "We're up here on top of a sand dune." And he waved both arms over his head.

This time they heard his voice but apparently not his words. Instead of looking up they glanced from side to side as if trying to locate the voice. Then they looked straight ahead. Brent called again, louder and slower this time. The man raised his head, glanced up at us, turned and spoke to his companion. They looked around the beach as if trying to find the person to whom Brent was speaking. No one else was nearby so they shuffled toward us.

"Do you have a cellphone?" Brent's voice boomed as if speaking in a megaphone.

"We don't have one. We don't have a computer either." The man's response was loud but his voice was shaky. He bobbed his white head up and down.

"There's been an accident," Brent yelled.

"What did you say?" the man asked.

"Someone is seriously hurt. When you get to your condo, could you please contact the police for us?"

The man and woman both responded by shaking their heads from side to side, shrugging their shoulders, and raising their arms with palms up. Brent might as well have been speaking Greek to two dolphins.

"When you get to your condo, would you phone the police? There's a dead body here." They responded with another enactment of puzzlement and Brent turned to me and muttered, "They just don't get it. They have no idea what we're dealing with." One more time he loudly asked them to phone the police. One more time the couple shrugged and held their hands with palms up. Brent shook his head and tightened his jaw into a grimace. "This is hopeless," he muttered. But he called out with frustrated politeness, "Thanks anyway."

Oblivious to our stressful predicament, they shuffled away. They had not recognized the panic in Brent's voice, nor had they noticed the stain on the sand.

"They were no help at all," Brent said.

I wondered why the twosome seemed familiar.

"We have to do something," Brent said. "But what?" He promptly answered his own question: "If no one else appears, I'll climb down the dune and run for help."

CHAPTER 4

I had seen the elderly couple before—but where? My mind struggled to grasp the location and circumstance and came up empty. They resembled hundreds of other elderly, rotund, white-haired vacationers. Their main distinction had less to do with their white hair and their fleshy figures and more to do with their manner of moving. They didn't walk; they shuffled as if having difficulty carrying their excess weight. I had seen those precise movements before.

"The couple had no cellphone," I murmured more to myself than to Brent.

"They didn't have a clue. When they get to their condo they won't phone the police."

Our predicament again filled me with a hopeless, helpless, frightened feeling. My legs felt like two rubber bands so I leaned against Brent. Together we stood near the rim of the dune and watched the white-haired twosome shuffle on the sand, increasing the distance between us. Also increasing were the nerve impulses leaping across the synapses in my brain. They suddenly flashed with new information.

The couple and I had eaten breakfast in the same restaurant on my first morning on Maui.

* * *

The condominium at *Hale Sun and Surf* was as expected. Attractive.

My sister's choice of colors and interior design outshone the practicability of furniture and fabrics. The unit was clean, thanks to a good maintenance staff. To my relief all things mechanical and electrical—shower, toilet, stove, fridge, lights, TV, radio—were in good working order.

The master bedroom's mattress had been comfortable enough to enhance my first night's sleep, and the small closet had more than adequately housed my minimal holiday wardrobe. The turquoise sofa in the living room looked long enough for Brent to stretch out on, and the easy-care glass table and metal chairs in the eating area were serviceable. The white upholstery on the chairs contained triangles of warm turquoise and circles of cheery yellow that matched cushions scattered on the sofa.

A few cracks in the wall, no doubt caused by a recent earthquake, had been repaired but not repainted. Procne, co-owner of the unit with my almost-ex-brother-in-law, Larry Ellis, liked her personal belongings and public surroundings kept in shipshape condition, so for her the unfinished repairs would be worrisome. For me, they served as enlightenment that even in paradise things were not always perfect. Everything else, general upkeep and practical utility of the unit, was more than satisfactory.

Adorned in my skimpy nightgown, I opened the gliding door to the lanai and walked outside. I immediately realized it was the best feature of the entire unit.

My elbows rested on the white railing and my lungs breathed in the soft moist air. I gazed down at a kidney shaped swimming pool, a neat lawn embroidered with oval flower beds, and four groupings of three palm trees. A row of low, vine-covered sand dunes guarded the beach, and beyond the dunes the Pacific Ocean rolled in from far away. I sat down on a green plastic chair and watched the water wash the sand. I listened to the rhythmical surf and admired subtle changes in water color. The shallow area was beige; a bit deeper the colour shifted to turquoise; farther out it became navy blue that ended in a horizontal straight line. Above the horizon the pale blue sky was cloudless.

Yesterday afternoon I had flown from leafless trees, below zero temperature, square car wheels, and fleece-lined boots crunching on snow-covered sidewalks. The dramatic contrast made everything here warmer and more spectacular. My eyes feasted on the summery sights, my skin absorbed the tropical moisture, and my muscles melted like butter in the heat. I felt at one with the world, content to stay on the lanai and retain this peaceful feeling forever.

Hunger dictated otherwise. The only way to relieve hunger pangs was to exit the lovely lanai and search for food.

Dressed in green T-shirt that matched my eyes and brown shorts and sandals that matching nothing, I went outside. After locking the door I walked down two flights of stairs to my sapphire blue rental car. The drive to the outdoor mall and food market that I had noticed en-route from the airport took about two minutes.

The proximity of the shops, closer than I had initially thought, was within easy walking distance of *Hale Sun and Surf*. For the next two weeks I would get healthy exercise while hunting and gathering for the necessities of life. I drove past the food market and pulled into one of the outdoor mall's spacious parking spots.

A restaurant called *The Wave* caught my eye. I walked over to it, went inside and for two seconds felt right at home. The wooden tables and chairs could have been located in the heart of anywhere in the Great White North. That, however, was where all similarity ended.

The scantily clad servers and the equally scantily clad cliental sitting out on a large patio could never have survived the weather at home. In a matter of minutes their bare arms and legs would have become frozen meat. December in Calgary and December on Maui were eons apart.

A sign invited customers to seat themselves, so I glided through the restaurant to a set of open double doors. Outside on the patio, I walked on blue and white tiles past three occupied white plastic tables, stopped at an empty one and eased onto a white plastic chair. I glanced at my close neighbours.

On my right, eating bacon and eggs and toast, sat a man and a woman. Their white hair was abundant and so were their figures. They both wore knee-length shorts and colourful shirts. In age they looked at least seventy, which in my estimation approached ancient. I glanced to the left at two men wearing shorts and golf-shirts; they sipped coffee and ate fruit while quietly conversing. The patrons on both sides of me seemed to bask with pleasure in the warm air.

My interest shifted from my neighbours to a hedge bordering the patio; the ubiquitous Hibiscus had earned the right to be Hawaii's state flower, and this hedge with its blood-red blossoms was truly breathtaking. Beyond the hedge, groups of palm trees stretched to the cloudless blue sky. Everything except dull traffic noises on a nearby but unseen road lived up to my expectation of paradise.

A waitress holding a pot with a large spout stopped at my table and offered coffee. I nodded and watched her pour the dark brew. She gave me a menu then moved over to the two men beside me and refilled their coffee mugs. They smiled and thanked her. At the other table, the elderly man and woman laughed at a private joke and their happiness made me smile; they may be ancient but they still enjoyed life. I opened the menu, focused on its printed words and mentally debated the yummy pros and the fattening cons of a full, hearty breakfast. Hunger ruled and when the waitress returned I ordered appropriately.

For several minutes I sipped coffee and gazed contentedly at the sky, the palm fronds, and the blood-red flowers. The waitress brought cereal and yogurt to the two men seated next to me, and then in record speed set a large plate heaped with papaya, bacon, eggs, and hash-browns in front of me. I sat up straight as she placed a small plate of toast beside the larger plate. Like a famine victim I dug in and relished each bite.

"Hello there!" the strident voice clanged like a jackhammer.

Startled, I dropped my fork with a clatter on the table and looked up, expecting to see a long lost acquaintance. Instead, I saw an unknown man smashing through the waist high hedge. He pushed aside branches, broke off leaves and blood-red flowers, and seemed totally oblivious to the damage he was causing.

With a beer can held high in the air in one hand and a cigarette in the other, he stepped on the blue and white patio tiles. He paused a second and then moved forward. A grungy shirt with pink and turquoise flowers clung to his chest, baggy khaki shorts drooped over his lower body and hung almost to his knees, and flip-flops protected the soles of his feet. His appearance was so unattractive and his actions so destructive that I wished I could summon Zeus and his thunderbolt to make the man disappear.

I couldn't replicate Zeus, but the gods were partially with me—the man directed his attention to a table other than mine. His flip-flops slapped loudly on the tiles as he closed in on the two men sitting next to me.

"Good to see you again," he pronounced, and his voice boomed disruptively around the entire patio. "I was hoping you'd be in Maui during the next few weeks. When did you arrive? Was the weather rainy and cold when you left Victoria? Bet you're glad to be here. Ha ha ha." His legs stopped walking but his mouth kept talking. He asked question after question and waited not one second for answers. "Isn't this warm air nice for a change? And the flowers, too, eh?" He sniffed briefly as if smelling their perfume then babbled on. "Is this restaurant still an okay place to eat?" Finally he paused for a deep breath.

"We find the food here consistently good." The soft, velvety voice contrasted sharply with the newcomer's booming monologue.

Out of the corner of my eye I peeked at the man with the velvety voice. He appeared older than both his companion and the newcomer, possibly because a thick thatch of white hair crowned his head. His companion's hair was a modest shade of light brown whereas the newcomer's hair was spiky and artificially coloured a bright orange. Of course hair style and color are poor indicators of age, the dye bottle and the hair stylist being so readily available in every village, town and city.

My two male neighbours failed to invite the newcomer to join them, but undeterred by this oversight he plunked himself down on a vacant chair. He set his elbows on the table and took a sip from his can of beer. The two men surreptitiously glanced at each other then looked at the newcomer and smiled politely.

"What's new?" the newcomer asked. Before anyone could answer, he asked another question. "Is the condo still in good shape? I was just leaving the tattoo parlour over there," and he waved toward a group of stores across the parking lot, "when I spotted you two sitting here. Good luck and good timing."

"You must have excellent vision." The soft voice of the man with white hair carried clearly through the air waves. He reminded me of a well trained actor who could whisper on stage so that each word would be clearly distinguished by every member of the audience.

No longer peeking, I gazed openly at the threesome and for the first time noted that the older speaker wore glasses. The newcomer again spoke and my attention shifted to him.

"Yeah. Good eyesight and good hearing. Birthdays keep coming, eh, but so far my eyes and ears are okay." He roared with laughter at his clever witticism and waved his arms wildly, possibly proving that they too were in good working order.

That was when I noted his upper appendages. I stared unabashedly, not at their gestures, but at their colourful squiggles and pictures. The artwork left very little flesh unadorned. His two companions were equally fascinated by the rippling art show. With wide eyes they watched his arms rise and fall but said nothing. They pretended to concentrate on their cereal and every so often nodded their heads amicably. The intruder rambled on and on about being physically fit.

I mentally christened the talker, "Motor-Mouth". His relationship with the other two men resembled mere acquaintances rather than close friends. His continuing monologue obviously had little impact on his listeners, though they attended to his words with polite nods and occasional smiles that failed to reach their eyes.

The speaker, however, had great impact on me, at least his tattoos did. I kept looking at his arms with their masses of colourful designs gone awry. To my eyes they resembled meaningless graffiti or black and blue bruises or unhealthy varicose veins. Both his arms, from shoulders to wrists, writhed like snakes as his hands accentuated every second word.

I looked from the arm art to his bright spiky hair. No wonder the color appeared artificial, the lower hair being beige and the top orange. I suspected it was not a temporary cool-aide prank but a dye job from hell. It had the unfortunate effect of reminding me that my own red hair was fading and on more than one occasion I had studied displays of hair colouring.

A rock and roll musical interlude shook my thoughts and put them in momentary disarray. The sound came from Motor-Mouth's cell phone. I stared in amazement as he put it to his ear and proceeded to broadcast his side of the conversation to everyone within a radius of three kilometres. His two companions squirmed in their chairs, glanced over at me, lowered their eyes and picked up their coffee mugs. Motor-Mouth finally ended his conversation with a loud, "Yeah, she'll be there." He clicked his cellphone shut and announced to the world that he and the caller were discussing an important business transaction. "It sure interrupted my breakfast," he said and laughed loudly.

I glanced at the can of beer on the table and the half smoked cigarette in his hand. That was breakfast?

He punched in some numbers on his phone and again put it to his ear. Though trying not to stare, I noted a few wrinkles on his face and concluded he was not as young as he pretended. He appeared about my age, which was near the mid-century mark. The recipient of his call answered, and he spoke authoritatively, albeit in a slightly softer tone than before. I tried not to listen, but when he mentioned the name of my condo complex, *Hale Sun and Surf*, my ears perked up like those of an alert cat.

"Go there now, Marlene," he ordered. "He's waiting for you. I'll see you later." Tucking his phone in the belt of his shorts, he turned to his companions and grinned. "I have a friend who works at the tattoo parlour over there," and once again he pointed across the parking lot. "His name is Jake and he has my cell number and through him you can contact me at anytime." He lowered his voice and said, "If you want the liveliest companions on the planet, the best B.C. bud in the world, or even just a snort I have them all. And they're the greatest." He reached out his hand, made a fist and gently jabbed the arm of the younger of his two companions.

The man cringed slightly, shifted position and gave a smile that looked uneasy and forced. He then gazed directly at Motor-Mouth and asked, "Do you remember any of the conversations we had last year?"

Motor-Mouth frowned, obviously puzzled.

The younger man said something in such a soft voice I couldn't make out his words.

"Oh yeah, I remember. I'll give it some thought." Motor-Mouth guffawed then continued to expound, "My friend at the Tattoo Parlour trimmed and dyed my hair early this morning. Very fashionable, don't yah know." He laughed again, turned and waved at the waitress and called out, "Bring me a glass of water and a cup of coffee. I'm real thirsty." Turning back to his companions he resumed his monologue.

His words were so repetitive, so boring, and so loud that I tried to tune them out by concentrating on the white-haired couple sitting at the next table. They kept looking from Motor-Mouth to each other. They too seemed entranced with him and, like me, in an unfavourable manner. The waitress set a bill on the table and the elderly man picked it up, studied it then placed cash on it. He stood up and helped his companion rise from her chair. Together they moved stiffly away from the table and shuffled toward the doorway. She seemed to have a sore left hip and he favoured his right knee. Watching them shuffle their way across the blue and white tiles, I suspected they suffered from forms of arthritis. Their ample bodies and white heads finally disappeared into the main part of the restaurant.

I concentrated on my good but no longer hot food. Keeping my head bent, I removed the view of Motor-Mouth's gesticulating arms. I slathered guava jelly on a slice of toast and chewed as loudly as possible, but the sound failed to tune out his penetrating voice. His words continued to flow like a thundering waterfall.

After paying the waitress, I glanced over at Motor-Mouth and saw him scratch his shoulders and neck as if he were being bitten alive by insects. These actions surprised me because I had seen no sign of flies or mosquitoes or any other insect since arriving on Maui. Normally, all biting creatures adored me, and I once told Brent it was my sweet disposition that attracted them; he expressed doubt about that theory.

I sipped the last of my coffee, set the mug down and once again gazed at the vociferous creature at the next table. At that precise moment he turned and looked at me. Our eyes met. My abdominal muscles twisted in alarm.

I averted my eyes, snatched my purse and stood up. I couldn't get away fast enough.

CHAPTER 5

"Good grief." I raised my eyes and looked at Brent. "No one else is nearby. I've never seen the beach so empty of people."

He shook his head and pressed his lips into a sombre line. "Just when we need help."

"Murphy's law. Anything that can go wrong will go wrong." I stepped away from the edge of the dune and felt thankful my rubber band knee joints and leg muscles were strengthening. My stomach stopped flipping flapjacks and my heartbeat slowed to a regular pace. I drew closer to the dreadful scene, fully expecting to experience a repeat of the untoward symptoms. None appeared.

Was I getting used to the unnatural death? Was I becoming immune to horror? In one way, the questions suggested relief, in another, they suggested disapproval. Coping with a horrid situation with skill was good; accepting a horrid situation with ease was insensitive.

Brent joined me and we stood side by side gazing down at the dead body.

"I wonder what happened," I murmured.

"Maybe death resulted from a diabetic coma or a heart attack."

"More likely from an accidental fall on the beach."

"On the beach...?"

"Brent, it must have happened on the beach. Remember the blood stains on the sand? And the trail of blood that led to this dune?"

"Why would an injured person climb up here?"

"I bet a couple of people carried the body up the dune."

A refreshing breeze frolicked around us. The garment on the body fluttered, minimizing the splatters of blood and maximizing the large pink and turquoise flowers. The colourful floral designs reminded me of the shirt Motor-Mouth had worn at breakfast on the restaurant patio. His shirt had been wrinkled and grungy, but if it had been neat and clean the flowers would have been a perfect match to the fabric fluttering in front of me.

My mind's eye reverted to the grungy shirt on the patio and my emotions re-lived my frantic urge to get as far away as fast as possible from that awful man

* * *

Hurrying away from Motor-Mouth, I neared the patio door and muttered, "What a boor."

A startled patron gave me a puzzled look, doubtless wondering if my hallucinations were visual as well as verbal. Preferring to appear sane, I slowed my pace and walked sedately through the open door into the restaurant; I pursed my lips to prevent any more unkind words from escaping from my mouth and made my way to the front entrance.

Outside on the sidewalk I tried to calm myself. Though warm sunshine beamed from the sky, my body shivered as if surrounded by swirls of freezing draughts.

It wasn't only that Motor-Mouth spoke loudly, behaved thoughtlessly, and looked uncouth, though those qualities were enough to make anyone uncomfortable; it was his resemblance to the solid citizen of yesterday that truly disconcerted me. The man wearing a long-sleeved blue shirt in the Calgary departure lounge and in the business section of the airplane had appeared ordinary and quiet, and his longish brown and white hair had been neat and tidy. Of course, the main reason I recalled him so accurately was because of his companion, the drop-dead gorgeous girl.

I stood on the cement and shivered. I gulped in three deep breaths of fresh air and felt a little better. The world around me grew warmer and lighter and a passerby smiled and said, "Aloha". I responded with a nod of the head. After all, I told myself, the unpleasant episode on the patio had not been life-threatening. Emotions had their place, but they were not supposed to rule every minute. A second passerby smiled and remarked on the lovely weather. The friendly cheeriness was contagious.

Maybe Motor-Mouth's boorish behaviour and gaudy appearance was nothing more than a middle-age holiday caper. Maybe it resulted from male menopause. I wished to believe that, but the wish faltered because something about him had seemed so sinister. Though no rays of evil emanated from him and no specific words and deeds denoted dealings with the devil, I still shivered at the thought of him. In sharp contrast were Motor-Mouth's two breakfast companions. Their refined appearances, cultured voices, and polite actions revoked evil and provided an impression of a world pleasant and safe. The breakfast scene was a complete conundrum. Were the three men best buddies? If so, why did Motor-Mouth's boorish actions make the other two behave in ways that portrayed discomfort?

Motor-Mouth himself was a paradox. How in the world had such an unsavoury person connected with the two quiet spoken men? And how had he latched onto the gorgeous, young girl? She too was a paradox—especially regarding her obsessive hand-washing. Would the girl and I reconnect? The prospect provided no cheer.

Like Atlas shifting the weight of the world, I shrugged. The girl was not my responsibility; her associates were none of my business; her obsessive hand-washing involved me not at all. What did we share in common? Nothing. What could I do to improve her life? Nothing. Even if she had been a close acquaintance could I have ended her relationship with Motor-Mouth? No. She made her own choices.

I shrugged again and the burden grew lighter. I glanced up at the blue sky, felt the sun's warm rays and started to move along the sidewalk. Passing a shoe store, I realized thoughts of the horrid man and the gorgeous girl were being replaced by attractive window displays.

After a quick overview of the mall, I walked to my rental car and drove the short distance to the supermarket. Though Sunday, the large air-conditioned store was open and filled with shoppers. I bought enough food to last a few days. I would stock up again before Brent arrived on December 24th.

Outside the building housing my temporary home, I parked the car in an empty space and carried three bags of groceries up two flights of stairs. The exertion tested my strength and endurance; with each flight the bags got heavier. Reaching the third floor I paused, puffing for more oxygen. Obviously regular exercise was needed to keep my no longer young body in reasonable shape. After catching my breath, I looked straight ahead and strode along the outdoor corridor toward Number 309.

A young woman breezed like a puff of air out of Number 308. She wore a white skirt that barely covered her buttocks and a sleeveless yellow top that barely covered her bosom. Her brunette ponytail swung back and forth in a youthful manner as she carelessly closed the door. She weaved in a staggering manner toward me. Her yellow purse hung from her left shoulder and with each step bumped her hip.

"Aloha," I said, thinking she was my new neighbour, someone holidaying from North America.

She did not respond.

I mentally gave her mother credit for having taught her to mistrust strangers, but the thought faded as she stared at my face with glassy, unfocused eyes. We passed each other and her movements resembled someone who had drunk one Mai Tai too many.

Like the proverbial curious cat, I turned and watched her weave down the first four steps. As she disappeared around the corner of the landing, I realized her right hand had been tightly clutching the railing, not unusual for an older person suffering from poor balance, but quite unusual for a younger person who seemed healthy and fit. Unless, of course, the one Mai Tai too many really was in effect. I dismissed her from my thoughts, unlocked 309 and went inside.

It was while putting groceries in the kitchen fridge that I experienced an epiphany. Stunned, I sat down on the nearest chair.

Could it be coincidence? Was it predestination?

Vivid violet was an uncommon eye color. The only other person I had ever seen with such irises was the drop-dead gorgeous girl in the Calgary airport. Our paths had just crossed again, but this time I experienced no feeling of mayhem and murder. If she was my next door neighbour, the odds of our meeting again were high.

Did that mean Motor-Mouth was my neighbour, too?

CHAPTER 6

"I'll climb down the dune," Brent said, and his voice gained strength with each word. No longer debilitated with shock he turned to me and added, "One way or another, I'll contact the police."

Though his ability to cope with the horrific situation had improved, he seemed powerless to walk away. He stood beside me, motionless and quiet. He stared transfixed at the corpse as if expecting to see a Lazarus style return to life. Of course it didn't happen. The corpse continued to lie deathly still. Finally Brent cleared his throat and took a step forward. He took another step, and another, and then he squatted on his heels and looked down at the inert form. Scrutinizing the head with the concentration of a surgeon, he slowly twisted sideways and leaned closer.

Suddenly he gave an audible gasp. "Gawd," he said.

"What is it?" I could tell by his voice that something new had shaken him.

"The head...look at the head. The right side has been damaged. Severely damaged."

I took a step forward, squatted beside him and leaned to the side. He was right; a deep abrasion caked with dried blood covered the temple area. I grimaced and reached out, intending to touch the edge of the wound with my index finger. Brent grabbed my arm and restrained the action.

"Don't touch anything. Police will test for fingerprints."

"Good grief," I exclaimed. I've already lifted an arm and held the wrist when trying to find a pulse."

"We'll explain that to the police when they get here...if they ever get here." To counteract his last words he nodded his head reassuringly and rose from his squatting position. "Just don't touch anything else."

"Okay." I continued to sit on my heels and study the damaged side of the head. What had caused such a deep cut and so much dried blood? A definite explanation evaded me, but two possibilities came to mind. I stood up and voiced them to Brent.

"Something hard definitely hit the temple area, maybe an accidental fall on a rock." I desperately wanted to believe it had been an accident. "Then again, maybe the side of the head was bludgeoned by a deliberate blow." With a shudder, I refrained from saying the unthinkable word.

Murder.

The end result of malice aforethought is murder. Momentary anger or fear of losing one's own life can also end in murder. Death of any kind is upsetting, but murder is worse because of unintended consequences: the perpetrator's relatives are dismayed and devastated, the victim's family, friends and acquaintances are dismayed and distraught; innocent bystanders are dismayed and shocked.

Brent and I, the innocent bystanders who happened to discover the body, suffered from shock. Who else would be affected? Families and friends of both the victim and the perpetrator. People working in Maui's tourist industry. Owners, guests and staff at *Hale Sun and Surf.*

I had met many of these people.

* * *

I gazed at the door of Number 308, but neither the gorgeous young girl nor Motor-Mouth appeared. I pondered the coincidence that my sister who owned Number 309 and the young girl in Number 308 were beautiful and connected with older men. Which of the unsavoury men was worse? Motor-Mouth or my almost ex-brother-in-law?

Leaving the answer unanswered, I sauntered to the stairway. A quick backward glance revealed nothing unusual so I walked down two flights and entered the dim passageway. Shade and cool air extended from the car-park-side of the building to the seaside, with rectangles of bright light shining at each end.

Halfway through the passage I stopped, took my sunglasses from my eyes and put them on top of my head. With improved vision I gazed at three washing machines and four clothes dryers, all of which seemed relatively new. If the necessity of laundering sheets and towels arrived this is where I would come. It would be easier to use the machines than to scrub bulky items in the bathtub.

Directly across from the laundry facilities was a bookcase containing used books, mostly paperbacks. They provided a handy and inexpensive book exchange for vacationing guests. After perusing the titles and finding none that caught my fancy, I decided to spice up the array by donating the mystery I had finished reading yesterday on the plane. Perhaps another bookworm could solve the fictional puzzle faster than I had.

Crablike, I stepped sideways and stopped in front of a wall-unit. Five sloping shelves displayed an amazing number of travel brochures whose superb designs would entice a travel-hungry tourist to part with wads of hard earned cash. One brochure, entitled *'Volcano Tours',* jumped out at me. I picked it up and scanned pictures and headlines. Phenomena such as earthquakes, hurricanes, and volcanoes always made me wonder if they were caused by nature, man's misdemeanours, or furious cosmic gods. Whatever the cause, they were scary and beyond human control.

My eyes moved from the large print on the brochure to a paragraph of smaller print. It gave details of the tour: a flight in a fixed-wing plane from Maui to Hawaii, the largest island of the archipelago; views from the air of agricultural land, flowing lava, active and inactive volcanoes. The tour appealed to me.

Hearing footsteps, I turned and saw a young man stride purposely from the seaside toward me. As he drew near, I noted a mop of fair hair, a determined expression on his face, a bare chest above tan shorts, and a set of muscles on his legs that rippled as he walked. He nodded at me rather curtly, making me think of the Greek sea-god Poseidon intent on causing a watery disaster.

"Aloha," I said, trying my utmost to keep my eyes from staring at his god-like physique. I opened my tote bag and with studied nonchalance dropped the volcano brochure inside, letting it settle near my suntan lotion, towel, and Mark Twain paperback.

"Aloha," he replied, and his voice sounded not like an annoyed sea god but like a herculean hero. He stopped in front of the middle washing machine and gazed at me. With a complete lack of subtleness his eyes swept from my head down to my feet and up again. The corners of his lips curved upward, exposing white teeth with a small, appealing gap between the two front ones. "You just arrived on Maui," he said.

Thankful for my lacy, menopausal mauve cover-up I sucked in my tummy and nodded affirmatively. How did he know of my recent arrival? Had we met before? Not likely. I'd remember meeting such a perfect specimen of manhood. With no clue to his identity, I admired his clean cut facial appearance and interesting grey eyes. His tanned face and body indicated his stay here had lasted longer than a mere two week vacation.

"Whose condo are you renting?" he asked.

"The Ellis condo."

"Ah yes. Larry and Procne's. Third floor. You're Ms Nightingale."

"That's right."

"Welcome to paradise."

"Thank you." I gave him a spontaneous grin. "It really is paradise, isn't it."

"So the adverts say." He glanced at the bountiful array of brochures then turned to the machines on the other side of the passage. He took a screwdriver from a pocket in his shorts and raised the lid of a washing machine.

I gazed at his back then watched him adjust one of the hinges. He seemed at home working with nuts and bolts and screws. He hummed a tune, immune to my presence behind him.

"Do you own a condo here?" I asked.

"I manage the building, the pool, and the grounds." Without glancing at me he continued twisting the screwdriver and said, "My pay includes the condo on the right side of this passageway."

"You live here all year?"

"I do."

"Lucky you."

He opened and closed the washer lid a few times as if testing it. Apparently satisfied, he closed it and turned to me. "I came here for a university reading break. They needed a handyman and I got the job."

"Did you return to university?"

"I intended to, because at the time my future looked bright. Then circumstances changed." He shrugged. "I liked the area, the work and the weather so I stayed on."

I nodded and thought of my own advanced education. With no definite destiny in mind, I had obtained a Bachelor of Arts. "What degree were you taking?" I asked.

"Electrical engineering."

"Will you ever go back and finish it?"

"I doubt it. After six years I still like the lifestyle. I no longer have any ambition to beat the books."

During his last statement his grey eyes seemed to grow dim and portray a strange sadness. Maybe he regretted the loss of a bright future. What else could make a handsome man, living and working in paradise, seem so sad? A chronic illness? A lost love?

I changed the subject. "Do you know Procne and Larry very well?"

"I know all the owners, but none of them well. I attend some of their meetings and help solve problems in their condos. Generally speaking, they're a good bunch." He turned to another washing machine and shifted the lid up and down. Seeming satisfied with its performance he lowered it and put the screwdriver in his short's pocket. Glancing back at me he smiled. "Enjoy your stay."

"I will."

"If you need any help, just ask for Andrew. That's me."

Grinning, I thanked him.

He turned to the third washer. I gazed at the back of his broad shoulders and his slim hips one last time then walked to the end of the passageway. Exiting into blinding sunlight I moved my sunglasses from the top of my head to the front of my eyes. The coloured glass cut the glare beaming down from the sky and reflecting up from the concrete floor.

I gazed at the terrace extending from one end of the building to the other then walked to a fence enclosing the kidney shape swimming pool. I opened the gate, went inside and dropped my sunglasses and wristwatch and menopausal mauve cover-up into the tote bag. I entered the warm water and lethargically floated on my back then leisurely executed an un-Olympian side stroke. I climbed out of the pool and picked up my belongings.

Pleasing though the UV rays felt on my body, I had no intention of allowing them to penetrate the skin whose dark Greek genes had been overpowered by fair Scottish and English ones. I was an exception to the prediction that the genes of people with dark hair and brown skin would overpower people with red hair and make them obsolete.

I grabbed the back of a chaise longue, dragged it across the grass to a grouping of three large palm trees and placed it near the trunk of the biggest one. I figured the fronds would provide shade. Though my desire was to look like a native Hawaiian, my lack of melanin forbade it from happening. Memories of severe burns and debilitating sunstrokes in my youth encouraged me to be careful. I slathered sunscreen over my exposed skin, dropped the tube of sunscreen in the tote bag and took out the book, *MARK TWAIN IN HAWAII*. The warm sun filtered gently between the palm fronds, a breeze tempered the heat, and the surf's rhythmical lullaby mesmerized my thoughts. My muscles relaxed, my eyes closed, my book lay unopened on my stomach, and I drifted off to the land of nod.

Regaining consciousness, I stretched like a satisfied cat and thought how lucky I was to be here. Not so lucky was my sister. The aphorism, *it's an ill wind that blows no good*, was holding true. The wind that blew ill to her blew good to me.

Early December Procne and Larry decided to split up. Or rather Procne decided to split up. Larry had triggered the decision with his usual desire to conquer everyone in skirts. This character flaw of his was well known, but his other flaws—deceits and bouts of violence—were less well-known. To me the man was unpleasant and unfathomable.

I once witnessed him purposely smash an irreplaceable Greek dish that had belonged to his deceased mother-in-law. He then ridiculed Procne because she was distraught. I told him off and Procne, bless her gentle heart, came to his defence. From then on I zipped my lips. His infidelities, including two efforts to use my body to satisfy his lusts, were appalling, but his constant criticisms that mentally and emotionally hurt Procne and his rough treatments that physically hurt her were worse.

Fortunately for all three of us, our lives failed to completely follow in the footsteps of Procne's and my mythical namesakes. Unlike the Greek myth, revenge and murder had not entered our lives.

When Procne phoned and said, "I'm tired," I knew something was up...she never complained. "I'm tired of pretending," she said. "What's love anyway?"

"It's passion, admiration, respect." The words flowed from my lips with ease.

"I loved Larry, but he never loved me."

"I wonder if he loves himself," I said.

For the next week our cellphones and emails burned. Ad nauseam we exchanged views on relationships in general and hers and Larry's in particular. To my credit, I refrained from offering advice. It turned out she didn't need any.

For twelve years Procne and Larry had jointly owned the Maui condominium. They had used it together and separately, mostly separately. Procne occasionally came by herself or with their two children or with female friends. Who knew who came with Larry?

This year they had planned to enjoy a family Christmas on Maui—until Procne reached her breaking point. The restful holiday plans were replaced by stressful activities such as visiting lawyers and putting their goods and chattels on the Vancouver market. Instead of relaxing together they were living apart and haggling hellishly.

Her collapsing world prompted Procne to suggest that Brent and I use the condo for the holiday season. Miracle of miracles, Larry agreed. So here I was, enjoying wonderful weather and anticipating the arrival of the man who for me made heaven on earth.

The downside was a twinge of guilt: first because Procne was sad; second because Brent was detained by an unexpected business commitment; and third because I was truly enjoying the quiet interlude.

A rumbling noise disturbed my rumination. Thunder? Surely not. I opened my eyes and gazed up at clear blue sky fringed between gently waving palm fronds.

"Aloha," a soprano voice said.

I jerked my head to the right and stared at a woman of indeterminate age. She wore a neon green bikini and her figure though not girlish was exceedingly trim. Her unwrinkled face was a pleasing colour of wet sand and her blond hair showed no strands of white. She adjusted the chaise longue that she had noisily dragged and parked beside mine. Then she inclined her head toward me and her dark blue eyes swept over my entire body. Her head bobbed knowingly up and down.

"Just arrived, didn't you."

I nodded and sat up.

"I can tell by your white skin."

So that was how the maintenance man knew of my recent arrival. I chuckled and slid my white legs over the side of my chaise longue.

She sat down on hers and smiled pleasantly. "It's obvious you're fresh from Amerreeka."

"Canada, actually."

"Where in Canada?"

"Calgary."

"Do you by chance know a realtor by the name of Tim Jones?"

"No, I don't."

"You're lucky." She pursed her lips, shook her head and changed the subject. "I'm from Vancouver. I own a condo here," and she waved her hand indicating *Hale Sun and Surf*. She leaned forward and gazed at me. "I haven't seen you before. Do you own a condo?"

"No, I'm staying in my sister's up on the third floor. She lives in Vancouver. Maybe you know her. Procne Ellis."

"Married to Larry?"

I nodded, wondering if she knew my almost ex-brother-in-law intimately, yet afraid to ask. Like a mind-reader she answered the unspoken question.

"I met your sister once and ran into Larry several times. I didn't have much to do with him, but he took quite a shine to my daughter."

"Your daughter was young and good-looking."

"Righto." She laughed. "At age seventeen she was a knock-out. That was six years ago, and she's still good looking. I once met your sister at an Annual General Meeting for condo owners."

"They're in the process of divorcing."

"A lot of it going around. Must be contagious." She shrugged and added, "It's tough. I've gone through it twice."

"Oh, that's too bad." I shuddered involuntarily. Losing Brent, whether to divorce or death, would be the most devastating thing that could happen to me. Politely, I asked, "Do you have other children?"

"Two boys. My daughter's in Calgary. The boys are younger and they're both in Vancouver."

"I bet the divorces were hard on them."

"My daughter found the first one difficult. She probably blamed herself. Kids do that you know. Her father, Jake Rathbone, was my first husband and that divorce was messier than the next one. The second one was easier to cope with. The condo here was part of my settlement."

"That's good, I guess."

"Righto. I've enjoyed having it. Have you been to the mall yet?"

"This morning I ate breakfast at *The Wave* and bought groceries at the supermarket. Their close proximity to the condo will make for good walks."

"Yes, they're close enough for that, provided you don't buy too much heavy stuff. The mall was expanded a few years ago. The shops are well stocked and well run."

"They seem to sell a wide variety of merchandise."

"Two years ago," she said, "I considered buying a ladies' wear shop in the mall, but decided against it. Green cards and tax laws were more than I wanted to cope with. It could've been fun. I get quite enthusiastic about clothes."

"Enthusiasm's a great asset for any business."

"A clothing shop might have been lucrative. People on holidays are inclined to spend money on unnecessary things."

I nodded, even though I had no intention of buying anything unnecessary. My money would purchase groceries and not much else.

A noisy engine blasted the peaceful ambience. My new friend sat up straighter and taller and gazed toward the sound. She waved an arm and said, "That's Andrew Strong."

My eyes followed hers and rested on a big lawnmower on which sat the fair-haired young man who had adjusted the lid on the washing machine. Leone and I watched him manoeuvre around palm trees and flower beds.

"Andrew's indispensible around here," she said. Her shoulders seemed to slump as she added, "I almost had him as a son-in-law."

"Really?"

"Really. Too bad it didn't happen."

Ever the romantic, I wondered if her daughter was the lost love who had changed Andrew's future, thereby causing the sadness that recently dimmed his grey eyes. Six years ago he had come to Maui and the future looked bright. Six years ago, according to his almost-mother-in-law, Larry Ellis had become interested in her daughter....

With a contented sigh my new best friend stretched her arms and legs and lay supinely on the chaise longue. "Well, I guess I'll toast my front. See you later." She put a towel over her face and that was that.

It was just as well, for I had gleaned the bottom of my conversational barrel. I lay back and pondered Andrew Strong and his almost mother-in-law. Both were friendly and pleasant, unlike the two people with whom I had flown from Calgary to Maui.

CHAPTER 7

$\mathcal{B}$rent's grisly discovery of the bashed-in temple proved to be a setback. Our mobility and clear thinking didn't actually reverse, but it did stop improving. As if visibly aging we moved slower, looked more haggard, and like zombies stared sadly down at the victim.

I tried to concentrate on the corpse's injured temple. The abrasions and shattered bone had been caused by a violent impact. The surface of the object that inflicted the wound must have been hard or sharp or both. From the amount of blood on the sand, the blow had been destructive enough to cause death immediately or soon after. Was the injury the result of an accident or an assault?

Finding the fatal instrument might answer those questions. Was the weapon lying on the beach right now? During my morning beach walks, I had never noticed rocks lying on the sand, but I had noticed a few hard shelled coconuts that had fallen to the sand from nearby trees. A fall on one could easily have caused the fatal injury.

An intentional injury was another matter. A vicious kick from a steel-toed boot could have caused the severe injury; a rock wielded as a weapon could have done the same; even a handy tool such as a hammer or a screwdriver could have struck the fatal blow.

Who had done the deed? And why had he done it?

The weapon question remained—where was it now? Had the killer buried it or carried it home? If steel-toed boots had been used, the killer might have discarded them in a garbage bin. If the weapon had not been washed to sea, would someone find it on the beach? I intended to climb down the dune and search.

First, however, the police must be contacted. Speed was not an issue because the victim was already dead and the perpetrator long gone.

With the weapon uppermost in my mind, I automatically started to search for it here and now on top of the dune. With little effort I proceeded to walk in ever-widening circles around the motionless body. With each step I closely scrutinized the groundcover.

"What are you doing?" Brent asked.

"I'm searching for a hard object, something that could be used as a weapon." I stopped walking and turned to him. "Do you think the injury could have been caused by a violent kick in the head by someone wearing hiking or work boots?"

"It's certainly possible."

"If that were the case, the weapon might be hiding on a shoe-shelf in the murderer's closet."

"Or still be on the murderer's feet."

"Hiding the weapon in plain sight." The idea almost made the corners of my lips curve in a smile, but not quite. Irony and humour were not on the agenda. It crossed my mind that a big belly laugh would relieve the tension and soften the lingering horror. Even a gentle chuckle would be better than no laugh at all.

The power of suggestion brought to mind Mark Twain's book and his amusing impressions of Hawaii.

* * *

'... large trees with funny names and shapes; fat cats of every variety lazing around; a few people with white skin and a lot of people with dark skin.'

Twain's humorous laments about being bitten by a scorpion, attacked by hordes of mosquitoes, and reconnoitring with a centipede and a tarantula made me laugh out loud. However, I was happy those insects no longer resided in hordes on Maui. Their loss was probably due to the killing miracles of modern insecticides

The book, *MARK TWAIN IN HAWAII,* had lain helter-skelter on my chaise longue until my new best friend had draped a towel over her face. With conversation eliminated, I picked up the book and flipped to the end, page 96. The book was short but the print was small. Returning to the beginning I rapidly discovered Twain's humour was subtle, his observations enlightening, and his insight and word combinations brilliant. He brought to life his 1866 visit to the Hawaiian Islands in an amusing yet informative manner.

His descriptions of various varieties of fresh fruit made my mouth water. Automatically I looked at my wristwatch and saw another reason why my mouth watered. It was an hour past noon.

Trying not to disturb my new best friend, I dragged my chaise longue across the lawn with as little noise as possible. Compared to the engine of Andrew Strong's grass-cutting mower, it made no noise at all, however, when it struck the cement terrace the sound sounded raucous. After placing the chaise longue in its original position near the swimming pool, I strolled into the welcoming cool air of the passageway, glanced at the colourful travel brochures and soft cover books and continued to the sunlight at the other end.

I climbed the two flights of stairs with ease and on the third floor paused, pleased to discover a lack of breathlessness. While admiring my improved lung capacity, I saw a man come out of Number 308. With his back toward me he locked the door. Was it Motor-Mouth? Identification was unclear because his hair was fair and not spiky. I walked at a snail's pace and with the disingenuousness of a snoop studied his back.

With the lock secured, he turned and I sucked in a big breath of air. He resembled Motor-Mouth not one iota, neither hippy nor businessman. He was taller, slimmer, neater, and better looking. As we approached each other I behaved with friendly Canadian candour and gave him a broad smile. "Aloha," I said, "another beautiful day in paradise."

"It is indeed." His response to my corny salutation was accompanied by a wide smile.

As we passed each other, I noted his fair hair was actually light brown sprinkled with white. He looked to be in his mid or late fifties. Of course age and appearance are often deceiving; he could have been years younger or older.

One thing was certain: like Motor-Mouth, he was much older than the beauty from Calgary. Her presence in the room earlier today still puzzled me. She obviously had a penchant for father figures; both Motor-Mouth and this man exceeded her age by twenty years or more. This one, however, seemed more personable, more gentlemanly, and more appealing than the tattooed loudmouth at the restaurant. I mentally hoped the girl had dumped Motor-Mouth and hooked up with this man.

Inside Number 309, I made a ham and lettuce sandwich, cut up part of a fresh pineapple and put everything on one big plate. I carried them out to the green plastic table on the lanai, sat down in the shade. While eating I read more of Mark Twain's amusing nineteenth century travelogue. If only I could write as well and as humorously as he had done.

At that moment I had a brilliant epiphany—for my quarterly magazine I would write an article comparing Mark Twain's Hawaii with mine. The one hundred and forty-four year difference could make it funny yet interesting. It would fit the magazine's eclectic format.

The contents of *The Integrator*, besides advertisements and local news, favoured no particular belief or philosophy. All subjects, within reason of course, could be included in the magazine. Sometimes I lamented that the diverse themes made me a dabbler in everything and a master of nothing.

The astounding thing was that my magazine had survived almost twenty years. Something was being done right. Its success, though limited, created little reason for change. It was not a fortune maker, but it covered the costs of printing, mailing, taxes, paying occasional writers and artists and other basic expenses. It also earned enough to keep me supplied with stylish shoes. Moreover, my work was play. How many people could say that about their nine to five jobs?

Brent could say it, and he often did. More than once I'd heard him brag that he seldom worked because he loved his daily engineering tasks so much. To his credit he also earned a fair amount of money doing it. He pampered me by paying for important things like housing and food. He also encouraged me to continue working, doubtless because he knew that satisfying my curiosity on various subjects and solving the challenges of writing, editing, and publishing kept me happy.

Sitting on the lanai for almost two hours, I giggled at Mark Twain's observations. Occasionally I jotted pertinent information on a sheet of paper for future use. When the western sun dropped low enough to send its beams onto me, a threat of sunburn warned me to escape its hot rays. Glancing over the railing, I noted all the sunbathers had disappeared, probably for an iced tea or a Mai Tai. The only human activity occurred in the swimming pool: a rotund granny wearing a one piece black swimsuit and three young children attired in matching yellow bikinis splashed and laughed. They were having a grand time.

I left them to their fun, went inside the condo and stretched out on the sofa. I perused more of Twain's Hawaiian travelogue. Fascinating though it was, a combination of yesterday's flight, the three hour time change, and the drop in altitude from Calgary's thirty-five hundred feet to Maui's sea level was more fascinating. Sleep came easily.

CHAPTER 8

𝒲alking at a slow pace I circled the body and studied it closely. I circled it a second time and closely examined the groundcover. During my third walk around it I bent over, locked my hands behind my back and tried to see under the leaves. Nothing untoward caught my attention.

Would a killer carry a weapon up the dune? Or would he throw it in the sea and hope the undertow would carry it to Japan? Would lugging a body be burden enough without adding the weight of a weapon? Was searching for a weapon up here a waste of time and energy?

The urge to search stayed with me. I widened my circle and with the toes of my flip-flops shifted leaves to see what lay underneath. Finally, feeling frustrated, I stopped walking and stared zombie-like at the green carpet.

In that split second the corner of my eye glimpsed a glimmer of white. The rising sun shone on something nestled amongst the greenery. I hurried over to it. For a solid second I behaved and felt like a real detective.

The object lay partially hidden under wide, glossy leaves. It was out of place, and if the sun had not gleamed on it at that precise second it would have gone unnoticed. With a sense of anticipation I squatted on my heels and stretched my fingers to pick it up. Fortunately, Brent's fingerprint warning leaped to mind and stayed my hand in midair. Plastic gloves would have been useful, but of course none were available. My fingers touched neither the white object nor the greenery growing around it. One groundcover leaf seemed a bit bruised; three other undamaged ones spread neatly over the object. It had been hidden with care.

The object was a lump of white coral about the size of a newborn's head. Several jagged points jutting from the centre would make it easy to grasp with one hand. There was no doubt in my mind—it could easily have created a head injury severe enough to cause death. I saw no blood on it. Doubtless the killer had wiped it clean.

"Brent," I yelled, "Come here!"

He had just started to go down the dune, so his legs were already on the other side of the rim. The excitement in my voice made him halt his descent. He gazed over at me and quickly reversed direction. He climbed back up and hurried toward me.

"What are you looking at?" he asked.

"A hunk of white coral. I think it might be the murder weapon."

He squatted beside me, peered under the greenery and studied the partially hidden object. "You may be right."

"Someone carried it up the dune."

"Mm mm. The million dollar question remains. Who did it?"

I had a million dollar answer, but I refrained from mentioning it because it was based on intuition. I understood that most violent murders are committed by members of the male persuasion, so my prime suspect was a man. Women, being wilier, subtler, and neater, usually choose weapons such as poison or a timely push over a cliff. However, I had to admit my expertise on the subject was limited. One could honestly say it was non-existent.

Since arriving on Maui, I had encountered several men, five of whom knew the victim and were fit enough to carry the corpse up the dune. Could one of them have committed the abominable act?

* * *

I was disappointed that my good-looking neighbour and the handsome maintenance man failed to appear. On the other hand I was relieved not to see Motor-Mouth.

It was Monday morning and tropical birdsong had awakened me, a much pleasanter sound than the screeching alarm clock at home. Cool juice had treated my morning hypoglycemia before I had donned shorts and T-shirt and flip-flops.

Traversing the stairs and passageway, I saw no sign of the three men. However, on the path I peripherally glimpsed a white rectangle sprinkled with black squiggles. I hurried past it but curiosity took hold so I stopped and stepped backward. Large black letters reminded me of signs in the Rocky Mountains warning skiers and hikers of snow avalanches. This sign, of course, was no avalanche warning. It was a water hazard warning, advising beach bums and swimmers to watch for unexpected dangers.

Giving the words little thought, I strode on the soft dry sand of the beach. Two people promenaded past me near the water and I copied them by taking off my flip-flops and moving onto damp sand where walking was easier. The sun had not risen above the dormant volcano, but the air was warm and the walk was enjoyable. It was a wonderful way to start a new day.

Early Tuesday morning I followed the same routine, except this time I stopped and read the entire warning sign. The hair on the back of my neck flicked nervously as I contemplated the meaning of the words:

> **WARNING**: *The Ocean is always hazardous under any condition and may cause serious bodily injury and sometimes death. At all times use extreme caution when approaching the Ocean. Anyone swimming in the Ocean assumes the risk with such actions.*

I absorbed this water wisdom and agreed that land lubbers like me needed to be reminded of ocean dangers. The Pacific appeared beautiful, soothing, and safe, making one forget that surprises lurked under the sea and on the shore. There could be man-eating sharks, stinging jellyfish, strong currents, and unexpected undertows, to say nothing of a swimmer's own physical limitations. On the shore other dangers existed such as sharp rocks, jagged coral, rogue waves, and gigantic tsunamis.

My thoughts lingered only a few seconds on tsunamis because they are monitored by trained human beings and scientific devices. Warnings are supposed to give residents time to dash from lower to higher areas before water engulfs them.

Stepping on a sharp rock or a hunk of coral could injure a foot and trigger a bad infection; that danger, however, could be avoided by visual attention. Rogue waves materializing from nowhere could sweep an unsuspecting beachcomber out to sea; but they seldom occurred, so why dwell on them? I forgot the dangers and once again enjoyed my beach walk.

On Wednesday morning I again awoke with the birds, drank juice, and on the outside corridor hoped to casually meet the handsome man from Number 308. Once again he did not appear. Nor did Andrew Strong or Motor-Mouth.

After exiting the beach access path, I admired the dome of blue above me and the ebbing water in front of me. High on the sand lay debris scattered from a recent high tide. I recognized green seaweed and small pieces of white coral. They were abundant, artistic, and not hazardous to walkers.

I strolled barefoot on the damp sand, greeted other walkers and avoided stepping on nature's works of art. The surf rose, broke, flowed up the beach, lost power and dropped under the next oncoming wave. It was mesmerising.

The hypnotic effect faded when an unusually large build-up of water sharpened my focus. This larger, non-normal wave crashed loudly on shore and with unusual force rose over my calves and splashed my knees. I almost lost my balance. I smiled. This may have been a rogue wave, but it was a small, harmless ones.

The sun peeked over Maui's extinct volcano and the increasing glare made me think about bringing sunglasses on my next promenade. Fellow walkers, male and female alike, waved and said "Good morning" or "Aloha," and their faces were wreathed in happy smiles. I cheerily returned their greetings.

Three people standing on the sand proved exceptions to these acts of friendliness. Two tall men and a slim girl adorned in a pink bikini failed to notice me at all. The two men stood side by side and gazed at the girl as if entranced by her. She stood with feet apart and hands on hips and listened with rapt attention to the words of one of the men.

The speaker's slim body, round rimmed eye glasses, and shock of white hair gave him a distinguished, intellectual appearance. His male companion had a more universal crown of brown hair, and though nice looking would fail to stand out in a crowd. The young girl caught and held my attention. I understood her companions' apparent interest in her. She was the drop-dead gorgeous girl with violet eyes.

I felt uneasy. Our paths had crossed in the lavatory, departure lounge, business class, third floor of *Hale Sun and Surf*, and now here on the beach. Five times in all. Maybe our destinies really were intertwined.

As usual, the girl was associating with father figures. I wondered if as a youngster her real father had somehow failed her, forcing her to a never ending search for a paternal substitute. The words of the white haired man must have struck an important chord within her for she moved closer to him, listened rapturously and slowly nodded her head, oblivious to the rest of the world. She was unaware of me, even when I moved closer and gave an unneeded throat-clearing and a loud, phoney cough. The white-haired man glanced briefly in my direction then turned his attention back to the girl. I leaned toward him, trying to hear his words, but his voice was too soft. The younger man gazed at the girl with nary a glance in my direction.

I took another step closer to them, but surf sounds obliterated their conversation. I coughed two more times to no avail. As far as they were concerned I might as well have been a grain of sand.

I lingered as long as seemed politely possible then walked on. Approaching the distinctive black rock point, I slowed my pace and glanced back. The threesome still stood on the sand, intent on their discussion. I sailed forward and left them and the black rocks in my wake.

Though the taller man had appeared familiar, actual memory of him evaded me. Then, at the end of the bay a bolt of recognition struck me. Both men had been at the restaurant on the first morning of my vacation. Sitting at the table next to mine, they had been joined by Motor-Mouth with his tattoos, beer and cigarette.

The two men knew Motor-Mouth. Ominously, they also knew the gorgeous young girl. I wondered if they knew the good looking man in Number 308.

I retraced my steps. Passing the point of black rocks I looked ahead. The chatting threesome had disappeared as if by a gust of wind. I walked to the area of their recent sojourn and found no footprints in the sand. A large wave had washed their prints from the face of the earth.

The rising sun cast its warm rays on the back of my head and shoulders and with a sprightly gait I walked toward *Hale Sun and Surf*. A handsome couple strolled gracefully ahead of me and I noted how the girl's suntanned skin contrasted nicely with her pink bikini. The two older men had been replaced by a fair-haired man who moved with the litheness of youth. The two young people made a cheery picture, glancing at each other and chatting.

Suddenly they stopped walking. They faced each other and I recognized Andrew Strong. Their bodies grew stiff and their gestures indicated annoyance. The relaxed picture they initially made changed to annoyance, tenseness then anger. Their voices increased in volume but surf sounds drowned out their words. She raised her right hand and angrily struck his chest with such force he jerked backwards. She struck him a second time and he yelled at her and raised his arm and his biceps visibly flexed; I feared he intended to strike her and his strength could have caused her severe injury. Fortunately, he refrained. Even at a distance their anger was something to behold.

I wanted to intervene and make everything right between them. With a touch of embarrassment I recognized my role as being that of a peeping Tom, not a fixer. I hated witnessing their emotional upset, but as adults they would seek help or solve the problem themselves.

I tore my eyes from them and entered the beach access path. When my bare feet reached the freshly cut grass I thought of Andrew, his muscular physique and his sad eyes. I washed my feet under the tap and admired the grass and flower beds. The condo owners were lucky to have such a capable employee. I hoped he and the girl would reunite and be as happy in their union as I was in mine with Brent.

The early morning promenades on Monday and Tuesday had left me feeling at peace with the world. Wednesday's walk left me thinking about the young girl and her acquaintances: the white-haired gentleman, his brown-haired friend, the youthful Andrew Strong, my neighbour in Number 308, and of course Motor-Mouth. The girl and the five men made for interesting rumination. Thoughts of them fell away as I ran up the two flights of stairs. I was physically fit and felt mentally at peace.

Thursday's walk, however, would produce different results, disturbingly different.

CHAPTER 9

𝓑rent leaned over the groundcover and examined the coral beneath the glossy green leaves. Sensing my scrutiny he looked up. "It's a miracle you saw this."

"Sunbeams get the credit, not I."

"Coral doesn't belong here. A rogue wave couldn't have washed it this high."

"No," I agreed, "but a tsunami could."

"When was Maui's last tsunami?"

"Centuries ago."

"Exactly. A bird might have carried it, thinking it was a shell with food inside."

"It's rather big for a bird to carry," I said.

"Well...that hunk of coral didn't climb up here on its own."

"You're dead on." The touch of black humour made the corners of my lips twitch slightly upward. Then I stated the obvious, "The murderer, or murderers, carried the coral up the dune and hid it under the leaves."

"It would have been easier to toss it in the ocean."

"Easier, yes. But a big wave could wash it ashore again, and the beach is a busy place. Hundreds of people walk on it every day. How many climb to the top of a sand dune?"

"One. And that one person has eyes of an eagle." Brent stood up straight and gazed directly at my face. "You'll have to show the coral and explain your suspicions to the police."

"Oh, the police." I had forgotten about them.

"I'll go and contact them right now."

"Do you think I have the makings of a detective?" I asked.

"Gawd, I hope not." He groaned and walked to the rim of the dune

The idea of a new career lingered in my mind. I had found the body and discovered the probable weapon. Could a real detective have done more?

But the mystery remained unsolved. Who had murdered the victim?

* * *

Early Thursday morning, murder was not part of my lexicon, but holiday relaxation was. As usual, the day started peacefully. I drank juice, donned clean khaki shorts and took my habitual route to the damp sand and sparkling waves. I greeted other walkers and appreciated everything around me.

Until I reached the black rock promontory.

On top of one of the largest rocks a man sat in a slouching position. He coughed loudly and repeatedly. His tight T-shirt might once have been white but now was spotted with dull grey smudges. His face, too, was grey, a ghastly, ghostly grey. His hacking coughs made me think of pneumonia, tuberculosis and his immediate survival. Because he seemed mentally dejected and physically incapacitated, I slowed my stride. Confident he needed help, I moved toward him.

He coughed again and then leaned forward so his head almost rested on a rock. A spasm shook his whole body and he retched. A second later vomit spewed from his mouth and sprayed nearby rocks.

Alarmed, I stopped in my tracks and stared at him. He needed help—that was for sure—so I again moved forward, intent on saving his life. Like a true heroine I reached the rocks and started to scramble on top of them. If nothing else, I could support his body and help move him to the smooth sand where he could lie down. But would I be strong enough to support his weight if his legs failed him? It crossed my mind that the prudent thing to do would be to dash off and find someone imbued with strength and knowledgeable in first aid.

He solved my dilemma by straightening his slouch, glancing over at me and shaking his head. He wiped his mouth on his arm and waved me away.

"Are you okay?" I asked.

"I'm fine," he replied.

"Maybe you should see a doctor."

"I don't need a doctor."

Reluctant to leave him, I waited. His cough had ceased, at least temporarily, and he no longer retched. I stood on a large rock and then, still worried about his welfare, moved forward again. The vomiting seemed to have settled his digestive tract and he looked a bit better, less grey, and he no longer coughed. He shifted position, sat upright and again shook his head at me.

"Go away," he said. His message was clear: he wanted me to mind my own business.

Twenty-four hour flu or bad food could have caused his stomach upset. A head cold or an itchy throat could have triggered his hacking cough. For some unknown reason none of my diagnostic suggestions rang true, but nothing else came to mind. Whatever his problem, my assistance was unwanted and probably unneeded. I scrambled off the rocks and slowly walked away. With a backward glance I saw him sit upright.

Following the curve of sand, I reached a long, flat area and looked back again. The rocky point and the man were no longer visible. I tried to focus on the pleasant people promenading on the beach and responded in like manner to their cheery "Alohas" and "Good mornings." My holiday spirit returned and I strode energetically toward a young girl walking awkwardly toward me. She moved as if the global positioning system in her inner ears was tuned to the wrong satellite.

Her movements consisted of unbalanced jerks. Her head bobbed from side to side and her arms swung askew except when she wiped her hands on the sides of her short, denim skirt. Her skirt had a frill on the bottom and her smudged sleeveless top had top buttons unbuttoned. Both shirt and skirt needed a good washing.

We came abreast of each other and I said, "Good morning."

She lowered her head toward the sand and a tangle of brunette hair that needed to be combed flopped over her eyes and hid most of her face. Barely glancing at me she stumbled and almost fell against my arm. She regained her balance, glared at me and moved on. She wiped her hands on her denim skirt as if trying to dry them. I wondered if she was hungover from too much partying the night before. I shrugged and continued walking.

Reaching the point of land at the end of the bay, I turned around and started to retrace my steps. At the straight, level stretch of beach I again saw the young girl. She too had turned around and was pacing awkwardly toward me. As before, she gazed down at the sand and gave little indication of seeing me. This time I refrained from speaking, but I slowed my pace and silently studied her. Her hair fell to her shoulders in a tangled mess; the skirt and top, though wrinkled and dirty, were well made and had once been a cute outfit. Her general appearance was dirty and unkempt. She continued to wipe her hands on her skirt. As we came abreast she raised her head and I noted sores on her forehead and cheeks. She looked directly at me. I stopped walking, intending to speak, but instead gazed speechlessly into her vivid violet eyes. They resembled two windows open to an empty room. It was as if no one lived there.

At that moment a large wave swept from the ocean and broke over the sand. Seeing it coming, I braced my legs and feet. It smashed against my calves, knees and thighs and almost knocked me down. I regained my balance in time to see the young girl, taken by complete surprise, topple sideways. Her outstretched right hand fell into the water and eased her fall somewhat. The wave receded and she staggered to her feet, apparently unaware her skirt was soaking wet. She glared at me and moved away.

I walked a bit farther, but curiosity got the better of me so I stopped and turned around. She also had turned around and was staggering toward me. Except for her unsteady balance she reminded me of a worried person pacing back and forth. Her hands wiped her skirt. Her bare feet indented the smooth sand as each step brought her closer. Watching her slim body approach me I felt an urge to run away.

"Good morning," I said and smiled.

She paused a second, took two steps closer and leaned forward.

I saw an oozing sore on her lower lip, another above her right eyebrow, plus the ones I had noticed on her cheeks and forehead. She stepped closer, invading my space until the gap between us almost closed completely. She peered into my face with eyes that were no longer empty. The formerly vacant eyes now flashed with fury.

"Why are you following me?" she snapped, and her voice was husky and threatening. "What do you want?"

Startled, I stepped back from her and said, "I don't want anything and I'm not following you." Feeling a pang of nervousness, I added, "Like you, I'm just out for a pleasant walk on the beach."

"I keep seeing you. Are you a policewoman?"

"Good grief, no."

She wiped her hands on her skirt then shook her right forefinger close to my nose. "Are you looking for ice?"

I chuckled. This was better, she was being humorous. "I left ice and snow in Calgary," I said.

"Ice is available on Maui. If you want some I can get it. I know someone who sells it cheap." She raised both hands. They glistened as though damp and sweaty. She lowered them and wiped them against the sides of her damp denim skirt.

"On a hot day, ice enhances a cool drink," I said.

"You're making fun of me."

"No I'm not."

"You are so."

With surprising swiftness her right hand doubled into a fist and shot towards my head. My alerted reflexes prompted me to lean sideways, but not quite far enough. With amazing force, her fist struck my left shoulder.

I gasped, jumped away and clutched my shoulder. "What's wrong with you?" I asked.

"You. That's what's wrong."

She pirouetted on the hard sand and stumbled away.

I watched her unsteady departure. Rubbing my sore shoulder, I puzzled over her behaviour. Why did she think I was following her? Why did she think I was a policewoman out to get her? Why did she want to sell me ice when I could get it from the condo fridge? Her accusations indicated mild paranoia. Her vicious attempt to strike my head was psychotic.

Several minutes earlier she had been pacing awkwardly back and forth like a person trying to solve a major dilemma. Then she had deemed ice as being important, Why would anyone worry about something as commonplace as frozen water?

Her appearance also disturbed me. Today she looked completely different from the girl I had seen in the airport. On that occasion she had been well groomed and her complexion had seemed clear and smooth, though it could have been enhanced with blemish-cover-up. In the airport lavatory she had washed her hands frequently in the sink and today she kept wiping them on her denim skirt. Even yesterday on the beach, while talking with the two men and then with Andrew Strong, she had looked attractive and neat, at least from a distance. Her behaviour had been polite until she and Andrew began to quarrel. Today, up close, she was not only unkempt and grubby, but she had sores on her face that were beyond the help of blemish cover-up; she behaved like a troubled, aggressive street person, or worse, like someone demented.

I watched her awkwardly walk away. She pirouetted with the grace of a toddler and proceeded to pace toward me. Having no desire to be accused again of following her or to risk receiving another blow, I turned and quick stepped in the direction of the black rock point. One strike on the shoulder was enough; it throbbed painfully. Feeling uncomfortable, dismayed and nervous, I shook my head and increased my speed.

Approaching the black rock promontory, I saw the weird man still sitting on top of one of the larger rocks. His facial complexion had lost its ghastly grey colour and looked reasonably rosy, his arms seemed tanned, and his digestive upset was in abeyance. There was no racking cough.

His right hand fluttered like a butterfly. His left hand held something, a wad of greenish paper, that his right hand flicked like an automatic money counter. At first I could not take my eyes from the US bills, but when I looked up at his rosy face I wondered if his flush resulted from good health and warm sunshine or from too much booze. Maybe a prescribed medication. Whatever the reason, his color and demeanour indicated a total recovery from his former illness. He stopped counting and called out to me.

"Did you see my girlfriend back there?"

Feeling a renewed twinge of nervousness, I slowed my pace. "Was she wearing a white top and a denim skirt?"

"That's her."

"She's walking on the beach." I refrained from mentioning that her movements resembled a troubled pacer rather than a healthy walker, and I certainly did not mention her illogical accusations or her act of physical violence. His nodded response made me shudder. My nervousness increased.

He said no more, just continued to sit and stare at me. Then he put the wad of US bills in the pocket of his shorts and tossed something in the water. The something resembled a syringe. That was when I knew for sure his arms were not tanned but were covered with tattoos. My heart beat louder and faster against my chest and the feeling of nervousness almost overwhelmed me. I resumed walking, faster and faster. Once again I wanted only to be far away from him.

How could the neat couple I saw in Calgary become so disreputable in such a short time?

Though the two people disappeared from my sight, they did not disappear from my thoughts. I especially worried about the girl...she was obviously in trouble and I suspected she knew it. Why else was she pacing and stumbling back and forth? Why was she suspicious of me? Why had she struck me? Reaching the beach access path en-route to my home away from home, I still thought about the weird couple. I stopped between the sand dunes and read the printing on the back of the ocean warning sign:

"SECURITY NOTICE: Video surveillance in use on these premises."

Below the words was a picture of the three story condominium in which I presently lived. The sign had been reassuring when I read it a couple of days ago. Today I found it troubling and rather ominous.

CHAPTER 10

"Here come some people," Brent said.

He stood with both legs over the rim of the dune, having already started his downward climb. A few minutes ago his descent had been thwarted by my discovery of white coral. Now it was derailed by the approach of two people walking on the beach.

"They look fairly young," he said, moving to the top of the dune. "Maybe they'll have a cellphone and be able to contact the police for us."

"Most young people do have them. Unless of course they're like us and leave them at home." I moved away from the well hidden coral, reached the rim and stopped beside him. Gazing down at the man and woman who walked with youthful vigour near the water, I said, "They're definitely younger than the couple whose help we tried to recruit earlier."

In a loud voice Brent yelled, "Hello you two on the beach. Hello. Hello" He waved his arms wildly above his head.

They stopped walking and in unison glanced at the empty stretch of sand.

Brent waved his arms and yelled again, "Hey you two. We're up here, on top of a sand dune."

The man looked up, saw us, and waved his right arm in response.

"Do you have a cellphone?" Brent called.

"Yes," the man answered.

"Do you have it with you?"

"I do." He walked toward us and the girl followed.

I felt incredible relief. The gods were with us. The man's voice sounded familiar and at first that seemed a good omen. From a distance he looked like thousands of other tanned, fair-haired, well built men. The girl seemed very young and her slim figure was neatly attired in fashionable red shorts and a red and white top. She could have been a sportswear model.

"That's great." Brent no longer yelled. "Could you call the police?"

"The police?" The man's surprise was apparent. He slowed his pace and repeated, "Why do you want the police?"

"We need the police to help us."

The man pulled a cellphone from his belt and asked, "What will I tell them?"

"Tell them we have a dead body up here."

"What?" The man stopped walking and stared up at us. He replaced the phone on his belt and stood still as a sandstone statue. He obviously doubted Brent's sanity.

"If you don't believe me," Brent said, "climb up and have a look."

The man maintained his statuesque pose and simply stared at us. I could almost hear his thoughts debating the pros and cons of getting too close to the two weirdoes on the dune.

"My wife found a dead body." Brent's tone of voice was gentler, softer, and more reassuring. Almost pleading, he added, "We really need help. We need the police."

"He thinks we're muggers," I muttered. "Or druggies."

* * *

The young girl was drugged or ill, or both. My mind's eye saw her pace desperately back and forth on the beach, glare angrily at me, and thrust her fist toward my head. No matter how hard I tried to get rid of the vision, it continued to torment me.

I tried to concentrate on the book, MARK TWAIN IN HAWAII, but the revolting scene on the beach kept superimposing itself over the author's sentences.

It was a sad state of affairs when Mark Twain's humour failed to banish an unpleasant thought. Visions of the girl faded slightly only to be replaced by recollections of the middle-aged man sitting on the big black rock, vomiting, counting wads of money, and tossing a syringe in the ocean.

The day-mare continued to blur letters of the book into meaningless gibberish. Were they enhanced by my recently consumed breakfast? Fruit, yogurt and toast had been eaten more for comfort than for sustenance and now they sat like a heavy lump in my stomach.

Was I becoming a compulsive eater as well as a reading failure? Would an obesity problem affect my happy marriage? Would losing the ability to read wreck my humble career? In the past, eating and reading were normal, enjoyable activities that I took for granted. One nourished my body and the other nourished my mind. Both provided brief escapes from mundane happenings.

Now my ability to concentrate was nil. Adult Attention Deficit Disorder as well as Dyslexia caused reading problems. Did one of them afflict me? I shrugged my burdened shoulders and leaned back in the green plastic chair. I tossed the paperback book on the table and closed my eyes. Jumbled thoughts, mostly negative, flitted amongst my little grey cells. Suddenly one thought made sense—attempt a different activity.

I opened my eyes and picked up pen and paper. Seeking inspiration, I glanced whimsically at the rolling sea then focused on the blank paper and started to write.

My intent was to write a scintillating article for *The Integrator*. I would bring to life my earlier idea of comparing Mark Twain's Hawaii one-hundred and forty-four years ago with my Hawaii today. It should be easy to write and the end result should be amusing to read. Black squiggles appeared on the white paper with what I hoped was logic and wit. With luck, the story-line would be perfect and no future revision or editing would be necessary.

A few minutes later I read what I had written: dots, dashes, and poorly constructed sentences. The muse had deserted me. My concentration had the lifespan of one of Zeus's thunderbolts. My breakfast still sat like a lump in the pit of my stomach and my mind's eye still saw images of two unsavoury people on the beach. Writing had not solved my problem.

Unable to read or write properly, I decided to do something radically different. Search for the distraction of other people and other surroundings.

Donned in a sundress, a pair of old sandals and a sunhat, I locked the door of Number 309, walked briskly down the stairs, through the parking lot, and crossed the street. I strolled on the sidewalk to the shopping mall.

At the big hardware store I paused and looked through a window. Everything a homeowner could possibly need was there. Approaching the front entrance, I noticed a man stride up to the open double doors and disappear inside. The reason he caught my attention was because his height, fair curly hair and purposeful movements created a powerful feeling of déjà-vu.

Was my imagination again running amuck?

He reminded me of Glenn Shaw, a man to whom I had been briefly engaged. Our relationship had ended abruptly, but my emotional suffering had lasted longer—a month. Then I appreciated my luck in being free of him.

Was Glenn on Maui? I sloughed the notion aside. Thousands of good-looking men resembled him. Besides, I was reaching the indeterminate age when complete strangers reminded me of past acquaintances. If Glenn were here, what did it matter? That youthful fling was long gone and so was any residual of love and hurt.

Leaving the hardware store behind me, I wandered past other shops and glanced at other people bustling about their business. Window displays abounded with evergreen trees and festive decorations, yet they failed to entice me to darken their doors. Suddenly, a particular window display caught my interest. Shoes were scattered strategically around a silver Christmas tree and the footwear looked too wonderful to ignore.

I was not a shopaholic, however, if the tendency developed, five hundred shoes would fill my closet. I opened the door of the shop and a bell tingled. I stepped inside.

A clerk responded to the warning bell by moving from behind a counter. She approached me and her face wreathed in a smile. "Good morning," she said. "It's another lovely day in Paradise."

"Indeed it is." I grinned, pleased to find someone who understood and spoke my language of mundane aphorisms.

Her smile grew wider. "If you need any help, just ask."

I thanked her and she returned to her place behind the counter. Left on my own to browse, I studied the merchandise. The enticing shoes, neatly displayed on shelves and tables, were of excellent quality with the majority appealing to my personal tastes. Absorption in footwear happily occupied my mind, eliminating the thoughts that earlier had been so disturbing.

My focus on a leather sandal with green and brown straps precluded awareness of another customer entering the store. My concentration shattered at the sound of a soprano voice.

"I've been thinking about those Birkenstocks."

The voice was familiar, but its owner was not. I studied the back of a blond-haired woman who was taller than me and was wearing an orange top and matching flared pants. She looked bright and dramatic but I was unable to identify her.

"So you've made a decision?" the clerk asked.

"Righto. A positive decision."

My memory twigged.

"Good for you," the clerk said.

"After leaving here yesterday I ran into my daughter's boyfriend. I didn't even know he was here." Her shoulders raised and fell in a shrug as if discounting the incident. "I don't like him much," she admitted, then with a chuckle that sounded more nervous than happy she added, "I decided I needed solace. Birkenstocks won't solve my problems, but they'll certainly divert them."

The clerk nodded sympathetically. "A new pair of shoes works every time. Not only do they beautify the feet, they lift the spirits better than alcohol or anti-depressants."

Alcohol I could understand, but to me anti-depressants were an unknown commodity. Both women laughed as if they knew both subjects well. The customer took a shoe from the display shelf, held it up and said, "I need a size eight."

"Coming right up." The clerk disappeared into the bowels of the shop and promptly returned carrying a box. She opened it and carefully took out two sandals.

I continued to study the back of the customer. Was she the sunbathing condo owner I had talked with on the lawn? My new best friend from Vancouver? If so, she looked vastly different. The orange outfit of flared pants and loose shirt contrasted sharply with that of the skimpy, neon green bikini. As she sat down on a small bench I glimpsed and recognized her profile.

"Do you still carry Roots shoes?" she asked.

"Sometimes," the clerk replied. "They're Canadian, you know."

"I know. So am I," the customer said.

Though not part of the conversation, I spontaneously piped up, "Me too."

The clerk glanced at me and smiled. The customer turned her head and with furrowed brows stared at me. After a few seconds the furrow faded and recognition spread across her face. "I met you someplace," she said.

I chuckled. "Sunbathing at *Hale Sun and Surf.*"

"Righto. You're the white-skinned lady. You look so different in a sun dress instead of a bathing suit. You're from Calgary."

"I am. And you're from Vancouver.'"

She nodded and asked, "Are you enjoying your vacation?"

Because the weird couple had been dismissed from my thoughts, I replied honestly, "Very much. I'm getting freckles and so far no sunburn."

The two women laughed. Even though both were brown as berries they seemed to understand sunburns and freckles.

I picked up the sandal with green and brown straps and looked questioningly at the clerk. "I can't figure out the size on this shoe. Do you have them in a seven?"

The clerk walked over and took the shoe from me, glanced at the tiny print inside and nodded her head. "This is a size seven."

I sat down, slipped my old sandal from my right foot, put on a nylon sock provided by the store, and eased my foot into the new shoe. It fit like a comfortable glove. I stood up, took a few steps, and it still felt comfortable.

"Earth shoes are great," my new best friend said while studying my foot. "You should buy those. The style looks good on your foot. Slim and neat. I wish I could wear that type of shoe."

In the end, we both bought new shoes, she her Birkenstocks and I my Earths. As we went out the door together she asked, "Would you be interested in joining me for a cup of coffee?"

"Yes, I'd like to."

"The coffee shop across the way is good." She waved toward a patio near the Tattoo Parlour.

"The Internet Coffee House," I said, having noticed it earlier.

"Computers. They're nothing but trouble. I avoid them as much as possible."

"A lot of people think that way."

"You don't?"

"I use computers in my business."

"What sort of business?"

"A magazine. Published quarterly."

"That sounds terribly intellectual."

"It's not." I laughed merrily. "I can hardly wait to tell my husband you think I might be intellectual."

We entered the shop, ignored the computers, and at the counter ordered coffee. She insisted on paying for both. After carrying our steaming mugs to a small table out on the patio, we sat down and looked at each other.

"You can buy next time," she said and raised her mug. "Here's to a great holiday."

"And to our new shoes." We both grinned and sipped the hot liquid. "Thanks for the brew," I said, "It's very good."

She took another sip then said, "If I remember correctly, you're related to Larry Ellis." I nodded my head and she continued speaking. "We didn't exchange names. Mine's Leone, Leone Humphries."

"Not Rathbone?"

"You have a good memory. That was my first husband."

"I'm Philomela Nightingale."

"Philomela? What an odd name. How did you get it?"

"It's based on a Greek myth. My maternal grandfather was Greek. In the myth, Philomela was a young girl who was transformed into a nightingale. My mother, after marrying a man with the surname of Nightingale, put the two names together and gave them to me."

"How interesting. So being turned into a nightingale was Philomela's claim to fame?"

"She was also an accomplice in a murder."

Leone's eyes widened and her mouth fell open, momentarily speechless. Finally finding her voice she said, "You mean you're actually named after a murderer?"

"That's right."

"How awful."

"Revenge is the basis of the myth and murder is its method."

She stared at me and then said, "With your red hair and light complexion I never would have suspected you of having Greek ancestry."

"My Scottish and English genes are predominant."

She chuckled. "My ancestors are boring WASPs. Four generations ago they came to Canada from London and Devon and who knows where else." She picked up her mug, took a long sip then set it on the table. She glanced at her wristwatch.

"You have an appointment?" I asked.

"Not really, not until seven this evening." She smiled. "I have a dinner date with a good friend. We're going to the Vietnamese Restaurant on the other side of the mall."

"Mmm, I noticed it on my way here."

"It's a nice place, if you like that kind of food."

"I do."

"My friend is another condo owner at *Hale Sun and Surf*. That's how we met. His wife of many years died of breast cancer three years ago. It was sad. They were devoted to each other. Their marriage was one of those rare, truly happy ones. The first winter after her death he wandered around like a lost soul, not interested in anything or anybody. He was better last year and he's even better this year. He's a broker in Vancouver."

I was tempted to ask if she was aiming to nab him as her third husband, but bit my tongue, unnecessarily as it turned out for she more or less anticipated the question.

"I'm not sure I want to marry again. If I was so inclined, he would be a good catch."

"Whatever will be will be." I tried to sound philosophical.

"There is one thing that worries me," she said, ignoring my philosophical foray. "It is running out of money. I'd hate to live my old age on the streets."

"I have that same concern. It's called the *Bag Lady Syndrome*. I think most women have it, including wealthy ones. I understand that Oprah Winfrey and Martha Stewart suffer from it, too."

"Really? And they're both so rich."

"A paradox, isn't it."

"Incredible." Leone seemed genuinely amazed.

"Apparently more elderly men than elderly women end up on the streets."

"Interesting. Probably because many well-heeled women keep working after age sixty-five. I think I'll get a job when I return home. If anyone will hire a middle-aged broad like me."

I smiled reassuringly. "A lot of firms prefer older women because they're less likely to move away or get pregnant."

"Maybe I'll get into fashion or tourism instead of the brokerage business."

"Well you certainly have style. And you said the other day you have enthusiasm for clothes."

"Righto." She chuckled then named the brokerage firm where her friend worked, but the name flowed in one ear and out the other and disappeared like email in cyberspace. "He works on Howe Street, the business street in Vancouver. That's where a lot of important companies have their offices. I worked as a clerk for Merrill Lynch after my first divorce. That's where I met my second husband who was very charming, very handsome, and oily smooth. I was quite smitten until after we married and he took up with my daughter."

I stifled a gasp and gulped a shocked response down my throat. Instead of placing my hand over my mouth, I picked up my coffee mug and slowly sipped the dark brew. Leone certainly led an interesting life.

"He sees his two sons quite regularly and I will say this in his favour... he never quibbles about child support."

"That must be helpful to you and the children."

"Yes it is. And I ended up with the Maui condo." Remembering that I, too, had a life, she asked, "What about you? What do you do with your time?" Before I could answer, she added with a chuckle, "When you're not holidaying in Maui."

"My life's not nearly as exciting as yours. Rather boring, really. Like I said earlier, I publish a quarterly magazine."

"Righto, so you said."

"Writing, editing, gathering adverts, publishing, distributing...it keeps me busy and out of trouble."

"Does it make a lot of money?"

"No. It pays its expenses and provides me with a small salary. Fortunately, thanks to my husband, I don't have to make house or car payments."

"Do you have children?"

I shook my head.

"That saves a lot of money."

"I suppose it does."

"Is your husband successful?"

"Yes. He's a petroleum engineer."

"Your husband and my friend, Fred, would probably enjoy each other's company. We must get together for dinner sometime."

She again glanced at her wristwatch. "I really must go. I want to buy a new dress for tonight. It'll probably take a bit of looking." She giggled. "Trying on clothes is fun, but time consuming." She drained her mug, set it on the table and stood up. "See you at the condo."

"Shooting the breeze has been fun. And thanks again for the coffee."

I watched her glide around a group of pedestrians and then like an orange phantom disappear, probably into a shop that sold female fashions. I sat back, sipped my coffee and thought of Leone's successful wardrobe and her unsuccessful marriages.

CHAPTER 11

With cellphone safely re-tucked in his belt, the man gazed up at us as if trying to determine our sanity. Finally he turned and said something to his young companion, and then with measured gait walked to the base of the dune. He clambered upward in slow motion. He paused part way up as if still doubting our sanity. He seemed reluctant to closely encounter the two weird strangers peering down at him.

A close encounter with him troubled me, too, not because we were strangers but because we were not. Recognizing him, I stepped backward until I could no longer see him. The young girl who stood on the sand watching his ascent was still in my line of vision. She glanced from him to the top of the dune and nervously wrung her hands as if expecting us to pepper her with bullets. When her companion reached the top of the dune she walked to its base and disappeared from my sight.

With sophisticated grace my former fiancé stood upright and turned to Brent. Then he spotted the motionless body lying on the groundcover. With an audible gasp he did a double take. Even in profile I could see the side of his jaw drop and his cheek pale.

Brent walked over to him. "We don't know what happened here."

Glenn Shaw nodded his head, no longer doubting Brent's sanity. He pulled his cellphone from his belt, punched some numbers then spoke into the tiny piece of equipment. He listened, spoke again and then replaced the phone in his belt.

I watched the two men move toward the body. Hearing a sound behind me, I turned and saw the girl climb to the top of the dune. She looked toward her companion and at the same time spotted the corpse.

"Omigod," she uttered, and her body convulsed in a tremor and her head turned from the shocking sight. As if seeking reassurance and protection she edged closer to her companion. She fluffed her hair and adjusted her shirt—even in the presence of death she seemed to want to look good.

* * *

Looking good can lift a woman's spirits. But could looking good sweeten a sour relationship? Leone had experienced more than her fair share of sour relationships and from all appearances had weathered them with the aid of attractive attire. Now she had gone to tour the shops and add another fashion statement to her wardrobe.

I set my empty mug on the patio table, rose from the chair and picked up my purse. I carried it in one hand and in the other carried the bag containing my new Earth shoes. Having received an adequate jolt of caffeine during my sojourn with Leone, I trotted energetically along the sidewalk, intending to study the lay of the land; in other words, to study more shops.

This endeavour began with an aimless stroll past a video shop, an electronic shop, and a dollar shop. They failed to interest me, but a tiny shop called Outer Fringe struck a chord of curiosity. I walked through the open doorway and a heady smell of incense swirled up my nostrils and made me cough. After blowing my nose and clearing my throat, I looked around. The shop contained an eclectic supply of merchandize, most of it in various shades of menopausal mauve.

I moved to a rack of ladies' clothes and flicked through garments that looked fanciful, flowing, and flimsy. Unable to imagine any of them adorning my imperfect figure at a public function or even at home alone with Brent, I moved on. At a series of shelves holding scented soaps, skin lotions, shampoos and conditioners, I stopped. All these items were mauve in colour and were advertised at 20 percent off the ticketed price. A saleslady glided up to me.

She smiled sweetly and asked, "May I be of any help?"

"I'm just browsing, thanks. But I confess to being curious about the predominance of menopausal mauve."

She frowned, raised her head in an imperious manner and corrected me, "Violet. Violet is a spiritual color."

"Oh, I'm chastened. I didn't know."

The saleslady studied me a second, then with a certain reluctance explained, "The colour violet is uplifting and not physically demanding or demeaning. In a person's aura it indicates immense spirituality."

"Really?"

"Yes, really."

"Do colours in an aura affect a person physically?" I asked. "Or is it vice versa?"

"Vice versa. An individual's health, emotions, and personality affect his or her aura."

Though I was not part of an outer fringe community, many aspects of the occult interested me. "I've seen auras a couple of times," I said.

She cocked her head and with an expression of disbelief studied me. I felt the need to elaborate. "I once fell while skiing and banged my head on some ice. I saw stars. A week or so later I saw a blue aura around my husband's head."

"Oh my dear." She drew closer to me and her expression changed from disbelief to concern. "I don't recommend head banging. A better way to develop the ability to see auras is meditation."

"I don't recommend head banging either. It hurts." Then, in a whisper I confessed, "To be quite honest, I know very little about auras or meditation."

"I suspected as much." She nodded wisely and said, "Every Wednesday we teach classes about both. The price is very reasonable."

"Thank you. I'll give it some thought."

Her spirituality was strong enough to recognize a touch of insincerity in my words. She bit her lower lip and turned around and glided back to the important cash counter. I returned to the less important display of soaps and shampoos and continued to be amazed at all the different shades of mauve. Oops violet.

I sidled up to another row of shelves. These were filled with books, none of which had violet covers. I checked titles on the spines and discovered why the shop was called "Outer Fringe." Most of the books dealt with weird subjects such as holistic health, spirituality, psychic experiences, astrology, numerology, and eastern religions—topics that most of my acquaintances would categorize as belonging outside mainstream knowledge.

I picked up a book entitled The Mayan Prophecies and turned to the back cover. I read that we are standing on the threshold of an extraordinary new world age. In December, 2012, civilization as we know it would change. I continued to read and discovered the authors had studied Mayan astronomy, mathematics, calendars, and prophecies. I was reading about the Mayan calendar when a voice spoke softly behind my left shoulder.

"Ma'am, I hate to interrupt your concentration."

Concentration? Indeed, concentrating was exactly what I was doing and with no sign of vile visions. I turned and looked up at a pair of round rimmed glasses and a shock of white hair. They belonged to the elder of the two men who I had seen twice before. His pale brown eyes resembled polished amber. Somehow he exuded warmth.

"No problem," I said, still secretly pleased that my ability to concentrate had returned. Lowering the book, I wondered if I should mention our mutual sojourn on the beach yesterday morning. I decided to refrain and instead beamed him a smile and said, "We ate breakfast at adjacent tables last Sunday."

With no overt sign of recognition, he studied me a moment. Vertical lines appeared between his eyebrows. He seemed genuinely puzzled.

Feeling quite unmemorable, I explained, "We were on the patio at the Wave restaurant. A man with colourful hair and art work on his arms joined you and your friend."

The frown lines between his eyebrows disappeared and his mouth curved into a friendly smile. "Oh, yes, I remember. You sat alone at the table next to us."

"I did."

"They serve a good breakfast there." His tone of voice grew softer as he continued, "Do you think I could impose on you for assistance? Advice, really."

"Depends on what kind of advice you want."

"I'm trying to choose a gift for my sister. She and I always exchange gifts after the beginning of the year. Christmas and Hanukkah are such busy times we settled on a later date." He smiled and then in three words described his sister: "She's a Pisces."

"Born in March?"

"You're a student of Astrology." He seemed relieved.

I shook my head. "No, my knowledge of the subject is minimal."

"Enough, I think, to understand my sister is sensitive, kind, and rather spiritual."

That word again. Spiritual. He and the owner of the shop should get along well together. Like a robot my head moved up and down and I waited for him to continue.

"We're what you could call Deists."

"Deists," I murmured. "You believe in God..." I hesitated, hoping he would fill in the blanks.

"Deists," he explained, "believe in a personal God based mainly on the testimony of reason."

"Interesting." Not wanting to delve into such a deep subject, I went back to Astrology. "Everyone I know who was born under the sign of Pisces is thoughtful and warm-hearted."

"That describes Rachel perfectly." He smiled again and his joy seemed to spread and encompass the entire shop. "Do you think a forty-eight year old woman would appreciate a gift like this?" He held up a bracelet made of wide silver links and from one link dangled a skilfully designed silver fish.

"It's beautiful," I said, studying the intertwining links and the sleek fish charm. The item seemed expensive and the price tag fluttering from one of the links confirmed it. I looked up at his golden brown eyes. "Not knowing your sister, I can't say for sure if she'd like it. Jewellery is such a personal thing. But how could a Pisces resist that gorgeous little fish?"

He grinned.

"Does she like clunky jewellery?"

"Sometimes."

"I suspect your sister would love this bracelet. In fact, I suspect she would love whatever you gave her simply because it came from you."

His eyes lit up like two bright lanterns. "How nice of you to say that."

"That's how I see it." I giggled, feeling embarrassed at having expressed an opinion about someone I had never even heard of before.

"Then this is it. Thank you very much for your help." He held out his hand.

Briefly taking his hand and shaking it, I said, "You're welcome."

"By the way, my name is Ezekiel Hoffman."

"Your ancestors must have been students of the Old Testament."

He chuckled and his eyes glittered like stars. "And I seem to be conversing with a student of both Astrology and the Bible."

"Not a very good student of either. My name is Philomela Nightingale. Does that tell you anything?"

"Well, the last name reminds me of Florence who was an innovative English nurse during the Crimean war. The first name reminds me of a Greek myth. According to the myth Philomela was transformed into a nightingale and her sister Procne was transformed into a swallow."

I burst out laughing. Not many people knew about the myth. My laughter must have been disrupting for my peripheral vision witnessed the saleslady pivot and glare with annoyance in my direction. Having ruined the shop's peaceful ambience, I put my hand over my mouth and managed to control my mirth. "You're quite right."

"I like the version on which Mathew Arnold based his poem, titled *Philomela*."

I nodded in agreement.

"Like most of us, I assume you're here for a holiday."

"Yes, from Calgary. And you?"

"From Victoria. Every winter I come for a month of sun and warmth. A friend usually comes with me."

"I'm here for a quiet week alone. My husband will join me on Christmas Eve and then we'll have nine days together."

He held up the bracelet and with an elegant bow, said, "I wish you and your husband a Merry Christmas. And thank you again for being so helpful." He turned and walked over to the counter.

I watched him take his wallet from his pocket and casually peel out enough cash to pay for the gift; his actions indicated financial security. He handed the money to the saleslady and chatted with enough humour to make her laugh. His pleasant manner and stately appearance made it clear why yesterday on the beach the violet eyed girl had been so taken with him.

Good grief. The troubled girl once again had paced unwanted into my mind.

To distract my thoughts from the girl, I opened the book languishing in my hand. The writing style was modern compared to Mark Twain's old-fashioned travelogue. It would add variety to my reading. I carried it to the counter, paid the saleslady and shook my head when she offered to put it in a violet plastic bag. With eco correctness, I dropped the book in the bag with my new shoes.

Leaving the incense aroma and the ambience of violet spirituality behind, I breathed in Maui's fresh soft air. I strolled on the sidewalk, passed other shops and then paused in front of a window displaying bright summery clothes. The shop was called *High Fashion*.

CHAPTER 12

*T*urning away from the corpse, our cell-phone rescuer quickly regained his sophisticated manner. He looked at Brent and his fingers rested easily on the cellphone attached to his belt.

"How did you happen to find the body?" he asked.

Standing off to one side, I studied the curly hair sprinkled with abundant strands of white. I also noted how well his physique carried a few extra pounds. After our last encounter on the beach access path I had not expected to see him again.

"My wife found it," Brent replied. "She saw stains on the sand and followed the trail of blood up here."

Our rescuer glanced over at me and gasped audibly. For the second time he did a double take. He seemed just as shocked at seeing his old flame as he had been at seeing the corpse, maybe more so. Before either of us could acknowledge knowing each other, his companion screamed.

"Look, the dead body's moving!" She threw her hands up to each side of her face.

She was absolutely correct, the corpse moved, or at least seemed to move. The life-like activity was caused by a slight breeze ruffling the flowered garment. I walked over to the young girl and spoke with reassuring matter-of-factness.

"It's just a breeze. It disturbed the clothing, not the body."

The girl's face paled to such an extent I feared she might faint. She turned away from the corpse, lowered one hand and put the other over her mouth as if trying to staunch rising nausea. Fortunately her stomach remained intact. She swallowed twice, cleared her throat once, and with both hands smoothed the sides of her designer shorts. She placed her hands on her abdomen and clenched and unclenched her fingers. Her nervous gestures diminished her urbane appearance.

* * *

Urbane was the perfect adjective to describe everything inside the *High Fashion* dress shop. Its shelves were alternately painted green and yellow and its contents made my sundress appear tawdry and outdated. However, none of this prevented me from admiring several garments hanging on green and yellow plastic hangers. I half expected to see Leone, but when she failed to appear I left the shop without buying anything. Inside a holistic health store I purchased a bottle of vitamin C simply because the price was right and dropped it into the bag with my shoes and book. Shades of being a shopaholic, this was my third purchase in one morning. Next I strolled up to a busy intersection, pressed the pedestrian button, waited for traffic to stop and walked across to the other side of the outdoor mall.

My energy level was fading. The breakfast of fruit, yogurt, toast and the later coffee with Leone kept me going for a while, but now hypoglycaemia was taking over. My stomach growled a message and I responded by entering the *Hole-In-The-Wall-Cafe*. The name proved descriptive—it really was a hole in the wall. A few steps took me across the tiny room to a tiny counter where I purchased a bran muffin and a glass of pineapple juice. I carried them to a tiny table in front of the window and sat down on a tiny chair. While taking my first bite of muffin I glimpsed a flurry of orange outside the window. It was Leone. Her shopping trip must have been successful for she carried her purse and new shoe bag as well as a larger bag with *High Fashion* emblazoned on it. Maybe she had been in the dressing room while I had browsed the green and yellow shop. She passed by the window and disappeared from view.

I chewed the bran muffin and sipped the juice. Thanks to the combination of rest and food and drink my lower appendages felt rejuvenated and my stomach stopped growling. My energy level rose and my little grey cells were energized.

I was sipping the last of my pineapple juice when a shadow fell across the tiny table. A voice said, "Philomela." I looked up. The recent nourishment prevented me from fainting with shock.

"Do you know who I am?"

"Glenn Shaw."

"After all these years you recognize me." He smiled and his teeth seemed whiter and straighter than I remembered. His skin had the look of a perfect spray tan.

"You haven't changed much, Glenn. A few white hairs, a few extra pounds, but neither detracts from your good looks." How could I be so pleasant?

"I recognized you the minute I saw you come out of that Holistic Health shop. You look wonderful, better than ever."

"Thank you. You still have a way with words." I smiled and wondered when we had parted company. Twenty years ago?

"Do you mind if I sit down?"

"Not at all." My politeness was nauseating. Was I being a hypocrite or just being socially pleasant? I certainly felt no attraction to the man. But then again, I felt no animosity either. In fact, I felt nothing.

"This is such good luck. I've thought of you so often that I couldn't believe my eyes when you appeared. You may not believe this, but I never truly got over you. Losing you was the worst thing that ever happened to me."

I snorted rather rudely. "That's a bit thick, Glenn. You made your choice twenty years ago. That reminds me, how is your daughter?"

"She's fine, She's studying to be a cosmetologist in Calgary."

"Ah, skin care. With the aging population she'll be kept busy." I wondered if she had sold him the spray-tan. "And your wife? Is she here with you?"

"We divorced six years ago."

"Sorry to hear it." Was I really sorry? I felt no love for Adele. She had been widowed a year before she took up with Glenn and I wondered if she even knew he was engaged to me. Perhaps he had neglected to mention such a minor detail.

"Our marriage struggled from the start, probably because I still carried a torch for you."

I swallowed an urge to laugh.

"I heard you married Brent Lark."

"Do you know him?" I stared at his face and saw two faint squint lines and a few crow's feet but no other signs of age.

"No, I don't. I just heard about it."

"He's arriving on Christmas eve."

"So you're on your own." He flashed his sparkling teeth and raised his brown eyebrows. With extreme nonchalance he suggested, "Why don't we have dinner together and reminisce about old times?"

"There's nothing to reminisce, Glenn."

"I disagree, Philomela. We had a lot going for us, and I think much of that feeling is still alive."

This time I couldn't swallow my laughter. It burst out my mouth and startled him. A crease formed between his brows and his eyes darkened with annoyance. Was his ego big enough to believe I pined for him? Surely he was mature enough to know better. His affair with Adele had wounded me; his announcement of prospective fatherhood had turned the engagement ring on my left hand into a meaningless trinket; his suggestion that I become his mistress just rubbed salt in the other two wounds.

As if yesterday, my reply came back to me: "A piece of tail on the side? You've got to be kidding. I never want to see you again."

But here we were, twenty years later, seeing each other again. Between then and now life had changed, giving this meeting as much meaning as seeing a cast-off kitchen chair.

"Where are you staying?" he asked.

"In a condominium." There were thousands of condominiums on Maui and I gave him no specifics regarding location. I purposely failed to mention the condo was situated on the seashore.

"We really could enjoy an innocent dinner together."

"No, Glenn, we couldn't. We have nothing to discuss." I wiped my mouth on a paper serviette and stood up. "It's been nice seeing you. I hope you have a happy holiday."

I stood up and marched out of the *Hole-In-The-Wall-Cafe*.

CHAPTER 13

$\mathcal{F}$our silent statues, that's what we resembled. My peripheral vision saw the other three gaze up to the sky, out to the sea, and down at their feet. Like me, they avoided looking at the body, hoping it would somehow disappear. Time crawled and after a never ending minute my legs grew stiff and uncomfortable.

"I wish the police would hurry," I said, and tried to relax by bending both knees.

"So do I." The young girl moved closer to Glenn.

My ex-fiancé put an arm around her shoulders and looked over at me. Except for a vague touch of arrogance, his facial expression was indecipherable. Our eyes locked and we gazed at each other as if alone in a room. Brent shifted position beside me and I looked up at him. His eyes were focused on Glenn.

* * *

Eyes pierced my back; I could feel them. A quick backward glance revealed that Glenn had exited the *Hole-in-the-Wall Cafe* and was following me. To avoid confronting him again, I stepped inside another ladies' clothing shop. I scurried past a rack of dresses and hid behind a rack of long gowns. A clerk studied me with suspicion, so I feigned interest in the merchandise by feeling fabrics, studying colours, and pulling out individual items that interested me not at all. My shopaholic ability waned quickly. I stepped from my hiding place, glanced out the plate glass window and saw no sign of Glenn. I thanked the clerk and walked out the door.

Though Glenn was nowhere in sight, I reduced my sidewalk presence by gracing the interiors of a flower shop and a dive shop. In the former I sniffed scents and in the latter I studied merchandise that would appeal to Brent. My final stop was the hardware store where I had first glimpsed Glenn. Needing no hardware items, I went inside anyway. It proved a lesson in global village: denizens of the great white north and denizens of this tropical island used similar fertilizers, insect repellents, rat poison, cleaning fluids, paints, and patio furniture. Over the centuries and across the oceans things changed yet remained the same.

I mused on how that phrase fit Glenn. Though older he remained the same; though thicker around the middle he retained a pleasing physique; though sporting many strands of white on his head he had hair that was still curly. His manner was still charming, sophisticated, and at the same time ingenuous—a Peter Pan personality, a boy who never grew up, a teenager masquerading as an adult. He was a male whose innocent and unctuous charm appealed to many women, but thankfully no longer to me.

I left the hardware store and walked toward my home away from home. The air was hotter than when earlier I had walked to the mall, so I took each step accordingly—fairly slow. Pavement on the road and parking lot radiated dry heat so my pace slowed to a snail's pace.

Gazing at the three story building in front of me, I glimpsed a female figure dashing down the two flights of stairs. At ground level she hurried across the pavement toward me, her silver shirt flashing in the sunlight and her short dark skirt swinging around her upper thighs. Aphrodite, the Greek Goddess of Love, popped to mind. From a distance the girl's youth, health, and sex appeal fit the mythical image. As she drew closer my assessment changed. Goddess of Love? Not in my estimation. To her credit two things appeared in her favour: her hair was combed and her hands no longer obsessively wiped her skirt. I studied her surreptitiously at first and then openly because she didn't so much as glance in my direction. We passed within touching distance yet her violet eyes looked down at the pavement and revealed nothing. I knew not if they were happy, angry, sad, or empty. I noticed ugly red sores on her chin, cheeks and forehead. Her body appeared anorexic, not thin. What had happened to the drop-dead gorgeous girl in the airport? One thing in her favour was she no longer resembled the unkempt witch who had struck me on the beach.

Was it just this morning that I had watched her pace back and forth on the damp sand? Was it just this morning that she had angrily struck me with her fist?

Slowing my pace, I glanced back at her and automatically stroked my bruised shoulder. It had stopped throbbing and now hurt only if something bumped it. She, unaware of my existence, hurried from the parking lot and crossed the street to the sidewalk. Heading in the direction of the shopping mall she stopped and conversed with a fair-haired man. They fell in step with each other and walked toward the mall.

At least she hadn't accused me of following her and hadn't tried to sell me any ice. I wondered if she had come from her holiday home, Number 308. What kind of a relationship did she have with the handsome man in the condo next to mine?

I shook my head in order to banish thoughts of the disconcerting girl and her mysterious relationships with older men. Clutching the bag containing shoes, book and Vitamin C, I slowly started up the two flights of stairs. The early afternoon heat drained my energy and at the top I paused to rest.

Angry voices assaulted my ears. The sounds, unpleasant in any location, were especially so in paradise. With heavy feet I moved slowly forward and tried not to listen. It was obvious a man and a woman were arguing and their words sounded repugnant. With no desire to be an eavesdropper, I tried to close my ears, but the argumentative voices continued to surge clearly through an open window. I stopped outside the door of Number 309, put the key in the lock, opened the door and raised my right foot to step inside. A voice I recognized slashed the air.

"You're as big a bastard as my second husband. He also took advantage of the inexperienced young girl."

I dropped my foot on the door sill and froze.

"She isn't young, and she certainly isn't inexperienced. She was in complete control of the entire activity. She even made me pay up front before anything happened. And her price was not cheap."

"You're lying."

"I'm not. I'm telling the truth. I didn't recognize her. How was I to know she was related to you? You certainly didn't tell me your daughter was a prostitute."

I heard the sound of a loud slap.

Envisioning his reddened cheek, I knew I should go into my unit and close the door and plug my ears. But I was unable to move. My muscles were immobile and my feet were glued to the floor. Nothing in my body worked except my ears. That wasn't quite true— my nostrils and lungs still breathed.

The sound of sobbing was infectious, making me want to cry, too. Through her sobs the female voice murmured, "I was afraid of this. That damn pimp has got her on drugs again."

There was no doubt in my mind...I knew the owner of the voice.

"There, there." The man spoke in such a soothing and comforting manner that I envisioned him forgetting his reddened cheek and holding her in his arms. "If she's addicted, she has to obtain money to pay for her habit. It's not really her doing these things. It's the drugs."

"Righto." The sobs slowly subsided. "Oh Fred, it's all so hopeless."

"I wonder if Marlene's on hashish, heroin, coke, or crystal meth?"

"What does it matter? They're all bad. She was on crystal meth before her last rehabilitation. I helped her that time. But will she let me help her again?"

"You can encourage her to go to a detox centre, but you can't force her to go. She has to want to do it."

"My poor little girl. I can't bear the thought of her existing in that awful lifestyle."

"Maybe we can think of some way to help her."

"Like paying her money for sex so she can buy more drugs?" Her voice dripped with sarcasm.

"Leone, that was the first and last time I ever resorted to paid sex. It didn't happen today and it won't happen again. I'll never contact any pimp again. From now on I'll look at Marlene as your daughter, an innocent young girl who was victimized and needs help."

I was in a state of shock. My new best friend was the mother of the girl who in less than a week had changed from a drop-dead gorgeous girl to a thin, sore-ridden hag.

The conversation continued but their voices faded. I realized they were leaving the bedroom area and walking toward the kitchen. Perhaps they were heading for the seaside lanai.

My feet unglued, my muscles flexed, and I stepped into Number 309 and closed the door. Shaken beyond belief, I leaned against the back of the door and stood stock still. I could not imagine living the awful life style of the girl with violet eyes. Neither could I imagine living in her mother's world. How could Leone bear to watch her child disintegrate, unable to help her own flesh and blood escape from a moral and physical morass? Neither situation was a good place to be.

In the past, I had sometimes felt unfulfilled because of never having produced a child. This especially affected me after being with two friends whose offspring provided them with great pride and joy. Unlike Leone, however, each of those friends had chosen a steadfast, loving husband who helped support and raise their children.

What I heard this afternoon was the dark side of procreation. For the first time ever I felt relieved to have missed motherhood.

Surely the pleasing ambience of paradise would return tomorrow evening when Brent arrived. In order to spend every minute with him, I must no longer procrastinate. I must forget Leone Humphries, her daughter Marlene, the man next door, the tattooed Motor-Mouth, and my old flame Glenn Shaw. I must write the article for *The Integrator*—not now, but right now.

I marched to the table in the sitting area and sat down, determined to write the entire first draft. I would emulate Mark Twain by making it interesting and humorous. Like him, I would write by hand. But I confess to wishing I had brought my laptop.

My reading skills and my concentration abilities were restored. At ten-thirty that evening I felt truly satisfied. The first draft was finished and the numbered sheets of paper sat on top of the coffee table. With luck, the manuscript would need only minor revisions and a bit of polishing.

I turned out the lights, picked up 'MARK TWAIN IN HAWAII' and carried it to the bedroom. I intended to reread the second last chapter that described his traversal of Kilauea's crater amidst black deserts, pillars of fire, and bubbling cauldrons. It was hard to believe that in 1866 the now active volcano had been dormant.

I hoped Twain's amazing activities would replace thoughts of today's disturbing happenings and allow me to sleep.

CHAPTER 14

"Where are the police?" Brent asked. "Why are they taking so long?"

Brent and I stood on one side of the corpse and Glenn and the young girl stood a short distance away on the other side.

The young girl muttered over and over, "Who would like do such a terrible thing? Like, who could actually kill her?"

At first I sympathized with her repetitious words. Then they became annoying. Hoping to soothe and quiet her, I finally replied, "A vicious, mean-hearted person."

"A drug lord," Brent said, "or an addict."

Less than thrilled with our answers she leaned against Glenn. Whether she really wanted to know who could do such a terrible thing was questionable. She closed her eyes and her breathing became shallow and loud, but to my relief she stopped repeating the questions.

Brent and I cleared our throats as if trying to compete with her loud breathing. Then the shrill shriek of an oncoming siren overtook the sounds of everything else. The welcome shriek drew closer and stopped with startling abruptness. All four of us scurried to the edge of the dune and looked down at the wide stretch of sand.

Two groups of people walked from the direction of our condo and their loud laughter identified them as vacationers. From an access path in the opposite direction, two people wearing dark blue pants and shirts appeared. They gazed from one end of the beach to the other, and as if pursued by drug crazed demons they ran to the water and stopped.

* * *

Two drug crazed people ran after me on the sand. My pursuers, a wide-eyed girl and a tattooed man, yelled like demons. I wore my menopausal mauve cover-up over my swimsuit and my legs pumped in slow motion while the man, who held a big syringe and needle in his right hand, kept gaining on me. Every so often he jabbed the long needle toward my arm and finally he caught up to me and plunged the needle through my lacy cover-up. The needle penetrated the muscle of my upper left arm. It hurt.

I woke up, a scream at the ready.

With no pursuer in sight, I kept the scream in my throat. Light shone through the window from the outside corridor and glimmered on the spine of Mark Twain's book. It pressed sharply against my upper left arm. Last night, I had turned out the bedside light but must have left the book on the bed. Doubtless the pressure of its cover on my arm helped trigger the nightmare.

The resemblance of the man in my dream to Motor-Mouth and the girl to Marlene upset me. I wondered if the dream was a subconscious warning. Of becoming addicted? Of being murdered?

Wide awake, I lay still and watched for movement inside the room and listened for sounds both inside and out. I kept telling myself the content of the bad dream was coincidental and meant nothing. Even so, it was a long time before sleep again enveloped me.

The next time I awoke, the sun was high in the eastern sky. My sleep pattern may have accommodated itself to the time change, but the nightmare had robbed me of an hour of sleep. Feeling un-refreshed, my body dragged out of bed.

It was the morning before Christmas and I tried to follow my established routine. Stepping on the beach, I looked left. A recollection of the unkempt girl and the vomiting man put my little grey cells in disarray. Did I want to follow yesterday's route?

Just thinking about the weird couple made me nervous, so I automatically turned right, the opposite direction of my previous walks. The likelihood of seeing the man and woman who had peopled my nightmare was minimal, but I wanted to do everything possible to reduce the chance of actually seeing them.

Carrying a flip-flop in each hand, I sank my bare feet in dry sand and headed for the water. Damp sand, low tide, and a lack of early morning walkers exacerbated my stride. My pace quickened into a lope as I gazed at new vistas—gardens, houses, and small condominiums. No sand dunes interrupted these residential views. Garish flowers, leafy trees and attractive buildings made my little grey cells happy.

The beach became rocky and difficult to walk on so I made a hundred and eighty degree turn and started to retrace my steps. After going a short distance I saw two other walkers coming toward me. I promptly recognized Ezekiel Hoffman's shock of white hair. He strolled beside his younger companion. They moved toward me and as we came abreast Ezekiel gently placed his hand on his friend's shoulder and slowed him to a stop.

"Aloha, Philomela."

"Aloha, Ezekiel."

"I'd like you to meet my friend, Daniel Epstein. Daniel, this is Philomela Nightingale, the young lady I met at the *Outer Fringe* shop."

"You're the one who helped Ezekiel choose the Pisces bracelet." I nodded and he said, "Rachel will adore that fishy gift."

"I'm glad."

Ezekiel explained to his friend the origin of my name and Daniel listened with apparent interest. When the account concluded he leaned toward me.

"I hadn't heard that Greek myth before. It's fascinating but a bit gory. Ezekiels' namesake is fascinating too."

"You mean the Biblical Ezekiel?" I asked. He responded with a nod and I said, "I read it years ago."

"Ezekiel prophesied to the people of Israel, warning them of the future fall and destruction of Jerusalem. A different part of his message is not so well known. He also emphasized the need for abolishment of evil and an inner renewal of each person's heart and mind. That part of the message needs to be heard today." His voice softened and the expression on his face grew serious.. "That's exactly where our present day Ezekiel shines."

Daniel seemed to shine, too, with admiration for his friend. I glanced over at Ezekiel who with a touch of embarrassment was studying the sand. I turned back to Daniel and asked, "How does one obtain a renewal of heart and mind?"

"With kindness and goodness," Daniel replied, "and with meditation."

The latter recommendation was rather outer-fringy so I made the conversation even more outer-fringy by zeroing in on UFOs: "I always thought Ezekiel's claim to fame involved seeing weird things in the sky, you know, unidentified flying objects." I sang somewhat out of tune, "a wheel within a wheel a-rolling, away in the middle of the air."

Both men burst out laughing.

Ezekiel controlled his mirth and with a shake of his head said, "I've heard that song more times than I care to count."

"From childhood until now," I said.

"The first time I heard it you probably hadn't been born."

"I doubt that. But thanks for the compliment."

"Many people take those Biblical quotes literally," Ezekiel said. "They believe he actually saw a real ship from outer space."

"You have to admit the Biblical rendition does describe the wheels as if they were part of an airship." Seeing the edges of Daniel's mouth form a happy face, I asked, "Were you named after another Old Testament prophet? The Daniel who interpreted the king's prophetic dreams?"

"No. Mine is just a common family name."

Marlene and Motor-Mouth came to mind so I said, "Going back to abolishing evil and opening a person's heart and mind...is that what illegal drug users try to do? Do they try to open their hearts and minds?"

Ezekiel, not Daniel, replied, "Some hope to do that, but it's a faint hope." His voice was soft yet firm and confident. "Illegal drugs dull the mind and open inhibitions, allowing users to do bad things they normally wouldn't do. At first a user thinks a drug sharpens his awareness, but it's an illusion. Drugs deaden the senses, especially the sense of right and wrong. They soon control his life...everything revolves around getting the next fix. A drug addict does not become alert."

Daniel nodded his head, confirming Ezekiel's pensive assessment. Then he grinned and said, "What the world needs now is more Lerts."

His remark took a second to register then I burst out laughing. The two men joined in. When our laughter subsided, I said, "If we find enough Lerts, we could weave a new myth around them."

For no good reason that started us laughing again. The three of us stood on the sand behaving as if we had not a care in the world—until an unexpected big wave almost knocked us down. The receding water sucked sand from under our feet and we struggled to stay upright.

"Speaking of myths," I said, regaining my balance, "do you think a myth or a semi-historical story can help an individual develop openness of heart and mind?"

I should never have asked, for it set Daniel on a lengthy explanation that was difficult to grasp. However, I sort of understood his final summary.

"The early Mayans are known for their mathematical skills. Their calendar ends on 22 December 2012. Some people think it foretells a shift in the earth's poles that will cause excessive earthquakes and volcanic eruptions. Some people believe it foretells that earth's path in the Milky Way galaxy will bring a time of peace and goodwill. Others think the Mayans simply got tired of working on the calendars so quit."

I chuckled and mentioned the book I had bought at the Outer Fringe shop. Daniel smiled and said, "I've read it."

"It may not be truly prophetic," Ezekiel said, "but it is interesting."

Daniel had surprised me. Of the two men he had seemed quieter and less intelligent. But once he started talking about the complicated Mayan calendar he expressed a good grasp of the subject..

"Miracles and optimistic prophecies," Ezekiel said, "resemble mass prayers and healing circles. Good results come from the positive thoughts and prayers of many people."

Daniel's attention was distracted by two young girls walking past us. His admiring glance disproved my supposition that the two men were lovers. Instead, I wondered if they had a father-son or a mentor-student relationship. I was too polite to ask.

"Right now," Ezekiel said, "it's time for us to continue our morning constitutional. It's been grand talking with you, Philomela."

"I hope we meet again," I said.

We parted amicably, they going one way and I going the other. I contemplated our discussion and regretted not asking them about their two acquaintances from Calgary. How had the two gentle scholars gotten mixed up with Marlene the prostitute and Motor-Mouth the tattooed creep? It was beyond my comprehension.

Maybe the two quiet men were not as they seemed. Maybe they were wolves in sheep's clothing. Maybe they secretly took drugs and bought them from Motor-Mouth. Maybe they were silent partners of the Tattoo Parlour. Maybe they were promiscuous perverts who partook of the pleasures of Marlene and other ladies of the evening. Maybe....

Enough. I could imagine more and more things and the mental images would just get stupider and less likely.

As I reached the access path to Hale Sun and Surf, a man who had been sitting on the sand a few feet farther down the beach slowly unfurled and started to walk toward me. Paying him no heed, I turned onto the path and walked between the dunes. At the warning sign a male voice startled me.

"Philomela."

I turned around and gasped. "Glenn, what are you doing here?" His sudden appearance and the closeness of his body to mine made me apprehensive.

"Philomela...." His breathing was deep and slow and his eyes were as pleading as a hungry child's. Sounding like a teen-age boy he murmured, "I just had to see you one more time."

"Why?" I was flabbergasted.

"Because...because we're destined for each other. I know it and so do you."

"I don't know it." I stared at him and my chest heaved indignantly.

"Yes you do, Philomela. Admit it. We had a lot going for us before it got messed up."

"Yes, it got messed up all right."

"A lot is still going for us."

I shook my head. "Nothing is going for us. Not one bloody thing."

"There's an attraction between us. I felt it in the cafe and I know you did too."

"Glenn, I felt nothing for you in the cafe and I feel nothing for you now. I doubt you really feel anything for me, either."

"Ah, but I do."

"I'm no longer a young, innocent girl. I'm a happily married, middle-aged woman."

"And your husband is a lucky man."

"And he flies in this evening."

"So this may be our last chance to be alone together."

"Why would we want to be alone together?" As soon as I asked the question, I knew I shouldn't have.

With his finger tips he gently stroked my cheek and before I knew what was happening both his arms were around me. I struggled briefly but he held me fast. He bent his head and kissed me fully on the mouth. To my amazement I responded.

As if that answered my question, he raised his head a few inches and smiled. "We'll find out right now why we want to be alone together. Let's go up to your place."

Before I could reply, his head again lowered and his lips touched mine. This time I responded differently. I jerked my head away and pushed the flip-flops in both my hands against his chest.

"Stop," I cried, struggling to get free of him. "This is ridiculous."

"You're fighting against your natural instincts."

"No, I'm not. I'm fighting against a would-be seducer."

"Philomela." His voice registered the forlorn sadness of a hero in a Greek tragedy, one who has yet to recognize his own hubris. "You do me an injustice. I love you. I always have."

I countered with the first words that popped into my head. "Love is only good when it abolishes evil and opens hearts and minds."

The words sprang from my recent conversation with Ezekiel and Daniel and they made no sense to Glenn and not much more to me. Their lack of logic made his eyebrows shoot up quizzically and he lessened his grip, allowing me to free myself from his embrace.

"Goodbye Glenn." Like a terrified rabbit I turned away from him and dashed between the dunes to the lawn. I ran past the foot washing tap without removing sand from my feet and continued into the dim laundry area. Reaching sunlight at the other side and with my heart beating like a petrified animal, I stopped and looked back. There was no sign of my potential seducer. I leaned against the wall and the frenzied beating of the blood-pumping organ in my chest slowed down. Putting the flip-flops on my feet I tried to make sense of what had just happened.

Glenn had obviously been waiting for me near the beach access path. I had not told him where I was staying nor even implied it was an ocean-front location. How had he known the exact building?

My emotions were unequivocal: his actions failed to make me feel like a femme fatal; his words failed to flatter my intellect; all he did was make me nervous, frightened and angry. Was he stalking me? Did he want nothing more than a roll in the hay? Or should I say sand? Or was there something more sinister involved?

Inside the condo, I prepared a light breakfast. Reluctant to take it out to the lanai, I sat at the inside table. Nibbling toast and sipping coffee, I recollected nearing the condominium yesterday—on the paved parking lot I had met the young girl, watched her cross the road and on the sidewalk chat with a fair-haired man. It could have been Glenn. Could he have followed me from the hardware store and watched when I turned into the parking lot of *Hale Sun and Surf*?

And did he know Marlene?

I washed my breakfast dishes then nervously ventured out to the lanai. With eyes wide I searched a hundred and eighty degrees for a glimpse of my unwanted stalker. There was no sign of him. I sat down at the green plastic table and heaved a long sigh. Being stalked was no fun. I was alert enough to know that.

Yes, I was a Lert. I grinned at the thought.

A few minutes later I got up, went inside to the kitchen, filled another mug of coffee and took it to the sitting room where I picked up the first draft of my article. I carried both out to the lanai and set them on the table. I leaned against the white railing and again scanned the lawn, the dunes, and the beach. There was no sign of Glenn.

I sat down and looked at the first draft. Concentrating on the work at hand I read:

HAWAII, THEN AND NOW
In 1866, Mark Twain sailed across the Pacific Ocean from California to Oahu. The journey took several days and nights. One hundred and forty-four years later, I flew in the sky from Alberta to Maui. The flight took less than six hours.

What a difference a century and a half makes.

I read the entire first draft and inserted a few differences that time had wrought: *Over the years much progress had been made, some good, some bad. Vehicles of transportation had improved and become more numerous; hordes of biting insects had been nearly eradicated; swimsuits now exposed more skin.* I removed my dissertation about natives sacrificing human beings to the god Lono and murdering Captain James Cook on the island of Kauai. Many forms of murder had occurred back then, but I considered the subject unnecessary. After all, few people were murdered on Hawaii today.

The revising and correcting of the article went well, possibly because my anger with Glenn had increased the flow of adrenalin throughout my system. My attention deficit problems were either cured or eliminated. Though not perfect, the manuscript would not have to be rewritten from scratch.

Two hours later, I set the draft aside, put on my purple swimsuit and slathered sunscreen on my exposed skin. Down on the lawn I noticed several people already well established on chaise-lounges enjoying the sun. I studied each of them and saw no sign of Glenn Shaw. Nor did I see Leone or the man from Number 308. The only person I recognized was Andrew Strong. He was at one end of the lawn cleaning a BBQ, and a blond haired girl wearing a flowered bikini was keeping him well entertained.

I adjusted the chaise-longue for the purpose of catching filtered rays of sun and slowly eased onto it. I put a towel on my face and let the sun warm my legs, arms and stomach. Lazily, I closed my eyes and dozed.

The laughter of young children woke me. Groggily, I sat up and looked at the granny attired in her black swimsuit in the pool with the three youngsters. All three children wore electric blue swimsuits. Granny was teaching the two oldest ones to swim while the youngest floated nearby in a plastic fish filled with air. Their joy increased when the mother joined them. Two generations became three and the scene was heart warming.

It brought me out of the funk that yesterday's eavesdropping had triggered. A snoop is bound to hear unwanted things. The jolly scene in front of me dissolved some of yesterday's unpleasantness and reminded me that happy families were not obsolete.

"Hi Philomela."

Leone Humphries' familiar voice interrupted my reverie. I looked up at the white bikini enhancing her curvaceous figure and accentuating her tawny skin. She stood beside my chaise longue, looking a picture of radiant health. Her sadness regarding her daughter's lifestyle was not apparent.

"I'd like you to meet Fred Pederson," she said, glancing at the man who stood a few feet behind her.

My handsome neighbour, wearing form-fitting swim trunks, stepped forward and extended his hand.

"We're neighbours," I said and shook his hand. "I live in Number 309."

"Ah yes." His face registered recognition. "We met on the stairs."

I nodded. "Are you two planning to absorb some rays?"

"We are. Then I intend to take Leone out for lunch."

"Did you go to the Vietnamese restaurant last night?" I asked.

"We did," Leone replied, "and the food was good."

"It wasn't busy," Fred said, "and the prices were reasonable."

"Perfect."

"Does your husband arrive tonight?" Leone asked. I nodded and she turned to Fred. "Philomela's husband is a petroleum engineer in Calgary. Maybe the four of us could go out for dinner some evening."

"Sounds great." Fred spoke with enthusiasm, smiled at me and then turned to Leone. "We'll make a date after he gets here."

"Not tomorrow," Leone said. "Christmas. Do you plan on roasting a turkey with all the trimmings?"

I shook my head. "I was thinking of frying two small beef steaks."

She laughed. "Good idea. We'll have to cook something, too. A lot of restaurants will be closed." She added pensively, "Eatery owners and their staff need family time, too."

I nodded. "That's true."

She turned to Fred and pointed to an area devoid of people. "Let's sun ourselves over there."

They dragged their chaises longue over the grass and settled side by side near a sand dune. Lying on their backs, they turned their heads toward each other and chatted quietly. The troubles with Leone's daughter seemed to have brought the two closer together.

For a while longer I toasted my body in the sun then went up to the condo, intending to spend fifteen minutes tidying and dusting and vacuuming. I was surprised when it took more than fifty minutes. I showered, dressed, and drove to the food market to stock up for Christmas. After putting groceries in the refrigerator and the cupboards, I checked the condo once more.

For Brent, I wanted paradise to be perfect.

CHAPTER 15

"Up here." Brent's voice boomed like a cannon:
The two people clad in dark blue shirts and trousers turned from the sea and scanned the wide expanse of sand. They looked everywhere but at the top of the dune.

"Up here," Brent called again. He waved his arms like a windmill.

Surf sounds must have twisted the direction of his voice because they looked everywhere but up. Desperate to get their attention I joined Brent and like idiots we both yelled and jumped up and down. Their heads turned in the direction of our voices but stayed on a level position so again they failed to see us. Our sad ordeal had already lasted too long and the police unintentionally were making it longer.

"Up here," we screamed in unison and wildly waved our arms.

Our unmusical duet must have resonated correctly or else our flailing arms entered their peripheral vision for they both looked up at us. They moved toward us in tandem and quickened their pace. Reaching the base of the dune they stopped.

I raised my eyes and looked at Brent. With a feeling of relief I inhaled loudly, exhaled more loudly, and murmured, "Praise the gods, and the police."

"They'll take care of everything." His eyes gazed into mine. Nodding his head with apparent optimism he glanced up at the clear blue sky.

* * *

The sky was dark and the road was shadowy. The headlights beamed a tunnel of light and a feeling of mystery engulfed me. Driving the rental car, I navigated the route in reverse that I had done on my initial trip to *Hale Sun and Surf*. It had been dark and shadowy then, too.

The drive to the Kahalui airport was trouble free until I approached my destination. A wrong turn provided a maximum of problems, making me drive around and around poorly lit roads. After what seemed hours the lot's entrance miraculously appeared on my left. I parked the car and hurried to the terminal.

According to the arrival monitor, Brent's plane was on schedule. I sat down on a hard bench near the carousels and watched people exchange warm greetings and obtain various suitcases. Christmas cheer was in the air and it increased exponentially when Brent's premature white hair, broad shoulders and tall frame came into view. I jumped up and ran to meet him and his long legs strode toward me. We met on the run and enveloped each other. Suddenly the world became brighter and better.

He retrieved his small bag from the carousel and hand in hand we skipped to my sapphire blue rental car. He noted the warm weather and while driving the car mentioned his drilling project.

"As much as I wanted to be here with you," he said, "I'm glad I stayed. We worked out the intricacies so both parties are satisfied. It's a done deal."

"That's great."

"Drilling will start next month."

"I hope it's a gusher. We need oil to fuel our cars and airplanes, to say nothing of making plastic dishes and furniture."

"I won't count on a gusher," he said, "but its proximity to other producing wells reduce its chance of being a dry hole."

I told him about the beach, the condo, and being unnerved by Motor-Mouth and his young girl friend.

In the condominium, he unpacked his bag and asked, "Have you heard anything from your sister?"

"Not a peep. Have you?"

"Procne phoned last evening. She sounded optimistic about everything. Everything except Larry."

"What's he doing now?"

"That's the problem. No one knows. A couple of days ago he disappeared."

"Good grief."

"Philomela, there's nothing good about grief."

I laughed. "Don't tell that to the characters in the Charlie Brown comic strip. But do tell me more about my sister."

"Procne said everything is falling in place, including legalities. They had a good offer on their house and the prospective buyers want to purchase some of their furniture."

"She's due for some good luck. Over the years most of her luck has been bad." I grinned at him and said, "Larry's disappearance may be the best piece of luck she could have had. He'd probably just muck up the house sale."

"You never know what he's going to say or do."

"I wonder where he is. Maybe the husband of one of his old flames shot him."

Brent gave me a reprimanding glance. To his credit he admitted, "He's a bad penny. He'll turn up when least expected."

We climbed into bed and forgot my sister and her almost ex-husband. With Brent here, I felt safe and happy. It was a wonderful Christmas Eve.

Unlike the previous night, I slept soundly, undisturbed by exterior sounds or interior nightmares.

CHAPTER 16

We watched the two policemen climb single file up the dune. They ascended with such agility I suspected they must work out regularly at a gym.

Glenn's girlfriend stood between him and me. She nervously flicked her hair, wrung her hands in front of her abdomen, smoothed the front of her red and white T-shirt, and then started to repeat her former mantra.

"Who could like do such a thing?" No one answered her question so she repeated it, "Like who could do such a terrible thing?"

"A so-called boyfriend," I replied, and with authoritarian succinctness added, "A pimp."

She jerked her head and glared at me. Her expression clearly accused me of profaning the poor victim, and in a way she was right. Earlier, Brent had answered that same question more diplomatically; he had avoided any implication that the dead woman was a drug addict and a prostitute. Now I, by merely mentioning a pimp, labelled the victim as a lady of the evening. The girl continued to glare at me.

"You're like cruel," she said.

"At least I'm not a murderer." To my own ears the remark sounded more like the words of a sharp defence lawyer than those of a distraught person who had just discovered a dead body.

"Relax," Glenn said and stroked his companion's shoulder. "The police are here. Everything will be okay." He gazed not at her but at me.

I felt Brent shift closer to me. I looked up and saw him again staring at Glenn. Did he suspect Glenn and I had had past dealings? He took hold of my hand and together we moved from the edge of the dune toward the body. We stopped at a respectful distance and gazed at the flowered turquoise and pink dress.

"Look at her arms," he said. "Skin and bones. Are those bruises on the front of her shoulders and upper arms?"

Sure enough, black and blue areas were apparent. Had firm hands grasped her arm pits and shoulders and caused the bruising? Earlier, I had noted the spaghetti straps of her dress but somehow had missed seeing the bruises. Now, gazing at the dress, I admired how it followed the slight hills and valleys of her body. Even in death the calf-length garment was unwrinkled and accentuated her pleasing but thin figure.

I noted that the dress, spotted with blood and sand, was made of the same material as the grungy shirt worn by Motor-Mouth on that first morning on the restaurant's patio. I found it a strange coincidence because Motor-Mouth and the gorgeous girl had not seemed the type who would wear matching shirt and dress.

"I don't see a purse," Brent said. "A purse could help the police identify her."

"Identification's not a problem," I said. "I know who she is."

"You do?" Brent stared at me, surprised. "You didn't mention it."

"No, I guess I'm stupider than dumb."

"Shocked," he corrected, "not stupid." He put his right arm around my shoulder. "Who is she?"

"She's the gorgeous girl I saw in the Calgary airport. She's the girl on the beach who struck my shoulder."

He leaned back and stared at me. Finally he asked, "Are you sure?"

"Absolutely. She's the daughter of Leone Humphries. Her name is Marlene Rathbone."

"How do you know that?"

"I overheard Leone talking to Fred and she mentioned her daughter's name. Earlier Leone had told me her first husband's name was Rathbone."

He shook his head. "She can't weigh much. The murderer must have carried her up the dune. If she had been dragged, more groundcover would have been damaged."

"I agree."

From the corner of my eye I saw the first policeman brush sand from his uniform and nod at Glenn and his companion. Seeing the corpse stretched out on the groundcover, he pursed his lips as if controlling tears or nausea.

The second policeman scrambled over the rim and stood up. The chest configuration revealed he was a she. My mental terminology changed from two policemen to one policeman and one policewoman.

The policewoman glanced at the young girl's body and stifled a gasp. She put her hand over her mouth and moved closer to her cohort as if trying by osmosis to gain strength. Together they viewed the scene then silently, almost reverently, moved closer to the corpse. They touched nothing.

The policeman asked, "Who found the girl?"

"I did."

"And you phoned?"

"No. My husband recruited this gentleman from the beach." I pointed to Glenn. "He has a cellphone."

His questioning was professional, polite, and to the point. When he stopped interrogating, the policewoman who had been quietly studying the victim turned to her cohort and said, "I'll call the C I D." He nodded his head and she punched numbers on her electronic device. She told the respondent she was investigating a suspected homicide and required the help of detectives, coroner and special equipment. Her message was clear and concise and needed no elaboration.

With hands clasped behind their backs, the two police officers slowly circled the body. The eagle badge on the left side of their shirts and the letters MPD (Maui Police Department) prominently displayed on both sides increased their appearance of professionalism. They studied everything about the body and occasionally bent down and examined a specific item more thoroughly. Their scrutiny and search for clues indicated nothing pertaining to the girl's death would be overlooked, but I had the distinct impression their experience with murder was minimal.

Was homicide uncommon in modern paradise? I had thought so when writing my article for *The Integrator*. Now I reconsidered the question and its answer.

CHAPTER 17

Standing at the edge of the dune, a fair distance from the disconcerting scene, Brent and I watched the efficient activity of the police. Glenn and his girlfriend stood nearby. All four of us shifted our feet, clasped our hands, and alternately watched the police in front of us and the beach access path below us.

After what seemed three hours but was probably three minutes, two heads capped with dark hair bobbed above the dune beside the access path. The heads came in full view and two pairs of legs strode onto the beach. Between heads and legs the upper torsos were covered with flowered shirts that contrasted sharply with the beige expanse of sand. Considering the circumstances, the colourful shirts seemed incongruously cheery. Could these two sporty, unprofessional looking men possibly be detectives? Just in case, Brent and I waved.

Both heads swivelled briefly from side to side and then with no verbal prompting from us looked up. They spotted our flapping arms and waved in response. Side by side they strode purposely along the beach to the base of the dune and proceeded to climb the slippery slope. On the summit they stood upright and their eyes swept the immediate vicinity and locked on the dead girl. They moved toward her, glanced at us and with brief nods murmured "Aloha."

Brent and I returned their greeting. My eyes focused on their bright shirts. Their attire, unlike the uniforms of the two police officers who stood near the body, resembled holiday outfits. I inanely thought that we had the makings of a merry sand dune survival party, not the beginning of a criminal case. The thought shattered as the policeman spoke to the two detectives.

"It looks like murder." The policeman proceeded to describe his version of the situation. During his short spiel he glanced occasionally at the four of us and concluded by pointing his index finger directly at me. "That red-haired lady found the victim."

Both detectives walked over to Brent and me. The shorter of the two stopped directly in front of Brent and said, "I'm Police Detective Kanui of the Maui Criminal Investigation Division and this is Police Detective Sanders." He spoke clearly and made sure all four of us heard his words.

The taller man nodded at us and took a notepad and pen from his pocket.

Detective Kanui stared at Brent and asked his name and local address then did the same with me. Detective Sanders stood at his side and recorded our answers. With preliminary questions out of the way, Detective Kanui scrutinized both of us. Brent managed to stand steadfast but I squirmed as the detective stepped closer to me. He was about my height so when he leaned forward his eyes gazed directly into mine. I felt like fainting.

"Can you relate exactly how you came to find the victim?" he asked, and his voice was soft, as if trying to reassure me.

I was not reassured, but I answered as best as possible. My voice cracked while explaining how I noticed the reddish stain on the sand, but it grew steadier as I described the telltale trail to the bottom of the dune.

He repeated several of my words in the form of a question. "You noticed a large reddish stain on the sand?"

"Yes."

"You followed a trail of smaller reddish spots to the dune?" I nodded and he asked, "Had reddish spots splattered the leaves?"

"Not that I noticed. A few damaged leaves prompted me to climb up the dune."

"This groundcover is hardy," he mused, "and highly resilient. Some leaves could easily have sprung back to a normal position."

I wondered if horticulture was his hobby.

"So the stains on the sand and a few reddish drops on the leaves were enough to make you expend energy to climb this dune?"

"Yes." I was getting used to his questions so my nervousness dissipated a bit. I managed to elaborate, "The spots puzzled me. I wanted to see what they were and where they ended. At first I thought they were spilled coffee, and then I realized the color was wrong and the consistency was too hard. I wondered if they could be blood." Suddenly remembering the importance of fingerprints, I confessed, "I'm afraid I touched the stain on the beach with the tip of my index finger. I also lifted the girl's right arm with my left hand, and used my right fingers to try and find a pulse on her wrist."

Detective Sanders stared at my face as if accusing me of behaving like an idiot, or worse, a criminal. He wrote something in his notepad and I hoped it wasn't too incriminating. Detective Kanui stepped backwards and with no hint of subtleness, studied me. To my surprise, he gave me an encouraging smile. "We'll take your fingerprints in order to eliminate them from any others."

I nodded, well aware that Detective Sanders was still jotting a jumble of words in his notepad. Were his words damning? I looked at Detective Kanui. His two eyes shone from his round dark face like two bright spotlights. They were more blinding than his colourful shirt and they looked around as if seeing everything and missing nothing.

He again leaned toward me and his eyes peered into mine. He stated what I already knew, "Detective Sanders will keep detailed notes. That way nothing will be misinterpreted or forgotten." Still probing my eyes, he asked, "Had you met the victim before?"

"Sort of."

"Sort of? That's rather ambiguous."

"Well, we were never formally introduced, but I saw her on a few different occasions."

"And those occasions were...?"

"Twice in the Calgary airport. Once on the airplane en route to Maui. Twice at *Hale Sun and Surf.* and twice on the beach. Her name, I believe, is Marlene Rathbone."

Detective Sanders wrote in a fast and furious manner. I wondered if his writing was readable.

"On each occasion she was alone?" Detective Kanui asked.

"In the airport lavatory she was alone. On the airplane she was with a man who might have been her pimp and drug supplier, but that information is hearsay. At the condominium she was alone, and on the beach she was talking with two men." The incidents involving Fred Pederson and Andrew Strong failed to enter my mind, but I did mention Leone. "I met her mother."

"Did you see the girl with her mother?"

"No. I never saw them together.

"Detective Sanders scrawled more words in his notepad and then, saying nothing, glanced at Detective Kanui. The latter raised his head and gazed thoughtfully up at the sky. He lowered his eyes and again studied my face. His eyes were hypnotic.

"Do you know where this alleged pimp and drug dealer can be located?"

"N-not really." I stuttered because Detective Kanui's sharp gaze disconcerted me. I swallowed and managed to say, "I don't know his name or where he lives. I nick-named him, 'Motor-Mouth'. He announced he has a contact person in the Tattoo Parlour at the mall. I have no idea who that person is."

"And the girl's mother? Do you know how to contact her?"

"Yes. Her name is Leone Humphries. She owns a condominium at *Hale Sun and Surf*. I don't know the unit number."

"Anything else?"

I tried to think, but nothing of any importance came to mind. I shook my head.

"You've been quite helpful," Detective Kanui said. He paused briefly before adding, "Mrs. Nightingale."

I didn't bother to explain that it was Ms. After marrying Brent I had retained my single name and at this moment the fact seemed unimportant. Brent, on the other hand, thought otherwise. When the tall detective mistakenly referred to him as Mr. Nightingale, he set everyone straight.

"I am Mr. Brent Lark," he announced. "My wife is Ms. Philomela Nightingale." Detective Sanders looked vaguely puzzled, so Brent provided more details. "Because of her successful career, she chose after our marriage to retain her maiden name."

I gazed with admiration at Brent. He had described the publication of my meagre magazine as a successful career.

"Perfectly understandable," Detective Kanui said, and his bright eyes resembled those of a wise old owl. "We have your temporary, Maui address. Could you give us your permanent phone number and home address?"

As Brent stated the address and phone number of our home in Calgary, Detective Sanders jotted the information in his notepad. Brent answered a few more questions, and then both detectives moved over to the other two witnesses.

Detective Kanui introduced himself and his cohort to Glenn and his companion. He asked questions of a general nature in a pleasant tone of voice and Glenn's answers were so soft I could barely distinguish his words. Detective Sanders jotted the replies in his notebook. Detective Kanui asked what they knew about the victim and instead of an answer he received blank looks. He repeated the question.

"We didn't know her at all," Glenn's companion replied. "I, like, had never seen her before."

Detective Kanui focused on Glenn who replied in a faltering manner, "Well, we, um, had never met the victim." His shoulders sagged and his self-confidence seemed to dribble down a drain. "We ah didn't know her, but we've seen her around."

"Where?" his companion asked, looking at him sharply.

Glenn ignored her and pointed to Brent, "This man called and asked if we had a cellphone so we climbed up the dune and saw this." He pointed to the corpse. "I called the police."

I watched my old flame, surprised at his sudden lack of sophisticated confidence. He had never lacked it in the distant past, nor had he lacked it two days ago at the *Hole-In-The-Wall-Cafe*, nor yesterday on the beach access path. But today, on top of the dune, he suddenly seemed unsure of himself.

Detective Kanui watched him closely then asked if they had been taking a morning walk on the beach when Brent called to them. Glenn replied affirmatively. The detective probed further about any previous contacts with the victim and Glenn shook his head. I thought his face reddened slightly and I wondered if he knew more about Marlene than he was willing to tell. Then again, maybe my imagination was on a roll.

Detective Sanders added his bit by mundanely requesting their permanent street address and phone number. He wrote down the answers. To the question regarding their local holiday address Glenn replied clearly, "A beach condo called *The Nest*." Detective Sanders wrote the name in his notepad.

Detective Kanui tossed out a few more routine questions and politely listened to Glenn's answers. None of the answers offered much that was new or enlightening. Detective Kanui again gazed pensively up at the sky and for a moment or two seemed to forget all of us.

I broke his rumination: "I think the murder weapon is here on the dune."

He turned quickly and his eyes dropped from the sky and pierced mine. Detective Sanders frowned at me as if I knew too much for my own good. It crossed my mind that the latter probably considered me not an innocent bystander but a murder suspect. It was an unsettling prospect.

I gazed at the inquisitors and tried to look exceedingly innocent, knowing full well it probably made me look guiltier than ever. I dropped my eyes and wished I had not mentioned anything about a weapon. But it was too late, I had to continue.

"White coral," I muttered. "It's under some groundcover leaves." Reluctantly, I moved toward the well hidden object, stopped beside it and pointed.

Both detectives walked over to where I pointed. Spotting the coral, Detective Kanui squatted down and scrutinized it. He pulled a plastic glove from his pocket, put it on his left hand and moved two leaves. He touched the jagged edges of coral gingerly then glanced at his cohort who had squatted close beside him. Without a word they nodded to each other, apparently agreeing it could very well be the murder weapon. The sound of new voices prompted them to stand up and look at the edge of the dune.

Three new people climbed over the rim. They carried cameras and assorted equipment and after greeting the police and the detectives proceeded to perform their magic. Detective Kanui instructed one of them to take the fingerprints of both my hands, and he did. When the task was completed, Detective Kanui gave the four of us permission to leave.

"We have your addresses here on Maui," he said. "We'll contact you in a few days, sooner if necessary. Are any of you planning to leave the island within the next four days?"

We replied with negative head shakes.

A few minutes later, down on the beach, Glenn regained his familiar self-assurance.

"Well," he said, "this has been quite a morning," He walked with his companion who maintained her innocent and youthful demeanour and repeated parrot-like some of Detective Kanui's phrases. Behind them, Brent and I strolled like silent ghosts. As we approached the beach path to our condo, Glenn turned to Brent and said, "I guess this is where we part company."

Brent studied Glenn, apparently wondering how he knew where we were staying. Then he politely nodded his head and said, "It's ironical and sad that we must deal with a death on a day that normally celebrates a birth."

"Yes," Glenn said, "it's very sad," But he didn't look particularly sad.

"Paradise can be deceiving," I said, and gazed pointedly at my ex-fiancée

Glenn took his companion's arm and turned away from us. "We'll see you around."

"Goodbye for now," Brent said, and entered the beach access path.

The recent tragic happening made the warning on the surveillance sign seem mundane and irrelevant. We walked despondently past it and stepped on the coarse green grass of the lawn.

"What's with that Glenn Shaw fellow, Philomela? You obviously know him."

My reply did not get past my lips. In stunned silence we stared at *Hale Sun and Surf.* The rising of a supine corpse could not have surprised us more.

CHAPTER 18

Shocked, speechless, and amazed, we stared at the scene in front of us. It contrasted so sharply with the scene on top of the dune that it was almost impossible to absorb. Going from sublime to ridiculous would have been easier than going from unbelievable horror to incredible joy.

Three children attired in pink shorts and pink T-shirts jumped up and down. They clapped their hands excitedly and gazed with pure pleasure at a large, imposing figure. The object of their attention was none other than a Maui version of Santa Claus.

He stood near the shuffleboard and there was no mistaking him for anyone else. His garb, compared to Great White North standards, was untraditional. A red sunhat crowned his head, a white moustache adorned his upper lip, a long white beard decorated his chin and cheeks and fell to his upper chest. In lieu of a red snowsuit trimmed with white faux-fur he wore a pair of red walking shorts, a red, short-sleeved T-shirt with a white stripe down centre front, and a brown belt with a big silver buckle. Bracelets comprised of bells circled his wrists and jingled every time he moved his brown arms. Instead of wearing snow boots and riding in a sleigh filled with gifts and pulled by reindeer, he wore flip-flops, walked on his own two feet, and over his shoulder carried a light canvas bag overflowing with gifts.

With a loud "Ho ho ho" he removed the bag from his shoulder and the children jumped higher and laughed louder. Their parents stood off to one side and clicked cameras, recording the happy Yuletide event for posterity.

Brent and I stood and stared. We were entranced by Santa's sartorial splendour and the cheery, tropical outfits worn by members of his appreciative audience. The horror of murder dropped into a hidey-hole of memory, replaced by the uplifting scene of joy and peace and goodwill.

Our minds cleared and we felt transformed. Grinning at each other, we moved forward, stopped at the tap and rinsed sand off our feet. We put on our flip-flops, gazed again at the happy people and walked on the grass toward them.

With a sharp intake of air I grabbed Brent's arm and forced him to stop. He had no comprehension of why I had halted him so abruptly

"What is it?" he asked.

"Leone," I whispered.

"Is she here?"

"The blond wearing green shorts and green and beige shirt."

He looked over at the group of adults and nodded. "I see her."

We silently studied Leone. Standing several metres behind the children, she was listening to the granny whose black bathing suit had been replaced by a red and white sundress. The granny apparently said something humorous for Leone laughed and politely placed her hand over her open mouth.

"Brent," I whispered, and clutched his arm tighter. "Is it up to us to tell her about her daughter?"

"Definitely not." His facial expression was stern and his voice was definite and reassuring: "The police will do it. They have experience with such things. They'll break the news in a gentle yet official manner."

"Good."

Side by side we skirted the happy group, hurried across the grass and headed for the passageway. With no inkling of what to say to Leone, I hoped to avoid her completely, and Brent, who had never met her, would be as much at a loss for words as I. We reached the entrance of the dim passageway and started to enter it. I heaved a loud sigh of relief. Escape was imminent.

"Philomela."

Oh no. That one word terminated our getaway. I stopped and stood deathly still. Like a robot I turned and looked over at Leone.

"Do you see Santa Claus?" she called, walking quickly toward us.

I nodded. "He looks grand and tropical and very Christmasy."

She reached the passageway and stopped beside us. Smiling up at Brent she said, "You must be Philomela's good-looking husband."

"I'm her husband, but the good-looking part is questionable."

"Not according to my eyes."

I performed introductions and she asked Brent if yesterday's flight had been pleasant.

"No complaints," he replied. "And now I'm enjoying the good weather."

"You and Philomela must have dinner some evening with Fred and me. There are some excellent restaurants nearby. We don't even need to drive. We can just walk to them." Brent nodded and she babbled on, "There's an Italian restaurant, a Vietnamese restaurant, a Chinese restaurant, and a Japanese one."

As she chatted in friendly fashion, I listened with increasing dismay. The poor soul was already coping with the sorrow of her daughter's drug addiction and unsavoury profession by putting up a brave front. And now she would have to cope with something far worse. I finally could not stand the subterfuge any longer; I felt obliged to speak of my dreadful discovery.

"Leone," I said, interrupting her flow of words. "Brent and I are harbingers of bad news. The police are checking a young woman up on a sand dune."

She looked at me blankly for a few seconds and then simply shrugged. "So what's bad about that?"

"She's a beautiful girl with brunette, wavy hair."

She looked intently at my face and I saw the blank expression slowly change to dismay. "Marlene?" she murmured. "You're not talking about Marlene."

"Yes, I am."

"Is she spaced out on drugs?"

This was getting worse with every word. Not knowing how to continue made me momentarily speechless.

"What's wrong with her? Is she behaving irrationally?"

"Oh Leone," I blurted, "she's dead."

"Dead? What are you talking about?"

"I know. It's unbelievable. But it's true. I was the one who found her body."

"You found her body?" She repeated my words as if too stunned to think of any words of her own. She moved to the wall outside the passageway and leaned against it. Her eyes gazed at the concrete terrace and she shuddered with disbelief. In her place, I probably would have reacted in exactly the same manner.

"Yes, I found her. The police asked me how to get in touch with you, so I told them about your condominium. I'm sure they'll be here soon."

"The police? Here?" She repeated my words as if unable to coin her own.

In the bright sunlight she looked pale and distraught. Afraid she might collapse from shock I walked over to her and put my arm around her. She lowered her head on my shoulder and sobbed quietly. I stroked her hair. Finally she raised her head and looked at me with tear filled eyes.

"My little Marlene." She spoke sadly and seemed in a depressing trance. Her words negated reality and it crossed my mind she might be in complete denial. She waved her right hand toward the immediate reality of Santa Claus and the laughing children. With a convulsive sob she said, "My little girl. It's Christmas and Santa's here."

Brent stepped close and asked, "Leone, would you like me to escort you to your condo?"

"It's just a few doors away. I can manage."

I shuddered. We should have been celebrating the anniversary of a wondrous birth, not the reality of a horrendous death.

CHAPTER 19

𝓑rent and I sat at the plastic table on our lanai. We tried our utmost to enjoy breakfast and failed miserably. Our first morning together on Maui bore no resemblance to the happiness I had imagined and anticipated. Peace on earth and good will toward men was replaced by horror and depression.

Paradise was lost.

Behaving like a person in deep mourning, I looked at the sea and found the wave action dreary and boring. Even the palm trees flicked their fronds with useless futility, and in the air birds squawked no joyous melody. I glanced across the table at Brent. Our eyes met but no words came forth. We both looked down at our plates, moved food around with our forks and ate little. What we did eat helped preclude conversation.

We set our half empty plates aside and silently sipped coffee. Brent made a supreme effort to start a conversation by saying the coffee tasted good. From there we ventured into the discussion of safe subjects such as weather and scenery. With the artistry of ballet dancers we skirted my discovery on the dune and our disconcerting revelation to Leone. The two awful subjects could not remain hidden forever, so finally they surfaced.

"If you hadn't followed the trail of bloody spots," Brent said, "Marlene might not have been found for days."

"That's true."

"Few people have your ungovernable curiosity." A few hours earlier that would have brought a smile to my lips, but now it did not. Brent continued, "Those who do have such curiosity seldom pursue it. A while longer and a high tide or a rogue wave would have removed the blood stain from the beach forever."

Once the floodgate of horror was opened, we sailed into its verbal depths with ever increasing detail. When the subject eventually seemed ready to sink, I changed tack and our conversational sails caught a different wind, a wind that blew us into the vital question of detection.

"Who did it?" I asked.

"I don't know." He shook his head. "I just hope the police find the killer soon." He leaned back in his chair and closed his eyes as if pondering the dreadful subject. A few seconds later he said, "It may have been a random slaying, someone out of his mind on drugs. Then again, it could have been a money-seeking purse snatcher who panicked when the victim fought back."

"It also could have been premeditated. Someone she knew. Someone bent on doing evil."

"Do you have a suspect in mind?"

After hesitating a few seconds I responded with a minimal shake of the head. I had no proof so my prime suspect's identity stayed sealed within my lips. "Speaking of suspects," I said, "Detective Sanders seemed to suspect me. After I mentioned the hunk of coral he glared and watched me closely. He hardly took his eyes off me while my fingerprints were being taken."

"I noticed that, too. But he has to be thorough." A minute later he elaborated and his tone of voice was clear and matter of fact. "As far as both detectives are concerned, we're all suspects, and we will be until the killer is apprehended. You just happened to find the victim, you also just happened to know who she was, and as it turned out you also happened to be the one who spotted what might be the murder weapon. I happened to be with you, so I'm as much a suspect as you are."

His words were reassuring, but not very. They didn't imply I was a murderess, but they did imply I knew more about the victim and her family than the average innocent bystander. The idea of my being a possible murder suspect remained.

"I dislike being a suspect," I said. "It's dreadfully disconcerting."

"The whole situation is disconcerting. I can't think of a worse way to start a holiday together." His eyes glanced out to sea, his body shifted in the chair, and his throat cleared away a frog. Looking again at me he forced a grin, albeit a superficial one, and tried to portray a positive attitude. He reminded me of a nervous chairman of the board taking control of a meeting.

"Philomela, we mustn't let this awful crime ruin our entire holiday. We're not part of the viciousness. We barely knew the victim and her mother. We're not involved in this case in any way except as innocent bystanders. You found the victim and I arranged for someone to call the police. That is all."

"So?"

"So who knows when we'll come again to Maui? I suggest we wash our breakfast dishes, go over to the dive shop and rent some snorkelling equipment."

I reached across the table and patted his hand. "Brent, that's a colossal idea. But there's a problem…today is Christmas and the shops are closed."

With the palm of his right hand he struck his forehead. "Partzheimer's."

"At least it isn't Alzheimer's." I managed a weak smile.

Our attempts at being funny, though feeble, were the first hint of humour that had risen since my discovery of the corpse.

"Well," he said, "we'll rent equipment tomorrow. The shops will be open. Unlike Canadians, Americans ignore the great English tradition of Boxing Day."

"Yes, instead of cleaning up gift boxes and dashing off to Boxing Day sales, they behave like normal human beings. But that doesn't matter because tomorrow is Sunday and most shops will be closed."

"Jinxed again. Monday will be the day. We'll go to the shops first thing Monday morning and rent snorkelling equipment."

My nod was agreeable, but my thoughts were not—they drifted back to earlier events and produced a picture of Marlene lying supinely on the groundcover. The victim would have looked attractive if her thinness and facial sores had not been so obvious. I tried to envision her as alive and drop dead gorgeous, but it was only wishful thinking. I shook my head to clear my little grey cells of dust and lint and mist.

"Brent," I said, and sat up straight, forced a smile, and tried to follow his optimistic lead. "You're right. We mustn't let the murder ruin our entire holiday. After all, like you said, we didn't know the girl or her family, not really. And it may be eons before we get back to Maui."

"Truer words were never spoken." The corners of his mouth curved into a wan smile then faded. He shuddered. "Until last night I had never heard of Marlene Rathbone. This morning I saw her for the first time."

"Brent, today we'll relax and enjoy the sun and swim in the pool." I picked up a piece of toast and with a knife spread guava jelly on it. "Dinner tonight will be steak and onions instead of turkey and cranberry sauce. Is that okay?"

"Perfect. I prefer steak to turkey any day."

Compared to the earlier horror, we managed to keep the rest of the morning relatively pleasant. We swam in the pool and played games of shuffle board and miniature golf. During our golf game Andrew Strong stopped by and wished us Merry Christmas. I introduced him to Brent.

"I'm sure you'll enjoy your time here," he said, smiling at Brent.

"I'll do my best."

Andrew seemed a trifle surprised at Brent's response; after all, most vacationers expounded enthusiastically about the island and its weather. As if Brent needed guidance, he proceeded to explain several pleasant activities available on Maui, all the time speaking and behaving as if the world and everything in it was normal and beautiful.

It dawned on me that he was unaware of Marlene's death. Because the victim didn't live at *Hale Sun and Surf,* the police had not bothered to contact the residential handy-man, even though the girl's mother lived here. Leone, after learning of her daughter's death, had quietly entered her condominium and closed the door and the drapes and spoken to no one.

A pause in the men's conversation gave me an opportunity to drop the bombshell. "Andrew, have you heard about Leone Humphries' daughter?"

He groaned, rolled his eyes and asked, "What's she done now?"

"She was murdered."

"What?" He stared at me, wide eyed. "Are you serious?"

"I'm perfectly serious. I found her body on top of a sand dune."

His attitude and demeanour changed from day to night. He stared at me with disbelief, his face paled and he was momentarily speechless. Finally his lips formed a soundless, "Why?"

"Nobody knows," Brent replied. "Yet."

Andrew's shoulders slumped forward and his face sagged. He seemed to lose four centimetres in height. "She had her problems, but she didn't deserve to be murdered." He gazed at me with eyes filling with moisture. "I once was madly in love with her. I even hoped she'd kick the drug habit so we could get together again." He moved his head from side to side. "Are you sure it wasn't a drug overdose?"

"Someone struck her on the head," I said, then added, "You've known her for quite a long time."

"About six years. She was the reason I stayed on Maui and didn't return to Berkley to resume my studies."

Empathy oozed from me. "Leone wishes you had become her son-in-law."

"I wished that, too, for a year or so. Unfortunately, another man entered the picture and dimmed that possibility. Tim Jones was the straw that broke the camel's back. He introduced her to drugs."

"I'm sorry." The two words were useless but true—I really was sorry. It crossed my mind that Tim Jones and Motor-Mouth might be one and the same. I let the thought drift away and asked, "Did Marlene's personality change after she started using illicit drugs?"

"Drastically."

"It must have been terrible for you, Andrew. It was terrible for Leone, too. Right now her daughter's death surpasses everything else. Happening on Christmas day somehow makes it worse."

"Poor Leone. Everything that could go wrong went wrong." He was pensive a moment then said, "The other day on the beach I ran into Marlene and for several minutes I actually hoped things might change for the better. I mentioned treatment for her addiction and that finished it."

"She refused," I said.

"In no uncertain terms. She flew into a rage, an unwarranted rage. It made me angry."

"She hit you," I said.

He stared at me in surprise.

"I saw her, Andrew. I was walking behind you. You know, she once got angry with me, too." I told him of her paranoid accusations and of her striking my shoulder.

"It's hard to believe she once was a gentle, fun loving person."

That, of course, was an aspect of the victim I had never witnessed. To more or less warn him I said, "I'm sure the police will want to talk with you."

He shrugged. "How can I help them? I have no idea who would commit such a crime."

Later that afternoon, Brent and I lay on chaises-longue in the sun and scanned several tourist brochures Brent had picked up in the passageway.

"We could rent a helicopter and tour Maui," I said.

"Or we could take the car and drive up island," Brent suggested.

"A short road trip would be nice."

"How about a flight in a fixed-wing plane over the active volcanoes on the big island?"

"Oh," I replied with a wide grin, "What a good idea. I'd love to do that."

"That appeals to me, too. I'll take this brochure when we go up to the condo. Tomorrow or the next day I'll phone and make a reservation."

"Sounds good."

The afternoon sun moved farther west. Brent's jetlag caught up with him and instigated a nap. I flipped through parts of Mark Twain's travel book and reread how Hawaiian priests sacrificed victims to the god, Lono. Then I read the brief account of natives murdering Captain James Cook on the island of Kauai.

Murders had occurred in 1866 and one had occurred today. I considered reinserting the sorry subject in my article: *Hawaii, Then and Now*.

After going upstairs to the condo, Brent put the *Volcano Tour* brochure on the coffee table and I took steak and vegetables from the fridge. I placed knives, forks, and serviettes on the table in the dining area and with a flamboyant flourish stuck sprigs of groundcover in a water glass as a centrepiece. Brent disassociated the greenery from the crime scene and remarked that it looked festive indeed.

The sun lowered to the horizon, so we went out on the lanai to watch it sink below the sea. A neighbour performed the conch shell blowing ritual and everyone standing on their lanais applauded his effort. The rusty orb disappeared from sight and miracle of miracles Brent and I saw a green flash. We both let out screams of excitement.

"I saw it!" we exclaimed in unison.

"It really does happen," he said.

We had learned about the green flash ten years ago on a Mayan cruise in the Gulf of Mexico. We had been on our honeymoon and because of other important activities had missed some lectures given by archaeologists and astronomers onboard ship. But we had managed to attend the lecture about the green flash. We soon discovered that learning about it was one thing and seeing it was quite another. Over the years at different locations we studied subsequent sunsets. Until this evening the gorgeous green flash had evaded us.

Thrilled with the discovery that it actually existed, we tried to remember details of the lecture.

"I think the flash briefly forms when the yellow sun and the blue sea blend together," I said. "Yellow and blue make green."

"True. The green flash is at the top of the setting sun and it's the last thing seen as the sun disappears into the water."

A short while later we sat inside at our festive little table. We sipped red wine from long stemmed glasses, ate delicious beef steak, Greek salad, crisp French bread, and chatted mostly about the green flash. Not once did we mention the murdered girl.

We went to bed early, appreciating the fact we were alive and well. We slept the sleep of the dead.

CHAPTER 20

𝓑rent and I sauntered onto the beach and with no questions asked automatically turned in the opposite direction from yesterday's walk. Discussion was unnecessary—we both lacked a desire to revisit the murder site. Strolling on the freshly washed sand, we admired the peaceful Pacific Ocean, the soft warm air, dawn's rosy glow, and the attractive beachfront buildings. We greeted other early risers but saw no one we recognized. Our morning stroll was pleasant, invigorating, and uneventful.

It was Boxing Day and we had no gift boxes to flatten for recycling. On the lanai we ate breakfast in relative silence, half expecting a visit from the detectives. They failed to appear.

"The detectives," Brent said, "have other people to question and other areas to search. Besides, they deserve holiday time with their families."

"It must be difficult to repress horror in order to joke and laugh with spouses and children."

He nodded. "A pleasant respite with loved ones should renew their vigour and enthusiasm for clue searching."

"I hope so. And we amateurs should help them as much as possible. But where can we start?"

"In the bathroom."

"What?"

He pushed back his chair and stood up.

Watching him leave the lanai I giggled. Murder or not, Brent made me laugh and it felt good. Sitting alone on the lanai I returned to the idea of helping the professionals search for clues. Where should we start to look for them? Answers underwhelmed me. Why should we look for them? An answer overwhelmed me—to help police speed up the wheels of justice.

Brent and I lacked the instinct of how a psychotic killer's mind worked. Nor were we educated in matters of motives, such as revenge, anger, greed or power. Methods of murder were not our expertise either. Nothing in the way of physical clues, psychological theories, history of the victim, or clever character analysis were within our grasp. The detectives knew everything we knew and everything we had done so our part in the investigation seemed more or less over. Should we just sit back and wait for them to solve the case?

It was mid-afternoon when Brent stretched out on the sitting room couch and dozed under his thrilling adventure book. I sat nearby at the table and added a few items to my article for *The Integrator*. The word flow was adequate but not stimulating, so I rewrote a few paragraphs with the hope of spicing up the article. The snippets I added here and there failed to enhance the article.

Would learning to meditate at the Outer Fringe shop inspire my writing skills? Not likely. Would refraining from drinking wine and eating meat and sweets purify my soul and enhance my ideas? Not likely. But the mere thought of food seemed to stimulate new ideas; they dripped from brain to fingers to pen to paper. The ideas related to wars, sacrifices, murders and they added a lot of zip. After quietly rereading my newly written words aloud I said, "Oh no." The words were not zippy, they were horrific.

My voice must have wakened Brent for he opened his eyes and looked around. "I think I dozed off," he said.

"You did. The cause is a one thousand and seventeen metre altitude change."

"That'll do it." He smiled and sat up.

I put my pen and paper away and challenged him to a game of miniature golf. He accepted with surprising alacrity. Maybe it wasn't so surprising, for down on the putting greens he trounced me badly. I managed to redeem myself by winning a game of shuffleboard. During both games we caught glimpses of no one we knew. Not Leone Humphries, Andrew Strong, Fred Pederson, nor thank goodness of Glenn Shaw or Motor-Mouth.

The day ended not with flattened gift boxes, but with another glorious sunset. Our neighbour with the conch shell must have been away for no sound signalled the sun's final descent. However, the gods and the weather conditions were with us. Once again we saw the fleeting green flash.

We felt blessed indeed, partly because we saw the green flash but mainly because we were alive and well and enjoying our holiday.

Was everything calm before another storm?

CHAPTER 21

Monday morning and the weather was more of the same—sunny and warm.

Instead of going for a beach promenade, Brent and I ate breakfast at our leisure then sauntered to the outdoor mall. We intended to wander aimlessly until everything came to life, however, wandering aimlessly proved unnecessary. Just as we approached the dive shop a man opened the door and bade us a cheery good morning.

"Do you work here?" Brent asked.

"Yes, I own this place."

"Are you open for business?"

"I am." He bent down, stuck a wooden wedge under the open door and said, "Now the door won't swing shut." He stood up and smiled at us. "Come on in."

We followed him inside and proceeded to study various displays of snorkelling equipment. Brent paid particular attention to specific brand names. He knew what he wanted whereas I was clueless. I had no idea what items would best serve our purposes. After a few minutes, Brent walked to the owner who stood behind the counter sorting merchandise and asked him a few brilliant questions.

I listened then eloquently said,: "For a person dedicated to skiing on snowy slopes you have great knowledge of snorkelling on silvery seas."

Brent stared at me a second and shook his head. His expression of mock sympathy was unable to hide a rumbling in his throat. It rose to his mouth and came out as a loud guffaw.

The owner, oblivious to the silly drama triggered by my awful alliteration, asked if we had seen a particular mask. Containing our mirth, we turned and watched him hold it in front of his face. We listened to him extol its virtues and when his sales pitch ended Brent pointed to a display of flippers on a nearby shelf. He and the owner walked over to them and discussed their pros and cons.

I moved to a display in the window and scrutinized a black and blue wetsuit. My attention switched to two pedestrians strolling on the sidewalk outside the window. Only the thick plate-glass prevented me from reaching out and touching them. They chatted with each other and then both laughed at a shared joke. The shock of white hair on the taller man and the crown of brown hair on the other left no doubt as to their identity. Ezekiel and Daniel were out strolling, either as a form of easy exercise or on their way home after eating breakfast in a local restaurant. Their carefree joy indicated a lack of worldly worries or undue sadness.

Would they be so happy if they knew about the death of their female friend? Probably not. I felt a sudden impulse to dash outside and pass on the tragic information. Because they knew the victim they might be of great assistance to the detectives. Or, and I shuddered at the thought, could they be the guilty parties? Could that explain their relaxed and happy behaviour?

Suppressing that unwanted thought, I hurried toward the shop's open door. It seemed vitally important that they learn of Marlene's death.

"Philomela." Brent's voice stopped me in mid-step. "Is there anything special you'd like to buy or rent?"

Though wanting to chase the two men, I let Brent's question take precedence and replied, "My knowledge of the equipment is meagre. I'll rely on your judgement." I gave him a big smile and stepped outside. Too late. The two men had disappeared, either around the corner or into the hardware store. I re-entered the dive shop and sauntered over to Brent.

He held a mask, snorkel and flippers in his hands. Satisfied with his choices he set them on the counter. He obtained a second set and put them on the counter also. Picking up the second mask he said, "You should try this one on."

I pulled the strap over my head and placed the mask so it fit snugly over my face. "It feels comfortable," I mumbled, but it felt a lot more comfortable after I removed it.

Brent took his credit card from his wallet and handed it to the shop owner. "If flippers were easy to take on the plane, I'd buy rather than rent them. It would be cheaper in the long run."

The owner nodded. "You could use them for years to come."

"It might be cheaper," I said, "but imagine the hassle of getting all that stuff through airport security."

Brent chuckled. "It could be quite entertaining."

"You mean confusing and frustrating and maddening. Security officers would confiscate them because flippers are weapons of mass destruction."

"How do you figure that?" he asked.

"With the swing of one flipper I could smack the heads of several people. Think what two flippers could do."

He grinned. "We'd end up in jail."

"Good grief." I closed my eyes because the word jail brought up a vision of the two detectives charging me with the murder. I sucked extra air into my lungs and opened my eyes. There were no bars in front of me.

Brent recognized my reaction to the unintended word association and smiled. "All is well," he said and turned to the shop owner. In a businesslike manner he signed on the dotted line of the merchant's Visa copy, politely accepted the customer's copy and tucked it and his credit card inside his wallet.

"I've not been to this shopping mall before," he said to the owner. "Could we leave our rental equipment with you for an hour or so while we wander around?"

"No problem, Sir. I'll keep them right here, behind the counter."

Brent thanked him and we went outside.

I looked again for Ezekiel and Daniel but they were long gone. The warm air enveloped me, inducing languid and lazy feelings. "I think I'm too relaxed to browse and shop," I said.

"That'll save us heaps of money."

The irony of his words made me smile; he was more of an irresponsible spendthrift than I. Looking up at the cloudless sky I squinted in the bright sunlight. Looking down at the sidewalk I admired feet adorned in sandals and flip-flops. Finally gazing at shoppers, I smiled at their happy faces.

It was easy to understand the basis of people's happiness. Decorations and cheerful messages such as *Happy Holiday, Happy New Year,* and even belated *Merry Christmas* were in windows everywhere. The festive words and sparkling lights spread through the entire area. They kept thoughts of murder at bay.

Hand in hand Brent and I wandered along the sidewalk, stopping every so often to admire specific window displays. We ignored the Tattoo Parlour, having no interest in receiving skin punctures or of reviving a conscious connection with Marlene and her decorated friend. Too soon for a coffee break, we bypassed the shop where Leone and I had enjoyed our caffeinated brews and friendly chat.

Needless to say, Brent showed a total lack of interest in ladies' fashions. Nor did he pay any attention to the shop selling *Outer Fringe* novelties. A gymnasium, however, caught his eye.

"Let's go in here," he said. "This looks interesting."

"For whom?"

"Come on, you'll love it."

With no desire to lift colourful weights, no urge to stride on a boring treadmill, no wish to glide on a soothing elliptic, no craving to ride a stationary bike, and no longing to row a pretend boat, I followed him inside. In my humble opinion, exercise was vastly overrated.

With enthusiasm bubbling from every pore, Brent gazed at the cavernous space. With increasing apathy I dragged behind him. A fit looking young man sidled up to us and smiled at Brent. He knew who might be a potential customer.

"Good morning, Sir. Can I help you?"

Brent looked at him and asked, "Could we check out the machines?"

"Certainly. Just follow me."

After what seemed ten hours of looking at torturous machines but was in reality closer to ten minutes, Brent said, "I might come here and work out. Do you charge by the hour?"

"There's a daily charge, and you can stay as long as you like."

At this point I noticed a young man lifting weights and flexing muscles. His back was to us, but I recognized the physique and fair hair of Andrew Strong. He, on the other hand, was so intent on his activities that he gave us not even a cursory glance. He appeared as strong as his name implied and my thoughts darkened as my little grey cells envisioned him carrying a limp Marlene up the sand dune. Could she have angered him enough on the beach to incite his killing her? I shivered.

The fitness salesman spoke to Brent and interrupted my rumination. "You won't regret it, Sir. Nor you, Ma'am. Exercising keeps you fit and healthy. Everyone feels better after a workout. As you likely know, exercise is the new fountain of youth."

Fountain of youth. Now that sounded encouraging. Maybe I should become a fitness guru myself—sometime in the far future. I turned and watched Andrew Strong pump iron as if there were no tomorrow.

"Strong and healthy muscles prevent injuries from falls and other accidents," the salesman said. His words, I knew, contained a ring of truth. I looked at him with new respect.

When his monologue ceased I turned to Brent. "There may be more to this exercising than I realized."

"Do you want to join me on a treadmill?"

"You build muscle and tighten butt. I'll exercise by hunting and gathering in all the shops."

Two vertical lines appeared in his forehead illustrating mock concern. "Bad idea. Our bank account...." His frown deepened and his voice faded to a low monotone: "Hunting and gathering could be expensive...."

"And fun."

The lines between his eyebrows disappeared and with a smile he thanked the young man. He took my arm and guided me toward the door. I glanced once more at Andrew Strong and wondered if he had heard our voices. He gave no indication of having seen or heard us.

After leaving the gym we toured a huge drug store and a tiny unisex beachwear shop, poked our noses in a few other places and then began to slow down.

"I feel gaunt," I said. "Are you hungry?"

"Starving."

We entered a small eatery. It was bigger than the *Hole-In-The-Wall-Cafe* where I had talked with Glenn Shaw, but less classy than *The Wave* where I had encountered Motor-Mouth and his two friends. At the counter we chose the makings for two sandwiches. After the chef piled mountains of meat and fresh veggies on slices of multigrain bread, we each picked up a tropical beverage. Brent paid for the lot and we carried them through the open door to a table on the wide sidewalk.

We sat down and for the hundredth time marvelled at the weather. The end of December and we sat outside attired in summery clothes. What an incredible treat.

Our breakfasts had been light so the sandwiches tasted all the more delicious. The nourishment in our stomachs improved our dispositions and revived our energies. With happy frames of mind we gazed across the table at each other and exchanged tales of two recent incidents: His had happened to a co-worker and mine had happened at the Calgary airport.

Brent told his story first. "Do you remember Jim, the geologist?" I nodded and he continued, "Well, a month ago he slipped on a banana peel and fell flat on his derriere in front of a young lady whom he had often admired from afar. He was extremely embarrassed. Concerned about his well-being, she offered to buy him a cup of coffee and he accepted. Last week they announced their engagement."

"Who would think falling on a banana peel could be romantic?" I grinned and related my tale about the customs' lady.

"A funny combination...not flossing teeth and not learning the computer." He chuckled appreciatively.

"That lady broke the ice and started my holiday on the right foot." My words were a bit of a mixed metaphor, but who cared? I was on holidays. I didn't even associate the word ice with Marlene.

A breeze passed over us and a nearby palm tree waved ever so gently. Brent gazed at it and sighed. "Can you believe the weather at home is freezing and the ground is covered with snow? I don't mean to harp on the subject, but the temperature difference between here and there is hard to grasp."

"Imagine living here all year with no perceptible change of seasons."

"Imagine not having to shovel snow."

I giggled and at that moment a person stopped beside Brent. I looked up and my mirth slipped like a slimy oyster down my throat. I swallowed hard and said, "Hi Leone." Fred stood behind her and I included him in my greeting. With extreme courtesy I asked, "Will you sit down and join us?"

"Please do." Brent gallantly stood up and pulled a chair from under the table for Leone. She thanked him and sat down.

Fred walked silently around the table, sat on a chair beside me, and I introduced him to Brent. My mind became as brilliant as an astronomical black hole. What to say? What to do? I wanted to ease Leone's pain, but knew not how to do it. Could a person's words extinguish another's grief? Could a person help ease another's pain? Should a sad issue be skirted circuitously as though it had never happened? Should words strike the target like Zeus's thunderbolt and face the grief dead on?

Fortunately, that inappropriate expression stayed within my lips. The phrase *dead on* was okay mentally but unacceptable orally. Brent came to my rescue.

He turned to Leone and pointedly asked, "Have the police come up with any clues regarding the death of your daughter?"

She mutely shook her head and Fred replied, "Nothing that we know of."

"I suppose fingerprinting results and other tests will take a few days," Brent said.

"No doubt." Fred spoke rather curtly, but who could blame him?

After a moment's silence, Brent said, "No purse was found at the scene. I wonder if the murderer was a purse snatcher."

Leone lowered her eyes as if in pain. A moment later she raised them and glanced at Brent. "It's quite possible. She often carried a purse."

"Maybe he was a drug addict," Brent mused, "looking for money to feed his addiction."

"When the detectives questioned us on Christmas day," Fred said, "they asked about drugs. But they didn't mention anything about a purse."

"Perhaps they think it's unimportant," Brent said. "Or perhaps they haven't even thought of it."

It crossed my mind that law enforcers could be suppressing evidence in order to weed out cranks and publicity seekers. Not being privy to such tactics I deigned to mention it.

Fred silently watched a few pedestrians stroll on the sidewalk behind Leone and Brent. Then, in a tone that conveyed annoyance, he said, "We've seen neither hide nor hair of the detectives since Christmas morning. I hope they're continuing their search and not slacking off. We want the murderer caught and dealt with as soon as possible."

"We do, too," Brent said. After a brief pause he added, "No doubt they'll question us again, soon. They'll want to know if we've thought of anything new that might help with their search."

Leone shook her head. "The only thing I can think of is Tim Jones. I'll stress the need for questioning him."

Fred nodded. "I suppose their first task is to eliminate everyone who was close to Marlene."

"That certainly includes Tim Jones." Leone's voice sounded loud and she spoke the name with bitter emphasis.

"Is Tim Jones a family friend?" I asked, remembering Andrew Strong's condemnation of him.

"He's no friend of mine," Leone said. "Marlene erroneously thought of him as a friend, but he wasn't. He's a drug pusher."

Fred's expression was sympathetic as he gazed across the table at her.

Tim Jones and Motor-Mouth were one and the same. Like Leone, I disliked the man. I knew too little of him to voice an opinion, but Leone had no such qualms.

"I'd wager all my money on Tim Jones," she said and pinched her lips together and nodded her head as if knowing for sure he was the guilty party. "The detectives should also check on workers at the Tattoo Parlour."

Beside me, I felt Fred shudder. Was it because he had talked with the contact person at the Tattoo Parlour? Or was it because his lady for hire had been Leone's daughter? I bit my lower lip and stopped a flow of questions that might incriminate him. I didn't want to make things worse. And maybe he hadn't shuddered at all; maybe it was my imagination again.

He surprised me by saying, "I've met Tim twice. Once he was pleasant and once he was revolting. He's a person I'd rather forget."

"Tim is a creepy devil." Leone spoke with the conviction of one who knew her subject well. "He encourages young boys and girls to try recreational drugs, and then he pimps for them after they're addicted. They pay him as their pimp and they pay him for their drugs. He's a real piece of work."

"He must be quite rich," I mused, remembering the black rocks and his wad of money. "Selling drugs is supposed to be lucrative."

"Criminals seem to find it financially rewarding," Leone said, "for a short while."

"I've seen Tim a few times." Without thinking beyond the moment I rambled on, "He looked and sounded fine the first couple of times. That was in the Calgary airport and in the airplane flying here. He looked dreadful and sounded horrid the third time at *The Wave* restaurant. I was so busy looking at his dyed hair and the squiggles tattooed on his bare arms I hardly recognized him."

Leone turned her head and studied me with intense interest. "You saw him on the airplane?"

"Yes, he and Marlene and I were passengers on the same flight to Maui."

"You didn't mention this before." Leone's voice accused me of the sin of omission.

"I didn't know she was related to you, Leone. And in the restaurant he looked so dreadful I wasn't positive he was the same man I'd seen on the plane. The only reason I remembered him at all was because your daughter was so drop-dead gorgeous." I could have bitten off my tongue. Why had that unfortunate word popped out of my mouth? I tried to smooth over the faux-pas by saying, "It all seemed unimportant until Christmas morning. Then of course everything changed. I've already told the details to the detectives."

That seemed to satisfy Leone, for she leaned back in her chair and sighed.

Thank goodness she didn't ask about the fourth time I saw him. I refrained from mentioning Tim's cough, stomach upset, and his wad of money and syringe.

We sat silently for a moment then Brent, who had never seen Tim Jones, turned the conversation away from murder. "Do you two like to snorkel?" he asked.

Fred shook his head. "You know the scoop...been there, done that, and bought the T-shirt. I have no desire to do it again."

"What about you, Leone?" Brent asked.

"I feel the same way Fred does. I prefer golf."

"Me, too," Fred said.

"Brent and I prefer swimming to golfing," I said.

"To each his own." Leone's lips almost smiled as she added, "I guess that means lying in the sun and eating dinner are the only two things the four of us have in common."

"I guess you're right." I smiled and hoped it looked reassuring.

"We still should have dinner together." Though her expression was sad, Leone glanced at each of us and added, "Everything is terrible, but we still need to eat. Will the detectives stop us from going to a nice restaurant?"

"I'm sure they won't." I was unsure if she was serious or not, so hesitated to suggest a specific place, day, or time. "Do you feel up to it, Leone?"

"I think so. It might take my mind from all the horror...." Unable to voice any specifics, she said, "Even if we go out for just an hour. A nice dinner with nice people in a nice location would be really nice."

"Okay with you?" I asked Brent.

"Sounds fine." He looked first at Leone and then at Fred. "How about Tuesday, tomorrow evening?"

Leone glanced at Fred who nodded agreement.

"Righto," Leone said, "It's a date then." Her lips turned up slightly at the corners. "Why don't you come to my condo for drinks first? Number ten on the ground floor. We can sit out on the lanai."

From then on our conversation focused on weather, shops, and local restaurants. We avoided subjects pertaining to drugs and the murdered girl. When the four of us slowly got up to leave, I said, "Tomorrow at six at Leone's place."

"Righto."

She and Fred wandered in one direction and Brent and I in the other. We stopped at the Dive Shop and picked up our rental equipment then made our way back to the condominium.

CHAPTER 22

"Our newest passion sounds super sexy."

Brent groaned.

His response was expected so I ignored it. "Of course it's not really sexy at all, it just sounds that way." I examined my clean foot, slipped it into a flip-flop then stuck my other foot under the tap.

Waiting for the cleaning procedure to finish, Brent said, "Super sexy is how you look in a swimsuit."

I giggled girlishly, flattered by his words yet at the same time disbelieving them. With mock seriousness I said, "Your praise is valuable, but it might make me vain and vacuous."

"Enough alliteration yet." He put his foot under the tap and in a serious tone said, "Snorkelling is a passion that involves good equipment—mask, flippers, breathing apparatus, etc. And the snorkeler must be able to swim and float. The coup de grace involves good coordination of eye and hand." He shook his foot, put it in a flip flop then placed his other foot under the flow of water.

"You're missing the point. A snorkeler seems super sexy because he floats on top of waves and views life beneath his body. It may sound silly to you, but a non-swimmer could easily misinterpret that description."

"This entire conversation is ridiculous." He stepped away from the tap and glanced at his watch. "Do you realize it's five-thirty?"

"Time flies when you're having fun."

The afternoon had been filled with fun. Brent and I found the snorkelling gear easy to adjust and easy to use. With the aid of masks and flippers we swam lengthy distances and viewed amazing sights. We saw colourful fish, abrupt changes in the sea bottom, and bits of plant life. Most of what we saw was beautiful and none of it scary, except for a big flat fish resting on the sand. Fearing it might be a sting-ray that could become aggressive if disturbed, we avoided it.

We snorkelled most of the afternoon and could have continued longer if hunger and exhaustion hadn't occurred. After cleaning our feet and finishing our discussion on the suggestive aspects of our newest passion, we walked side by side through the dim passageway, climbed the stairs and entered Number 309.

We showered off saltwater, put on dry clothes, and hurried out to our private lanai. We reached it just in time to watch another dramatic sunset, listen to our neighbour blow his conch shell and applaud his musical talent. Due to a slight haze on the horizon no green flash appeared. Night won the tug of war with day and in the kitchen under artificial light I prepared a light meal. We sat at the inside table and ate. Healthy fresh air and exercise had made us tired so we went to bed early and slept soundly.

Tuesday morning we awoke feeling refreshed. Attuned to holiday mode, we walked with enthusiasm to the beach then stopped. Instead of automatically turning away from the direction of the crime scene we admired the white surf in front and the blue dome above.

"Shall we be brave and walk past the site of horror?" Brent asked.

Reluctantly, I said, "Yes."

Drawing near the fateful dune we slowed our pace and looked up. Long stretches of yellow tape marked off the crime scene. Within the restricted area a policeman sauntered back and forth; either protecting the location from snoopers and desecrators or searching for new clues— or both. He paid us no attention. We lingered a minute then continued walking. In single file we passed the point of black rocks. Motor-Mouth aka Tim Jones slithered like a snake into my thoughts, but I managed to banish him. At the flat stretch of beach Marlene popped to mind and I got rid of her by concentrating on the beach attire of other walkers. Brent and I continued walking to the point of land at the end of the bay.

On our return trip we saw not one policeman but two, and they appeared to be taking down the yellow tapes. Trying to be normal and friendly, I waved at them. They either did not see me or chose to ignore my gesture. I moved closer to Brent.

"Once the yellow tapes are gone," I said, "the crime site will become history. Only a few people know about it now, and fewer will remember it later."

He shrugged his shoulders. "It will always be ghostly for us. We'll never forget it."

"Speaking of forgetting, we mustn't forget tonight's dinner date with Leone and Fred."

"To be quite honest," he confessed, "I had forgotten it. Maybe on purpose."

"A pleasant party it won't be. You and I will be tense and uncomfortable. And so will Fred and Leone."

He nodded. "All four of us will pretend we're having a grand time. But murder will be the elephant in the room."

"Is there any way we could get out of it?"

"No." He shook his head.

"You're right. Leone's already depressed and with good reason. If we cancelled we would only add to her misery."

"Like she said...it will be a diversion to have a nice dinner at a nice restaurant."

"With nice people." I grinned at him.

"That goes without saying."

As our condominium building came into view, I noticed two people walking ahead of us. They glanced back, reduced their pace and turned around. I recognized Glenn Shaw and his girlfriend. Brent recognized them, too.

"That's the couple who came to our rescue with a cell phone," he said. "I think they're waiting for us to catch up with them."

I deigned to reply. Seeing Glenn again was not my idea of a good time, not because I cared about him, but because my gut feeling indicated he was up to no good. With luck this would be our last meeting. We drew abreast of them and stopped walking.

"Good morning," Glenn said. His broad smile exposed his sparkling white teeth. Brent and I returned his greeting and he asked, "Have you had enough courage to approach the fateful dune?"

"We just walked past it," Brent replied. "How about you?"

"So far we've steered clear of the area."

The young girl took hold of Glenn's arm. Wide-eyed, she gazed at us. "I was like too upset to go. I couldn't possibly return to that awful place." She shuddered. "My husband agreed we could, like....."

Husband? I heard nothing more. I stared at Glenn. He pointedly turned away from me, seeming to have enough decency to be embarrassed.

"The entire experience was upsetting for both of us," he said to Brent. "It was extremely scary for Zelda."

"It was upsetting and scary for all of us." My tone of voice sounded sharper than I intended. Glenn's deceitfulness annoyed me more than I cared to admit.

He remarried. So what. The issue was not his new wife; it was his not mentioning her when we talked at the *Hole-In-The-Wall-Cafe*. My marriage was discussed and so was his divorce—after I asked about Adelle and their daughter. On the dune I assumed Zelda was his girlfriend or live-in-partner. Now it turned out she was his second wife, or maybe his third or fourth wife. It proved again that Glenn was sleek and slippery, a truth twister and a consummate liar.

His life, of course, was none of my business. But then again, maybe it was. He had invited me to share a meal with him before my husband arrived on Maui, and such a meal could have proved innocently nostalgic and pleasant. But there was no innocence or nostalgia involved in his stalking me, nor in his kiss and his effort to entice me into taking him up to my empty condo. What gall. His words and deeds illuminated his entire personality, brought his true colors to the fore—the leopard had not changed his spots.

My annoyance with him bubbled like boiling water and then burst into a steam of anger. For a second I wanted to kick him in the-you-know-where and tell him to go procreate with himself. Fortunately, the feeling faded as quickly as it appeared. I bit my tongue and remained silent.

"The police are in the process of taking down the yellow crime scene tapes," Brent said. "They must have collected all the evidence they could find."

"When we were, like, on the dune," Zelda said, looking at me, "I heard the detectives talking with you. You, like, know the victim's mother?"

"Yes, I do, but not well. She owns a condo at *Hale Sun and Surf.* I met her for the first time last week."

"She must be beside herself with, like, grief."

"There's no doubt this is a difficult time for her."

Brent stepped closer to Glenn and extended his right hand. "We haven't formally met. I'm Brent Lark and this is my wife, Philomela Nightingale."

Accepting the outstretched hand, Glenn said, "I'm Glenn Shaw and this is my wife, Zelda."

As the two men shook hands, Brent stared at Glenn and his expression was not particularly friendly. I nodded to Zelda, casually mentioned that Glenn and I had met years ago in Calgary, and then nonchalantly resumed walking. The other three followed. Neither Zelda nor Brent asked for details of Glenn's and my previous meeting.

Brent, who was walking between Glenn and Zelda, said, "I understand you live in Calgary. What part?"

"Mount Royal."

"Nice area. Do you own a condo here?"

"No. We're renting one for three weeks. The complex is called *The Nest*. It's farther down the beach."

"Three weeks sounds nice," Brent said. Then he added rather pensively, "We go back to Calgary on Sunday. I'll certainly miss the sun and warmth."

Zelda caught up with me and somewhat breathlessly said, "We arrived five nights before the murder. I was tired from the flight and all, but seeing that body was, like, awful. It made me feel ill at ease and unsafe."

I glanced at her youthful face and frail figure. She was almost as beautiful as Marlene had been, but not quite. Maybe that assessment had something to do with her relationship with Glenn. Did I criticize her for marrying the two-timing liar? He obviously had charmed her as he once had charmed me.

"I don't blame you for feeling ill at ease and unsafe." I figured a husband like Glenn would make any wife feel ill at ease and unsafe, but I kept these words to myself. She had referred of course to a murderer, not to her husband. "A welcome like that would be dreadful for anyone."

"I've never been here before," she said. "On Christmas morning I panicked and like wanted to fly right back home. I'm exhausted. For me the last three nights have been like sleepless in Maui, not sleepless in Seattle."

I smiled at her attempt at humour. She seemed an all right sort of person; too bad she had hooked up with Glenn. It crossed my mind that both attractive young girls who had recently entered my life were involved with undesirable, older men.

But were either of these two men capable of committing murder? That was the burning question. Tim Jones may have had a drug crazed reason to kill Marlene, but why would Glenn kill her? On the dune when the detectives had questioned him about the victim, he behaved in an uneasy manner. He said he had never met her before. I wondered about that. I also wondered if he knew Tim Jones.

"Nightmares wake me up several times a night," Zelda said. "I keep seeing that poor girl lying on top of the dune, like, over and over again. The result is I sleep quite a bit during the day." She glanced back at her husband. "Poor Glenn has to do things on his own."

"I'm sure he can manage that." To my own ears my voice sounded sarcastic.

She missed the sarcasm and smiled at me. "Yes, he's very capable."

My better nature rose to the fore and I sympathized with her tiredness. "Hopefully your nightmares will soon stop. Lack of sleep is debilitating because it makes thought and activity difficult. Look at the positive side...it was fortuitous for us that you two came along when you did, and that you had a cellphone."

"I suppose so." Zelda sounded dubious.

"It's a good way to look at a bad set of circumstances."

"Philomela's right," Brent said, coming up from behind us. He nodded encouragement to Zelda then changed the subject. "We're going snorkelling this afternoon. Do you two snorkel?"

"No," Glenn replied. "But we're both fairly good swimmers."

"There's a dive shop in the mall," Brent said and with nary a pause explained, "If you're interested, they have a good rental department. The equipment we rented is excellent and we found the snorkelling around here quite good."

"We might take it up sometime," Glenn said.

At the path to our condo we parted company, they to continue their walk to their rental accommodation in *The Nest*, and we to our free accommodation in *Hale Sun and Surf*. Brent asked if Glenn was my former fiancee and I nodded. Nothing more was said about him.

As we cleaned our feet under the tap on the lawn, I noticed Andrew Strong leaning against the fence at the pool. He was talking with an attractive, dark haired girl wearing a flowered bikini. The girl seemed quite entranced with him.

Did he still feel hurt by Marlene's fling with Larry? Was he angry because of her recent outburst on the beach? Could all this affect him enough to make him seek revenge and resort to murder? At the moment he seemed to be finding solace, not revenge.

"Come on, Philomela. I'm starving." Brent turned and started to walk across the lawn.

A short while later, sitting at the table on the lanai, we ate fruit, yogurt, and muffins and in a relaxed fashion discussed positive aspects of the island. Our walk past the crime scene proved therapeutic in that it helped remove our feelings of nervousness and revulsion for the area. The horror lingered, but our feelings of debilitation disappeared.

I was still galled by the fact that at the *Hole-in-the-Wall-Cafe* Glenn had withheld information about his marriage to Zelda. It made his subsequent stalking manoeuvres all the more appalling. His deliberate deceitfulness continued to nag at me. With such an attractive young wife, why would he waste time with a middle-aged old flame? I felt a strange twinge of fear.

Brent stood up. "Let's tidy our digs." He efficiently picked up our empty fruit bowls. I lagged behind him, picked up our cutlery and plates and carried them to the kitchen.

We washed and dried our few dishes, dusted and vacuumed, donned our swimsuits, and ran downstairs. For the next two and a half hours we suntanned, swam in the pool, played shuffleboard and miniature golf. After returning to our condo we ate lunch in the shade on our lanai. I stayed out there for an hour working on my article. Brent stretched out on the sofa in the living room and read an adventure novel.

It was two-thirty when we again made our way downstairs, anticipating a few hours of pleasant snorkelling. We looked forward to seeing more native fish and plants.

We did not expect to see a visitor from away.

CHAPTER 23

*B*rent's index finger pointed to a man standing alone on the sand. "Is that who I think it is?"

My eyes followed the direction of his pointing finger. The man in question wore swim trunks and his sturdy legs and thickening midsection could have fit a dozen sun-seekers. His back was toward us and his front faced *Hale Sun and Surf.* He made a forty-five degree turn and his profile and thinning hair struck me with a hammer of recognition.

"Good grief. It can't be." Still wearing flippers, I followed Brent out of the salt-chuck onto the beach. Our afternoon of floating on undulating waves and viewing underwater scenes had been wonderful. Not so wonderful was the man in question.

"What do you think? Is it Larry Ellis or is it his twin?"

"He doesn't have a twin."

"Then your sister's missing husband has been found."

"What's he doing here?"

"I have no idea. But I intend to find out." Brent stepped out of his flippers, dropped his mask and snorkel on the soft sand, and strode toward my almost ex-brother-in-law. His long strides quickly closed the short distance between them. "Larry," he said.

The man pivoted another forty-five degrees and looked straight at Brent. Even from a distance I could see his jaw drop. The sight of Brent surprised him, and not with pleasure. He put one leg forward and bent his knees as if preparing to dash away.

"I didn't expect to see you here," Brent said.

"Nor I you." Larry's voice sounded sour.

"Did you know we were staying in your condo?"

"Of course." He smiled and his attitude changed from vinegar to honey. "That's why I was looking at *Hale Sun and Surf.* Hoping to see you."

"And here I am." Brent held out his right hand and Larry to his credit accepted it in gentlemanly fashion. "Are you here to kick us out of your condo?" With no trace of dilly-dallying, Brent came straight to the point.

"Of course not. I'm renting a studio in *The Nest*. Like you, I just needed a short break from cold and snow. And, I might add, the slow stock market."

"Is the market falling?"

"Yes. Not unusual for this time of year."

Brent mused aloud, "Bulls and bears are taking a break from making money, and pigs are getting their throats cut."

Larry chuckled. "That's one way to say it."

"How's Procne?" Brent asked.

"She was fine when I left. As you know, we're making a few changes."

"I'm sorry about that. It's tough on both of you. And on the kids. But in the long run I'm sure it will work out for the best."

"Oh we'll get back together. That's not a problem."

"Not a problem?" I muttered aloud, then under my breath added, "Think again Larry." I stepped out of my flippers, picked up Brent's snorkelling equipment and carried it as well as my own over to the two men.

"Aloha, Larry," I said.

He looked at me and nonchalantly waved a hand. "Hi Philly."

I bristled. Larry always called me that because he knew I hated the nickname. Smoothing my bristles, I put my best foot forward and managed to smile and return his wave. It wasn't easy because my arms were burdened with snorkelling gear.

"Maybe we could get together for dinner some evening," Brent suggested.

Yuk, I thought, what a horrid suggestion. Being polite to Larry for more than a minute or two would be impossible.

"Can't tonight. I have a date with two friends who also are staying at *The Nest*."

"What a shame," I said, and my voice dripped with sarcasm.

Larry didn't seem to notice.

Brent was politer. "Well, it's good to see you. We're enjoying your condo. Thanks for letting us use it."

"You're welcome."

"How long are you staying?" I asked.

"A short while. Right now I have to attend a meeting. Nice to see you." He nodded to us, turned around and strode off.

Speechless, Brent and I stared at his disappearing back. Then we looked at each other.

"*The Nest*," I said. "That's where Glenn and Zelda are staying."

"That's right."

We stood and watched his retreating figure for a moment longer, then I gave Brent his snorkelling gear and we walked over to the beach access path. On the lawn at the condo I stuck my toes under the foot-washing tap and said, "Seeing Larry was quite a surprise."

"For Larry as well as for us. He was not pleased to see us."

"That's the understatement of the year. Do you believe he's here for a touch of sea and sun?"

Brent shrugged. "He said he came to get away from cold and snow. But I have a suspicion his reason for coming here is not so innocent."

"He seemed rather evasive. What do you think he's up to?"

"He might be trying to pull a fast one, like changing the joint title on the Maui condo. If he manages to put the condo in his own name, it would make things difficult for Procne."

"If it's a joint title how can he do that without the spouse's permission?"

"He can't legally. But with Larry, legality is unimportant. He might have figured a sneaky way to get around it."

I didn't want to believe it, but I had known Larry long enough to realize such deceitful action was not only possible, but probable. "Do you think we should phone Procne and let her know Larry's here?"

"Definitely. And I'll tell her to inform her lawyer—pronto."

Inside the condo, I phoned Procne long distance in Vancouver. She answered after the second ring and we discussed the weather and the progress of selling their house.

"It's a go," she said. "I can't believe how lucky we are to sell it so quickly and to get our asking price."

"That's great news. But I have news that's not so great. Guess who's renting a studio at *The Nest*?"

"Who?"

"Your almost ex-husband."

"What? He's in Maui?"

"No doubt about it. We saw him on the beach half an hour ago and spoke with him. He said he needed a break from cold and snow and the falling stock market."

She snorted.

"He said you and he will make up and get together again."

"Fat chance."

"He's having dinner tonight with friends."

"Did he say with whom?"

"No."

"I wonder what he's up to."

I shook my head, but to her the action was invisible so I said, "Who knows? But here's Brent. He wants to talk with you."

I handed the phone to him and he thanked her for the use of the condo. "It's comfortable and we're enjoying it," he said. He cleared his throat and proceeded to the crux of the call: "Procne, you and I need to talk seriously about Larry and his business dealings."

Although I heard only one side of the conversation, it was enough to know that Brent's concern about Larry's disappearing-act from Vancouver and his sudden appearance on Maui would get through to my sister. "Procne, he's up to no good. You must phone your lawyer first thing tomorrow morning and have him check your joint ownership of the Maui condo. Warn him that Larry is probably trying to do something illegal with the title, or worse. Whatever he does will benefit him and hurt you and the kids. Promise me you'll phone your lawyer first thing."

He was so emphatic and so insistent that I knew she would follow his advice. Like many others, she respected Brent's honesty and intelligence.

When Brent finished talking, I took the phone. My sister and I discussed the furniture the house buyers didn't want and she told me the children were doing fine. Then we mulled over what she would do in the future.

"I might move to Vancouver Island," she said.

Where had that idea come from? Was it because Brent and I had talked about buying property there? "Have you made any definite plans?" I asked.

"I'll rent until the school year is finished."

We pursued the subject no further and after discussing sundry other things we ended our conversation. A few minutes later I realized I had failed to mention Marlene's murder. Nor had I mentioned we were having dinner with two of her fellow condo owners. Oh well, I'd tell her next time.

I hustled to get ready. When Brent stepped out of the shower I stepped in. While he shaved I dabbed lipstick on my lips and mascara on my eyelashes.

Brent buttoned his bright Hawaiian shirt and muttered, "I wish I could figure out what Larry is trying to do."

"Do you think Larry knows Glenn and Zelda?"

Brent chuckled. "It's possible. The two men both have reptilian charm."

"Why do you think Procne was attracted to Larry?"

"For the same reason you were attracted to Glenn. They both have superficial charm and good looks."

"Good grief. You never cease to amaze me."

"Once Larry latched onto Procne, she helped him gain credibility. People who had doubts about him were reassured by her...he can't be all bad because he has such a nice wife."

I nodded and glanced at my watch. "It's time to leave. Brace yourself for an uncomfortable evening."

CHAPTER 24

At precisely five o'clock, adorned in formal holiday attire—flowered Hawaiian shirt and khaki pants for Brent, blue and green cotton dress with wide straps and short green knitted sweater for me—we walked sedately downstairs. We went through the passageway and out to the cement terrace and when the miniature golf course appeared on our left we stopped walking. To our right was the ground floor patio of Number 10.

Leone saw us and quickly stepped through the open gliding door. "Welcome," she said, "Nice to see you again." She extended both arms and hugged me like a long lost lover. By osmosis her body seemed to absorb strength from mine, making me feel weak and wondering if she would ever let go. Finally she did, and her arms fell to her side and her feet stepped backward. "Come in," she said.

We followed her into the living room where Fred sat comfortably in an armchair. He stood up and raised the glass clasped in his hand. "Greetings. I'm the new bartender."

I cocked my head and asked, "Are bartenders allowed to drink on the job?"

"They are in this joint." He grinned and to prove his point took a sip.

"You'd better order before he has another one," Leone said. "Who knows how long he'll be able to pour."

Fred gave Leone a pretend grimace and turned to me. "Philomela, what's your poison? A Mai Tai?"

"I'd prefer white or red wine, if you have it."

"We do. And you, Brent?"

"Gin and tonic please."

"We have no tonic. How about sprite?"

"That's fine."

I knew Brent was being polite because his favourite warm weather drink was gin with tonic water, preferably Beefeater gin with Schweppes tonic. For ten years I had been trying to convert him to Canada Dry tonic water because it cost less. So far I had not succeeded.

"Sorry about not having tonic," Fred said.

"No problem." With feigned seriousness Brent added, "I really don't need it because my malaria is in remission."

Fred missed the feigned part of Brent's seriousness. "Are you troubled with malaria?" he asked.

Brent laughed. "No, it's just that tonic water has quinine in it and quinine is a treatment for malaria."

"I didn't know that," Leone said.

"Quinine comes from the bark of a tree," Brent said. "And for centuries it was used in the tropics, especially India and Africa."

"Female mosquitoes distribute malaria." Fred said, adding information about the illness. "Gotta watch those females," Everyone chuckled, encouraging Fred to expound, so he did. "The mosquito that transmits malaria from one person to another is called *Anopheles*. It comes out in the evening."

Brent nodded. "That's why mosquito netting over beds is a good prevention for malaria. Other preventions are personal insect repellents and mass spraying."

"Unfortunately," Fred said, "no vaccine is currently available, but there are pills that reduce the risk."

"Hawaii is tropical," Leone said. "But there are no mosquitoes here." She looked around as if trying to find one.

It was my turn to impart knowledge, so I mentioned what I had learned from Mark Twain's book: "A hundred years ago Hawaii had lots of mosquitoes as well as centipedes and scorpions and tarantulas."

"Scorpions and tarantulas?" Leone looked surprised. "Here?"

In wise woman manner, I said, "Before the onslaught of spraying, all those nasty creatures were in Hawaii. In 1866 Mark Twain wrote a book about his visit to the islands and he frequently mentioned numerous creepy-crawlies. But he never mentioned anyone ever getting malaria. Maybe the special mosquito didn't live here."

"That's possible," Fred said, handing us our drinks. "Shall we go outside and sit on the lanai? Out there we can search for mosquitoes, scorpions, and tarantulas."

"What fun," I said.

Leone led the way and indicated four chairs around a table. "Make yourselves comfortable."

The men and I sat down and Leone hospitably passed around a bowl of macadamia nuts. I clasped a couple in the fingers of my left hand and in my right hand held up my glass. I intended to say, "Happy holidays," but instantly realized happiness would be impossible for Leone. I changed the toast to, "Here's to our good health."

"And to finding the murderer of my daughter." Leone raised her glass and her hospitable smile faded.

"I'll drink to that," I said.

"So will I," Fred and Brent said in unison.

We sipped our drinks in silence. Our initial efforts at achieving good cheer had been dampened by Leone's reference to Marlene. Sooner or later the subject was bound to come up, so I was relieved that Leone had been the one to do it. What better way to bring the tragedy to the fore than as a toast? What better way to express the hope of bringing justice to the person who had caused her daughter's untimely demise? From now on, if one of us slipped up and mentioned murder, a pleasant evening would not be suddenly shattered.

Brent changed the direction of our conversation and focused on our snorkelling experiences. He explained our rental equipment and described some of the fish we had seen. When he finished, I initiated a discussion of miniature golf and shuffleboard. Then Fred asked if anyone would like a second drink. Brent and I declined but Leone and Fred had refills. They needed stimulants more than we did.

"Leone and Fred," I said, "you'll never guess who we saw on the beach this afternoon."

Leone shook her head and shrugged her shoulders. "I have no idea."

"Larry Ellis, my almost ex-brother-in-law."

"Really?" Leone raised her eyebrows.

"The owner of your condo?" Fred asked.

"The same. He and my sister are parting company."

"Procne is your sister?"

I nodded.

"What a small world." In wonderment, Fred moved his head from side to side. "My wife and Procne were good friends. They saw each other here on Maui and occasionally had lunch together in Vancouver. We never did get to know Larry all that well, though at social functions he was amusing and gregarious. He always had some big deal ready to happen."

"That was and still is Larry," I said. "For better or worse he and Procne are going their separate ways."

"Too bad," Fred murmured. "But it doesn't surprise me."

Brent gazed intently at Fred as if willing him to elaborate. When nothing more came forth, Brent said, "I don't understand why he's here. He should be at home attending to their house sale and other legalities. He disappeared a few days ago from Vancouver and no one knew where he went. Then today we happened to run into him on the beach."

"Serendipity in reverse," I said.

Fred chuckled. "In other words, a lack of good fortune."

Brent looked Fred a query and asked, "Do you have any idea why he might be here?"

"I haven't a clue," Fred said. "But if he's in the middle of a divorce...I wouldn't want to be his wife."

Brent nodded. "Exactly."

After we finished our drinks, Leone locked the condo and the four of us strolled toward the outdoor mall. We amicably discussed safe, uncontroversial topics such as Maui's fine beaches and great weather. Fred, it turned out, was a master of irrelevant yet interesting trivia.

"It's the Trade Winds," he said, "that keep Hawaii's weather so perfect. Without the winds the islands would get unbearably hot."

In what seemed no time at all, we reached our destination, a Japanese restaurant. We entered a medium sized room with oriental decor and a subdued and meditative atmosphere. An attractive dark-haired hostess greeted us, and Brent immediately complimented her on the lack of loud raucous music. She smiled knowingly as if the compliment of peace and quiet had surfaced from other satisfied customers.

She turned to her left and gracefully led us to a table near the front window. She pulled out a chair for Leone and pulled out the chair beside it for me. We sat in comfort with our backs to the window while the two men sat down across the table from us.

We continued our conversation about Maui in particular and Hawaii in general— beautiful scenery, good weather, interesting and sometimes bloody history. Fred elaborated on the latter by mentioning Captain Cook's fatal visit to the island of Kauai. Fortunately he didn't dwell on the details of the great explorer's murder, but instead turned the conversation to the early missionaries. The rest of us listened in a relaxed, appreciative manner because he was in fact a fascinating raconteur.

A waiter came to our table, helped Fred choose and order a bottle of white wine then moved away. When he returned, he opened the bottle with dramatic flourish and poured a small amount in Fred's glass. Fred examined the colour, followed the procedure of swirling and checking for legs, sniffing the aroma, and swilling a small amount in his mouth for taste. Finally he nodded approval. The waiter smiled and half filled all four stemmed glasses.

We toasted the weather and each other and sipped the fermented grape. The evening was proving far more pleasant than I had expected. Though none of us forgot Marlene, we concentrated more on the living than on the dead. We enjoyed the nice wine, the nice atmosphere, and each other's nice company.

Nice food, attractively served, lightly spiced, and very tasty added to our enjoyment. There was no need to pretend about having a good time because we in fact were having a good time. Brent and I often glanced at each other with amazement at how the evening was unfolding. I could tell that Leone and Fred were enjoying themselves, too—they were experiencing a pleasant distraction from the horror and sadness of the last few days. Having dinner together was a grand way for all of us to relax and get to know each other.

Then came the voice. It shattered the peaceful atmosphere like a breaking mirror. Motor-Mouth spoke as he had at *The Wave*—loud and uncouth. I would have recognized the strident, raspy voice anywhere, even without his announcing his identity to the hostess and to everyone else in the restaurant.

"I'm Tim Jones and I have a reservation for three."

Yuk. The man who probably murdered Leone's daughter was here in this room. Why did he have to come to this particular restaurant at this particular moment? I glanced at Leone. The gods were with us: she was talking with Brent and was so absorbed in their conversation that she failed to notice the newcomer. Relieved that she was unaware of his presence, I glanced over at the owner of the loud voice.

He stood at the small desk near the front entrance. Even if I had not recognized his voice, I would have recognized his tattoos. He was wearing a short sleeved Hawaiian shirt that exposed the wild decorations on his arms.

I also recognized his two companions: Ezekiel Hoffman and Daniel Epstein. They both wore conservative Hawaiian shirts and dark blue trousers. Until tonight, the only other time I had seen them with Tim was when he had joined them for his so-called breakfast. Since then, having chatted with the two genteel men on the beach and with Ezekiel in the *Outer Fringe* shop, I could not understand the trio's friendship. What did the two soft spoken gentlemen have in common with loud Motor-Mouth?

With a sigh of relief I watched the hostess lead them to a table near the rear of the restaurant. All three looked straight ahead as they followed her, so were unaware of our presence near the window. Tim sat down facing us and the other two sat facing Tim. Tim spoke to the hostess and though I could hear his voice, his individual words were indistinct.

Ezekiel and Daniel behaved in the manner I had come to expect of them, unassuming and quiet and polite. I saw Daniel turn to Ezekiel and watched in profile the movements of his mouth. His soft voice was aimed for the ears of his companions, not for every patron in the restaurant.

It was unlikely the two gentlemen would turn around and notice me, and Tim was too full of himself to pay attention to anyone else. His loud voice made him hard to ignore and most patrons, including Brent and Fred, glanced briefly toward him.

Leone remained unaware of Tim's presence. Relieved that she had failed to recognize his voice, I chatted a bit louder than normal about other restaurants in the area, knowing full well my words were inconsequential and unimportant. Leone knew the restaurants better than I, so she explained some of their good and not so good features. Thankfully, she remained oblivious to the rise and fall of Tim's raspy voice. All went well until we started to eat dessert, green tea ice cream.

"This rice is bloody cold!" The complaint boomed like a bass drum from the back of the restaurant and reverberated around the room.

Peripherally, I saw Leone turn her head sharply in Tim's direction. Her right hand tightened around her spoon and her knuckles whitened. I could almost feel her body stiffen. There was no question, she recognized the source of the voice and knew it belonged to her daughter's boyfriend, pimp, drug supplier, and suspected killer.

"He's here," she whispered, "inside this restaurant." Then louder and with more venom, she added, "He's the one who started all Marlene's problems." Looking dazed and frantic, she rose from her chair.

For a minute I thought she was going to march to the back of the restaurant and confront Tim. It would have been a bad scene all around, mainly because Tim Jones was obviously high on something—a form of alcohol, a type of hallucinogenic drug, or both. Fred glanced over his shoulder at the complainer and then his right hand stretched across the table and grasped Leone's arm. He had met Tim twice before and knew what could happen. He shook his head at her and gently eased her back down into her chair.

"Ignore him," he said and gently patted her arm. "The creep is stoned. He probably won't even recognize you. Let him be. Talking with him right now would be a complete waste of time."

Leone pursed her lips, closed her eyes and placed her clenched fists on the table. Her pain was real and emanated from every pore of her body; it spread outward and somehow began to penetrate the pores of my body. If this was my way of helping to soften her sorrow and alleviate her pain, so be it.

Brent waved to our waiter and asked for the bill. With no fuss or muss he and Fred evenly split the cost of wine and food and paid with their individual credit cards. Unable to bear being in the same room as Tim Jones, I stood up, leaving my partially eaten green tea ice cream to melt in the bowl. I led the way to the front entrance and the others followed. At the door, Leone abruptly stopped, turned around, and with an expression of malevolence stared at Tim.

As if feeling her eyes on him, he shifted his attention from his friends and stared directly at her. My heart missed a beat. She took two steps forward and I felt sure we were going to witness a dreadful confrontation. But nothing happened. Maybe she realized he was too out of this world to even recognize the mother of his dead girlfriend.

Tim's scrutiny made Ezekiel and Daniel glance around. They recognized me and waved. I waved back. At our other meetings they had been so amicable that under other circumstances I would have gone to their table for a brief chat. But with Leone standing beside me, miserable and morose, and Tim sitting across from them, stoned and stupid, I did not dare do so.

The two older men had known the deceased, but they obviously had not met her mother. Did they even know of the girl's death? Maybe they did or maybe they didn't. Nevertheless, they remained on friendly terms with my prime murder suspect. In the dive shop I had wondered if Ezekiel and Daniel knew of Marlene's death and now I continued to wonder. Perhaps the police were unaware they knew Marlene so had not questioned them. And the murder, as far as I knew, was not headline news. I made a mental note to inform Detective Kanui about the two gentlemen. They might be able to give him some new leads, unless, of course, they had somehow participated in her death.

Brent took my hand and led me out the door. At a slower pace Fred guided Leone, who kept stopping and looking back, but he finally got her outside.

"That man," Leone muttered venomously and glared through the window at him. "I despise him."

"Do you think Tim's a front man for his two friends?" Fred asked

The expression on Brent's face registered surprise and doubtless mirrored mine. I had considered the three men as acquaintances, not business partners.

Brent turned to Fred and said, "It's possible they've worked together. Maybe those two bought real estate from Tim before he became a serious addict."

"They might work as behind-the-scene people," Fred suggested. "Maybe they scout schools and colleges for future drug victims. Maybe they reap some of the rewards from Tim's drug and prostitution sales."

Fred's suggestions disconcerted me more than I cared to admit. Every time I saw Ezekiel and Daniel the more I liked them as persons and disliked their involvement with Tim Jones. These new suspicions cooled the warmth I felt for them. I glanced over at Leone and asked, "Have you ever seen Tim's two dinner companions before?"

She shook her head. "Not to my knowledge."

"They knew Marlene," I said. "I saw them talking with her on the beach."

Leone's eyes were moist and a tear slid down one cheek. "In the past few years I haven't met any of Marlene's friends." Her voice was low and sad.

"At least the arms of the two men aren't covered with tattoos." I hoped my remark might add a touch of lightness. It did not.

"Tim looks dreadful," Fred said, "worse than when I saw him last year. Tonight his voice blared like a siren and his behaviour was strange and aggravating. The whole scene was weird. Neither of his friends behaved like space cadets."

"Maybe," Brent said, "they acted too smoothly. Maybe they behave urbanely in order to fool future victims."

Brent's words distressed me. I found it hard to believe Ezekiel and Daniel could possibly be involved with Tim in any type of business venture, legal or illegal. An association based on mutual social interests also was out of the question. What would they do together, other than eat, and what would they talk about? I tried to imagine the three of them having a philosophical discussion and almost burst out laughing. If they were not Tim's business associates and not his social friends why else would they suffer his company?

Could it be that financial rewards were involved? Could the two men benefit monetarily from Tim's illegal activities? Could they be subtle users of drugs themselves? Could they be clients of prostitutes? Or could they be up to no good in some other manner?

The evening air was warm, but I shivered.

CHAPTER 25

"ACTIVE VOLCANO AIR TOURS." Brent read the words loud and clear. Then he glanced at me to make sure I was paying attention. "Listen to this: 'See Maui and the Active Volcano Area on the big Island from the best vantage point—THE AIR.'"

"I hear," I said. "And my eardrums are still intact."

He lowered the brochure and across the table our eyes met. In a softer tone of voice, he said, "That's the tour I'd like to take."

I shifted my eyes from his steady gaze to the back of the brochure. I chewed a bite of toast and it slide down my throat, preventing a giggle from rising to my mouth. His enthusiasm with this spectacular tour mirrored my own when a week ago I first perused the brochure. Refraining from mentioning that fact I merely chuckled and said, "It's amazing how great minds think alike."

With a broad smile he read aloud a few highlights of the tour. He wet his lips with a sip of coffee, silently studied the glossy paper for a few seconds, and then explained: "Weather permitting, we fly over Haleakala, the extinct volcano here on Maui, and proceed to Kilauea, the active volcano on Hawaii. We also fly over Mauna Loa and Mauna Kea to see the world class observatories. We even fly over the Parker Ranch and some agricultural areas." He pronounced the strange names reasonably well and his enthusiasm knew no bounds.

"Fascinating," I said, and meant it.

"I'm going to phone and make a reservation right now."

"Do you have enough cash to pay for it?"

"I'll buy now and pay later." His lips became a crescent moon and his body unfolded into a standing position. He walked to the door of the lanai and paused. "I intend to use my credit card." Exiting the lanai he called over his shoulder, "What day would you like to go?"

"Anytime they have seats available."

"You're very agreeable."

"We're on holidays. Remember?"

Sitting alone on the lanai, I let my skin absorb the tropical warmth. There was no worry of burning because the eastern sun had not yet risen over the roof of the condominium. The blueness of the western sea and sky soothed my eyes, the soft air relaxed my muscles, and the rhythmical surf removed worries from my brain. I leaned back and listened with delight to Brent's side of the telephone conversation; he was so polite and so pleasantly excited.

"A cancellation this afternoon? That's great." As he spoke those words, a loud knock sounded on our main door.

I leaped to my feet, dashed from the lanai through the living room, passed Brent who was leaning on the kitchen counter talking on the landline, and in the hall beside the bedroom stopped at the front door. Opening it, I stood face to face with Detective Kanui.

"Ms Nightingale," he said and bowed graciously. Like an automaton I started to bow in response, but his next words stopped me. "May I come inside?"

"Of course." I stepped aside and ushered him into the small hall.

"I hate to disturb you, but I'd appreciate a few moments of your time."

I nodded, closed the door and moved in front of him. "Let's go out to the lanai. It's the nicest place in the condo." I led the way past Brent, who was still talking on the landline in the kitchen, and walked through the living room. Out on the lanai I indicated a green plastic chair. "Please make yourself comfortable." As he sat down I asked, "Would you like a cup of coffee? It's fresh and ready to drink."

"That would be nice, provided it's no trouble."

In the kitchen, while I poured coffee into three clean mugs, Brent hung up the phone and whispered in my ear, "We fly this afternoon." He preceded me out to the lanai and greeted Detective Kanui.

The detective stood up and politely shook Brent's hand. "Good morning, Mr. Lark."

Their hands separated and both men sat down. Brent studied the newcomer and asked, "Is all well with you, Detective?"

"Very well, thank you."

"And is your murder investigation progressing?"

"Yes, slowly."

I set a tray containing three mugs, cream pitcher and sugar bowl on the plastic table. Placing a mug in front of each of us, I suggested they help themselves to the accoutrements. I sat down facing our guest, picked up my steaming mug and took a small sip of the hot, black brew. Detective Kanui did the same and so did Brent. Setting his mug on the table, the detective looked first at me and then at Brent. He was a master of the art of silence.

Brent and I waited in wary anticipation. We looked everywhere but at the penetrating eyes that seemed to miss nothing and understand everything. Apparently we, too, understood the art of silence.

Finally our guest's words filled the air. "The purpose of my visit is to ask if any new recollections have come to mind since our first meeting."

We had expected words to that effect, so Brent and I glanced at each other then gazed over the railing at the ocean.

"I would like you to probe your memories," Detective Kanui said. We remained silent, trying to follow his suggestion, and finally he asked, "Has any new incident, major or minor, entered your thoughts? Anything at all that might pertain to the case." He looked directly at Brent.

Brent's eyes turned from the ocean to our guest. He slowly shook his head. "Sorry, Detective, I can't add anything to what I've already told you."

Detective Kanui nodded then focused his dark mesmerizing eyes on me. "Ms Nightingale, have you thought of anything that might shed new light on the murder? Anything at all, no matter how trivial?"

Looking directly at him, I squirmed uneasily in my chair. The role of witness made me almost as uncomfortable and nervous as the role of suspect. Feeling stupider than dumb I slowly admitted, "Well...there is one thing. But I don't think it's pertinent or even helpful. That's probably why it slipped my mind before."

"Yes?" Detective Kanui nodded his head, leaned patiently back in his chair and placed his hands on his lap.

"A few days before the murder, I saw the victim talking on the beach with two men. One of the men I've seen on five different occasions and the other one I've seen four times."

"You counted the occasions?"

"I did."

His casual attitude dissipated and leaning forward he appeared expectant.

Feeling more nervous than ever, I swallowed, cleared my throat and proceeded to describe how I first saw the two men with Motor-Mouth, aka Tim Jones, during breakfast. "The second time I saw them they were talking with the victim on the beach. The third time, I ran into one of them at the *Outer Fringe* shop where he asked my advice regarding a gift for his sister. We chatted and he introduced himself as Ezekiel Hoffman. Do you know him?"

"No, I don't." He took his small notebook and pen from his pant pocket and started to write. "Was that the extent of your conversation?"

"Pretty much. We discussed gifts and a bit of trivia and a bit of religion and philosophy, and then we went our separate ways."

"You didn't ask him about Tim Jones?"

"No."

"And the fourth occasion?"

"On another of my beach walks, I happened to meet the two men who also were out walking. This time Ezekiel introduced me to his friend, Daniel Epstein."

"Did you come away with any lasting impression of these two men?" He jotted down the new name.

"Only that they were very pleasant, very polite, and very well-spoken. I would describe both of them as intellectual gentlemen. To be quite honest, I liked them."

"You said there were five occasions."

"I saw them again last night at the Japanese restaurant at the mall."

"Let's go back to when you saw them with the victim on the beach. You did not speak to them?"

"I would have, but neither Ezekiel nor Daniel noticed me. The girl apparently didn't see me either. All three were too intent on their conversation to pay attention to anyone else, so I walked on."

"I see. And they were just talking?"

"Yes, an intense discussion, or at least that's how it seemed."

"Mmmm. Do you think the men were trying to pick her up for sexual favours?"

I shook my head. "I honestly don't think so. At least that was not the impression I got. Quite the contrary in fact."

"They were behaving like old friends?"

"I don't know if I'd describe their behaviour as that of old friends. It's possible though." I raised my shoulders and let them fall. "They certainly didn't behave like enemies. Ezekiel did most of the talking and the other two listened with great interest."

"You did not hear what was being said?"

"No. The surf was too loud. But for some reason I had the impression the two men were encouraging her to do something.

"Something in the line of, ah, her work?"

"I don't think so. If it had been something involving sex, I think she would have appeared more confident and been more in control of the situation. As it was she looked interested but puzzled. She actually seemed unsure of herself. I wish now I had moved closer and eavesdropped like a snoop."

Detective Kanui once again leaned back in his chair. He placed his hands flat against each other in front of his heart as if preparing to pray. Then he closed his eyes. For several seconds he sat in relaxed meditation.

I refrained from interrupting him, as did Brent. We surreptitiously glanced at each other and then looked back at our guest who suddenly opened his eyes and dropped his hands in his lap.

"You said you saw the two men last night."

"They were dining with Tim Jones at the Japanese restaurant."

"Ah. Tim Jones. Not an easy man to track down."

"Apparently he has a contact at the Tattoo Parlour."

Writing that information in his notebook, he asked, "Are the three of them good friends?"

"I don't know. It seems unlikely because Tim appears to have little in common with them."

"I see. Do you think these two men are members of a club or a cult, or a particular religious faith?"

"In the Outer Fringe shop, Ezekiel told me he's a Deist. Apparently Deists believe in God by way of reason, not based on faith alone."

"Not Muslim, Sikh, Christian, Jew, or pagan?"

I shook my head.

"Not Atheist or Evolutionist?"

"No."

"Would you say he believes in some kind of cosmic design?"

"I think so." I was duly impressed with the detective's litany of various religions, but failed to see what bearing they had on the case.

"Do you know where they are from and where they are staying on Maui?"

"They live in Victoria, Canada."

He nodded, "I know the city. It is quite English in style. I visited one of its wonderful gardens. Butchart Gardens, I think it was called. Coming back to the two gentlemen. Where are they staying on Maui?"

"In a condo somewhere on this beach." I pointed and said, "In that direction, but I don't know exactly where. Apparently they often spend a month here during the winter."

"You have been helpful, Ms Nightingale. If you think of anything else, absolutely anything, please contact me. You have my card?"

"Yes, I do." Recalling Marlene's unexpected and violent behaviour on the beach, I proceeded to relate the incident to him. I concluded by telling him I thought she suffered from paranoia. "You see, she accused me of following her, and before aiming her fist at my head and striking my shoulder she even asked if I was a policewoman."

"Were you injured?"

"A beautiful black and blue bruise."

His head bobbed up and down like a yo-yo and he jotted words in his notebook. "Her paranoia and violence could have been a reaction from drugs."

"She seemed nervous and her hands were damp. She kept wiping them on her denim skirt. Is that a result of drugs, too?"

"Sweaty hands is a side effect of crystal meth."

"Detective Kanui," I said, "does the word ice mean anything other than frozen water?"

"Yes. A form of crystal meth that can be smoked is called ice."

"That explains it." I actually smiled. "Marlene asked if I wanted ice and I said I had lots in the condominium freezer. I stupidly thought she meant small cubes of frozen water that can be served in drinks."

He laughed, apparently as pleased with my ignorance as with my revelations. "Anything else?" he asked while jotting down a few more words in his notebook.

I shook my head, secretly pleased with my ability to give him some new information.

"In a day or two I'll check with you again. Maybe your subconscious will spew forth more helpful tidbits."

I giggled. "I wouldn't rely on it. I'm afraid my subconscious is sometimes quite unconscious."

"So far it has done very well. I thank both of you."

He put the pen and notepad in his pocket, stood up and shook our hands. He turned and marched through the condo to the main door and I trotted after him. Just before he closed the door I touched his arm.

"There's one more thing, Detective Kanui. My brother-in-law, Larry Ellis, and my sister, Procne, live in Vancouver and own this condominium. They are in the middle of a divorce. Larry disappeared from Vancouver a few days ago and no one knew where he went. We ran into him on the beach yesterday."

Detective Kanui looked puzzled. "And why do you think this has anything to do with the murder?"

"It probably doesn't. But when I first met Leone Humphries, she told me she knew Larry. She was not thrilled with him because apparently he had a fling with her daughter, the murder victim, when she was a teenager."

"Do you know how I could contact your brother-in-law?"

"He's renting a studio at *The Nest*."

Detective Kanui pulled his notebook and pen from his pocket and jotted down this new piece of information. He looked at me and asked, "Anything else?"

"I think that's all."

"Your recollections are interesting. Thank you again, Ms Nightingale." He stepped outside and closed the door.

Back on the lanai I gazed at Brent and asked, "What do you make of all that?"

"I have no idea. He seemed pleased with you, though."

I shrugged my shoulders. "All in a day's work."

"You just gave him three new contacts, four counting the Tattoo Parlour. One of them might lead to something important like a motive or a new suspect. I think he's eliminated you as a suspect."

"I hope so."

Brent glanced at the never ending motion of the sea then turned his gaze on me. "Let's forget about Detective Kanui and the murder for the rest of the day. We'll have an early lunch and get ready for our tour."

I said okay but my thoughts lingered on our discussion with the detective.

Brent noticed my preoccupation. "Philomela, don't forget we're here for a short holiday and a happy one."

"A happy holiday it is." I stood up, shook thoughts of murder from my head and grinned. I put the three mugs on the tray and carried them to the kitchen.

After a quick lunch we dressed for our Volcano Tour. Brent picked up the car keys and glanced at me. "Are you ready?"

"I'm good to go," I replied.

CHAPTER 26

*W*ednesday afternoon we headed toward the town of Kahului. The drive started pleasantly, mainly because thoughts of Detective Kanui's visit and murder in general had been pushed aside. A few fluffy clouds increased our positive attitude by shading the sun's glare from our eyes. As usual, the scenery was lovely, even though the upper half of the extinct volcano, Haleakala, was shrouded by heavy clouds. Sugar cane fields bordered the highway and traffic was light.

"Look at that silver car," Brent said. "It's tail-gating us."

I cranked my neck around and looked through the rear window. Sure enough, a silver vehicle drove so close it almost slammed into the trunk of our sapphire blue rental car. Brent gently hit the brakes three times, hoping the brake lights would deliver a message to back off. The driver either ignored Brent's message or failed to understand it; he continued to drive too close for comfort or safety.

Brent muttered, "What in Hades is that idiot doing?"

He braked briefly two more times and the tailgater ignored both messages. Brent braked a third time and again the message failed to connect with the driver. Like a silver monster the car continued to snap at our rear bumper.

The opposite lane opened free of oncoming vehicles and the driver behind us pulled sharply into the oncoming lane and zoomed forward. He sped abreast us and I glared through Brent's window at him. To my surprise I recognized his profile. My eyes studied the upturned nose and the brown hair with its receding hairline. My mouth formed a large o. Before I could speak or shake my fist the car shot forward and left us in its exhaust. The driver had not glanced in our direction.

"Guess what," I said. "The driver of the silver menace was Larry Ellis."

"Really?"

"He had no idea who he was passing."

"I'm not surprised. At that speed he had to concentrate on the road, not on the occupants of other cars."

"I wonder where he's heading," I said.

"Not to the airport. Look, he's signalling to turn into the town of Kahului."

The silver bullet turned off the main highway and eventually disappeared behind some buildings. We continued toward the airport.

"Why would he go to Kahului?" I asked. "The town is not particularly scenic."

"He's probably going to consult with a shyster lawyer about illegal land documents. Or he could be going to visit a land-title official to discuss changing the joint title of the Maui condo."

"Oh, poor Procne."

Brent shook his head with moral umbrage.

"What if he's hiring a criminal lawyer to defend himself from murder charges?"

"Philomela, Larry can be quite malicious. But murder? That's pure speculation on your part."

"I may be dredging the bottom of the barrel for clues. But from what Leone told me, the dredging may be worthwhile."

"I don't know about that. I doubt if Larry is capable of murder. Then again, I don't trust him as far as I could throw him. Let's forget him and the murder. We're on holiday mode. Remember?"

"Of course." I smiled and pushed lousy Larry from the surface of my mind. I concentrated on other things, admiring the scenery and anticipating our flight over the island of Hawaii.

The road grew busier so Brent slowed down. Signage was good and after only one minor glitch he entered the lot and parked the car.

On the phone the agent had told Brent the *Commuter Terminal* was just past the parking lot, but she had neglected to mention the size of the lot. Though I had been in it twice before, by parking near the main terminal I had been unaware of its hugeness. Now we walked, and walked, and walked. Just as we were about to give up, the end of the lot came in sight and so did the sign: *Commuter Terminal*.

The roof of this side of the building was supported by pillars and devoid of walls. Walking up to the airy structure, we spotted another sign, *Fixed Wing Volcano Tours*. A counter and a few benches assured us we were in the right place, even though no one else was in sight. With the entire place to ourselves we sat down on a bench and waited.

After about ten minutes a man wearing a pair of shorts and a flowered shirt appeared from somewhere in the back of the building. He greeted us and said, "I'm the pilot," and proceeded to check our names and reservations. A few minutes later several other people straggled in and he did the same with them.

He led all of us on a circuitous route to the back of the building and ushered us through an open door in its back wall. Outside, on a grassy field sat a sparkling white plane, a twin engine Piper Chieftain. We braced our bodies against the heavy wind and walked up to it.

Brent looked at the pilot and asked, "Will the wind hinder your take-off?"

"Not a bit. This is normal. The Trade Winds blow almost constantly. Because of them, Hawaiians are able to boast of their pleasant climate."

I nodded, remembering Fred's similar explanation last night.

The pilot checked his clipboard and called out two names. A young man and woman came forward and he told them to sit behind the pilot's seat. His roll call continued until everyone was seated. There were ten of us in all—nine passengers and the pilot. Brent and I sat at the very back. Our seat numbers were nine and ten.

The pilot explained the headsets and started the engine. The aircraft roared to life and moved slowly to a runway. By the time it took to say, 'Bob's Your Uncle', it zoomed a short distance on the tarmac and before you could say, "And Fanny's Your Aunt," it flew in the air and soared along the north shore of Maui. It turned slightly and flew toward the dormant volcano and heavenly Hana, the town whose alliterative description greatly appealed to me.

"Because of the clouds," the pilot said, "we are unable to fly over Haleakala. But the ancient black lava runs can be seen lower down."

We gazed out the window at curving bays with black beaches. Black streaks stretched down the side of the extinct volcano and heavy clouds still covered its top.

We glimpsed heavenly Hana and then flew amongst scattered clouds over the Halenuihaha Channel. The water churned with whitecaps and I visualized Mark Twain bobbing on those rough waters in a schooner in 1866. His trip from the island of Oahu to the island of Hawaii had taken a few days; his sleep on board the ship had been disturbed by roosters crowing, rats galloping over his body, cockroaches camping in his hair, and natives spitting at his feet. In comparison, we sat in clean, comfortable seats free of undesirable creatures and viewed the world through a clear glass window. Our flight from the Island of Maui to the island of Hawaii took less than an hour.

We reached the north shore of the big island by flying under a blanket of white clouds. We passed a series of steep cliffs dotted with flowing water falls then approached the town of Hilo. The pilot landed the plane and told us to disembark. He helped with refuelling while we wandered with other passengers around the runway.

I heard someone say, "Ezekiel," and my ears perked up like a hunting cat's. Brent walked on and I shifted close to the speaker, the young man who sat behind the pilot. The name Ezekiel was uncommon enough that I immediately suspected the passenger could be talking about my white-haired acquaintance. I gazed up at the cloudy sky and listened with innocent intensity.

"I was surprised when we ran into him yesterday," the man said. "I didn't know he was here."

"His buddy is very good looking," his young companion said. "Do you know him?"

"Only by reputation. He has a history involving drugs. In my opinion he makes Ezekiel appear more dangerous than ever."

"I wonder why Ezekiel gets involved with those people. What's the point?"

"Maybe he likes living on the edge," the man replied.

"I heard Ezekiel was engaged to a girl who died in a skiing accident."

"That was a long time ago."

"What about his buddy? Are they lovers?"

The man shrugged. "I don't know. All I know is his buddy was once involved in a fight over a girl in some nightclub."

Scotch mist started to seep from the sky, making everyone look warily up at the claustrophobic grey clouds. My eavesdropping ended as the couple hurried toward the plane. Refuelling, fortunately, was finished. Rain drops pelted down harder and faster so Brent and I scurried to the steps and gratefully followed the couple inside. While we hooked our seat belts the pilot informed us that Hilo gets a minimum of 160 inches of rain a year.

The plane took off and flew over a cruise ship. In short order we gazed down at huge areas of black lava; the lava must have arrived recently for nothing grew on or near it. One wide stretch must have been older than the others because it contained a bit of greenery and several newly constructed houses. I doubted the wisdom of building a house there, but Hawaiians were a daring people who liked to play with fire.

Farther on, we saw streams of fresh lava flowing down a cloud-crowned hill. The hill was in fact Kilauea, the active volcano. Hot lava flows hit the water and columns of white steam rose in the air. Several flows were red hot and according to the pilot were ten feet, approximately three metres, in width. Two people walked near one of the new flows and the pilot grew quite agitated.

"If a crater under those two people collapses," he announced, "they'll be toast. The temperature of the molten material is 1500 degrees."

He specified neither Fahrenheit nor Celsius, but at that temperature it hardly mattered. Who could imagine such heat? If the path collapsed under the adventurers' feet, I suspected they would be crisper than toast.

Mark Twain again came to mind. In 1866, he and his companions had travelled up to the top of this very volcano. They had perched in a lookhouse and gazed down into the crater to a path winding near bubbling magna; later that night Twain and a male companion had descended into the huge crater and walked along the dark bottom amid streaks of fire. No one could do that today, not while the volcano was erupting.

Mark Twain related in the book that in 1840 Kilauea had burst a passage through its side and sent a river of fire five miles broad and two hundred feet deep to the sea. It had swept away forests, plantations, huts, and everything else in its path. Fish had been killed and the atmosphere had been poisoned with sulphurous vapours and falling ashes and cinders. Earthquakes and tidal waves had added to the devastation. Twenty-six years later, when Twain visited the area, the volcano had resumed a restless sleep.

The current volcanic eruption sent lava down the mountainside but was not as severe as the one in 1840, but it was lasting much longer. Steam and clouds forbade flying over the crater, so our plane left the lava flows and soared over the ocean where we witnessed surf reaching ten metres in height. We turned and ascended through misty clouds until reaching the top of Mauna Loa. We admired Mauna Kea with its famous star studying observatories that gleamed like domed white castles in a mystical fairyland. A few minutes later we searched in vain for cattle grazing on the lands of the Parker Ranch. Other agricultural areas came into view and we identified crops of sugarcane, macadamia nuts, and grains.

Entranced by the sights below, I paid little attention to a voice saying: "Traffic. Traffic." It took several minutes before I realized the computer was warning the pilot of nearby airplanes.

After flying back over the churning channel of water, we skirted along the southwest coast of Maui where I recognized the areas of Wailea and Kihei, their shapes were exactly like those on the maps. Before we headed east to the city of Kahului, the sun disappeared in the Pacific Ocean and no conch shell sounded and no green flash appeared.

The plane landed at the Kahului Airport and everyone seemed sorry the flight was finished. Brent and I disembarked and thanked the pilot who stood near the bottom step. The young man and woman who had discussed a person called Ezekiel came out a minute later. They, too, thanked the pilot. As they walked from the plane I approached them.

"Do you by any chance know Ezekiel Hoffman?" I asked. The man's eyebrows rose and his eyes widened so I explained. "I heard you mention the name, Ezekiel. The name is unusual so I wondered if you meant the gentleman I know."

He nodded and studied me uneasily. "Are you a friend of his?"

"I've met him a few times."

"You heard me talking about him in Hilo."

"Yes, briefly."

"He's not a bad sort, but he gets involved with weird activities and unsavoury associates. A lot of people suspect his motives so don't trust him," He ended our conversation by abruptly taking his girlfriend's arm and saying, "Goodbye. Have a good day." They walked quickly away.

The man had not been rude, just extremely brusque. It was obvious he did not wish to discuss Ezekiel with me. I learned nothing more than what I had overheard in Hilo. None of it was particularly reassuring.

Our walk back through the parking lot seemed shorter than the one to the commuter terminal. We climbed inside the rental car and Brent drove to the highway. The surrounding countryside was dark and dreary. Fortunately, the silver bullet and its driver were busy elsewhere.

We decided to stop and eat dinner at one of the outdoor mall's numerous eateries. A Chinese restaurant caught our fancy and inside it we found the service fast, the food tasty, and the price right. After dinner we strolled to a Baskin Robbin's outlet, bought a small carton of ice cream and carried it to the parking lot.

"Today was great," Brent said, remaining in true holiday mode.

"It was an adventure. I wouldn't want to build a house near one of those lava flows."

"Me neither."

Brent eased the car from the parking space and started to enter a small road. He jammed on the brakes to avoid hitting three pedestrians: They were none other than Tim Jones, Ezekiel Hoffman, and Daniel Epstein. They had stepped on the pavement directly in front of our moving car. Unaware of how close they came to being run over, they strolled three abreast across the road to the sidewalk on the other side. Somehow Tim waved his hands as he talked and the other two listened to his words with what seemed dazed politeness. None of the three paid any attention to the car that had almost run them down.

Our holiday mode was put on hold.

"I could have killed them," Brent said.

"Were they drunk or stoned or what?"

"Who knows? They are the most unlikely threesome I've ever seen."

"I don't know what holds them together," I said.

Brent's foot touched the accelerator and he turned the car onto the main road. "Tim is so sleazy and the other two are so proper." He shook his head in slow motion as if searching for an answer.

We discussed their different personalities, their apparent interests, and a few possible reasons for the strange friendship. We came up with nothing that was edifying.

Inside the condo, we sat side by side on the sofa, ate ice cream and watched a light-hearted movie on the Classic Movie Channel. The day had been so interesting and so enjoyable that even Larry's speeding silver bullet, my snoopy eavesdropping at Hilo, and Tim and his two friends stepping in front of our rental car could not mar it. We were back on holiday mode.

If only it could last until Sunday.

CHAPTER 27

Our departure date drew closer and Brent and I did our best to enjoy every remaining moment. On Thursday morning, hand in hand, we quick stepped along the beach until the dismal dune came in sight. Then we slowed down.

"Two days ago," I said, "the police officers finished their search for telltale clues and removed all the yellow tapes." I looked up, expecting the area to be devoid of human activity.

Not so. Someone stood with his back toward us on top of the dune, apparently studying the crime scene. With head bent he took two steps forward, squatted on his heels and brushed his hands over the groundcover. He turned slightly and we recognized Detective Kanui.

Was he looking for clues? Or was he trying to see the murderous act in his mind's eye? Did he expect the gods to enlighten him with an intuitive message? Whatever his aim, the crime scene was not yet delegated to the halls of history.

"Is he searching for something that might have been missed earlier?" I whispered.

"Maybe," Brent replied.

"What do you think he's looking for? A fingernail? A footprint? A purse? A strand of hair?"

"Philomela, I have no idea what he's looking for."

"He could be searching for bits of clothing. Something that might identify the murderer."

Before Brent could reply, the detective stood up, turned around and gazed out to the ocean. His peripheral vision apparently glimpsed us, for he turned suddenly and looked directly down at us. He waved his right arm.

"Good morning Philomela and Brent." His voice was clear and cheery.

I was amazed—he had used our first names. Did that mean we were now his buddies instead of his suspects?

We returned his wave and watched him scramble with amazing agility down the dune. He walked across the soft sand, reached us and stopped. I watched his face and the impression I received was that he looked terribly pleased with himself.

"How's the case coming?" Brent asked.

"It's progressing."

"Does that mean you have a suspect?" I asked.

He smiled enigmatically. "Well, let's say we have a couple of interesting leads."

"We're due to depart for home on Sunday," Brent said. "If no one is apprehended by then does that mean we'll be detained?"

"Not as long as we can contact you if necessary."

"The other detective," I said, "wrote down our Calgary phone number and our house and email addresses." I looked at him questioningly. "Is that enough?"

"That's all we need. Detective Sanders has recorded everything of importance." He looked directly at my face and frowned slightly. "Ms Nightingale, I must confess I'm glad you came by. I have a few more questions. Could you take the time to answer them?"

The hair on the back of my neck prickled: He had reverted to using my surname. Was I again being treated as one of his major suspects? "Go ahead," I replied, and with a nervous smile tried to look nonchalant and innocent. "Ask away."

"Can you expand on your knowledge of Tim Jones?"

I bit my lips pensively then said, "My knowledge of him is limited. We were never formally introduced though I've seen him four, um no, five times. Leone Humphries told me a bit about him and none of it was good. I think you know everything I know. There's nothing more to add."

"Do you have time to go over it again?"

The process seemed a complete waste of time. However, what did I know? I was not a detective. Besides, time was not an issue: my morning agenda consisted of a leisurely walk and breakfast.

I nodded, closed my eyes and for several seconds tried to visualize Tim Jones. I couldn't do it; doubtless my subconscious wanted nothing to do with him. After a few more seconds I began to reiterate my knowledge of him.

"Well, I first saw him in the Calgary airport departure lounge, and then I noticed him in the business section of the airplane sitting beside Marlene. I only noticed him because earlier I had admired her gorgeous appearance. Sitting together, they looked like father and daughter. Then I thought maybe she was his secretary, trophy wife or mistress. He was dressed quite conservatively in a long-sleeved pale blue shirt and he looked like a businessman starting a holiday. His hair was longish and brown, white at the temples, but it was clean and neat. His manner was reasonable, his voice was quiet, and his general appearance was normal. I heard and saw nothing out of the ordinary."

Detective Kanui nodded. Brent stood silently beside me and gazed at the water. Our fingers unclasped and we dropped each other's hands.

"The third time I saw Tim was the next morning at *The Wave* restaurant. I was eating breakfast on the patio and he climbed through a hibiscus hedge and joined two men at the table beside me. The two men knew him, but greeted him with minimum enthusiasm. They turned out to be Ezekiel and Daniel. At first I didn't recognize Tim. His hair was wild and part of it had been dyed a shocking orangey-red. He wore a grungy pink and turquoise flowered shirt with short sleeves that exposed decorative tattoos on both arms. He was loud and talked incessantly to the two men and also on his cellphone. I think one of the people on the other end of his phone was Marlene. I got the impression he was giving her instructions to meet a man. He drank beer and smoked cigarettes for breakfast. Maybe the cigarettes were marijuana, I didn't recognize the smell. Oh, and he mentioned he had just come from the tattoo parlour. He said he had a contact there. He also mentioned B.C. bud."

"Did you know what he meant?"

"Marijuana." I wasn't completely naive about social drugs.

He nodded.

I took a deep breath and the detective patiently waited. Finally I continued speaking: "Our fourth encounter was over there," and I pointed at the rocky point. "He was sitting on one of the large rocks. He wore a dirty T-shirt and shorts. He looked grey and he coughed and retched and vomited. I started to walk over to see if he needed help, but he waved me away and said he was fine. A short while later I returned and he looked better because he had more color in his face and no longer coughed or retched. He waved at me and asked if I had seen his girl-friend. I told him she was walking on the beach behind me. In actual fact she had been pacing awkwardly back and forth in what I thought was a distraught and sickly manner."

"Did you tell him that?"

"No. And I didn't mention that she had struck my shoulder."

The detective nodded his head, encouraging me to continue talking.

"Like an automatic counter, Tim's hands flipped paper money. I don't know what denominations they were because US money is all the same color. He tossed what looked like a syringe in the ocean and I walked on rather quickly. The suggestion of addiction and drug money made me anxious to get away from him." I looked at Detective Kanui and said, "I suppose it's possible that drug use attributed to the girl's violent behaviour and to his stomach illness."

"It's not only possible, it's probable."

"What a horrid life Marlene must have led." I cleared my throat then continued with my recollections: "I saw Tim Jones for the fifth time at the Japanese restaurant at the mall. He came in with Daniel and Ezekiel. Brent and I were dining with Leone Humphries and Fred Pederson. Leone blames Tim for getting her daughter on drugs and forcing her to work as a hooker to pay for them. She also suspects he murdered Marlene. As a result, after seeing Tim she behaved like a churning volcano ready to erupt. We managed to get her out of the restaurant before anything happened. And those are the only times I saw Tim Jones."

"There was another time," Brent said. "We saw him last night, but we didn't speak to him."

"That's right." I smiled at Brent, appreciating his help. "On the sixth occasion Tim was walking on the sidewalk at the mall with Ezekiel and Daniel. They crossed the road in front of our car and Brent jammed on the brakes to avoid hitting them."

"Would you say," the detective said, "that they were high on drugs?"

"I don't know. But I do know they weren't alert to cars." I almost grinned.

"Did Tim appear sloppy and uncaring?"

"That's an understatement. He looked unsavoury, but not as dreadful as that morning on the rocks."

"My next question may seem irrelevant because your answer will only be a guess." He paused and cocked his head at me.

I waited.

"From the little you've seen and heard of Tim Jones, do you consider him capable of committing murder?"

"Yes," I replied. Without hesitation I elaborated, "Because of hearsay, because of seeing him in unflattering situations, and because of my gut reaction. His presence makes me feel uncomfortable, suspicious, and nervous. He scares me. From drugs and pimping, murder could easily be the next step. I'd say he's the likeliest suspect around."

"What about the two gentlemen, Ezekiel and Daniel?"

"They're a real puzzle. I cannot believe they're Tim's close friends. How they became friends with Tim and Marlene I don't know. The idea of them being murderers is beyond my comprehension."

I refrained from mentioning the suggestions made by Fred and Brent outside the Japanese restaurant. The idea of the two men being in business with Tim seemed too absurd. My curiosity had been aroused by the overheard conversation in Hilo, but it also seemed unworthy of mentioning. Minor personality clashes between two people often occurred.

With no prompting from me, Detective Kanui thought of a business connection on his own. He casually asked, "Do you think your Deist friend could be associated with Tim in some sort of business venture?"

"No," I replied. "Maybe that's wishful thinking on my part, but if they do have a business involvement with Tim, I'll be the most surprised person on earth."

"Do you think they knew Tim because they were Marlene's friends?"

"I don't know." I shook my head. "Then again, she certainly had a serious conversation with them that morning on the beach." I helplessly flung out both hands with palms up. "It's a conundrum."

Detective Kanui agreed. "Yes, a conundrum that must be solved sooner rather than later."

"That reminds me of my brother-in-law. This may have no bearing on the murder, but I'll mention it anyway. On our way to the airport yesterday afternoon, Larry Ellis passed us on the highway. He was speeding in a silver car and he turned into the town of Kahului. Brent thought he might be on his way to visit a lawyer or a land-title agent."

"Your regard for this man is not high."

Brent groaned.

With gross understatement I said, "You could say we've experienced his prevarications."

Detective Kanui smiled. "This man is proving to be very interesting. When Detective Sanders and I visited him at *The Nest* yesterday evening, I asked him about the Christmas morning murder. He said he knew nothing about it. I asked him when he came to Maui and he said he arrived here Christmas day at nine p.m."

"On Thursday, December 23rd," Brent said, "I talked on the phone with his wife. She said he had disappeared a day earlier. If he wasn't in Vancouver and he wasn't here, where was he between Wednesday afternoon and Saturday evening?"

"We checked the airlines," Detective Kanui said then added with a touch of smugness, "I can assure you the results were enlightening. Much to our surprise, we learned he had arrived on Maui on December 22nd, not on December 25th."

"So," Brent said, "he was here when Marlene was killed."

"Yes, according to the airline records." He grinned at me and said, "The records seem to confirm that he is more than a prevaricator, he is an out and out liar."

"Why would he lie about his arrival?" I asked.

"That's a good question." Detective Kanui shrugged and after a brief silence said, "If I remember correctly, Philomela, I believe you said Mrs. Humphries told you that several years ago Larry Ellis had a fling with her teenage daughter."

"Yes. Needless to say, Leone was less than thrilled about the relationship. She thought Larry had taken advantage of the girl."

I again thought about Marlene's fling with Larry triggering the demise of her relationship with Andrew Strong. It was irrelevant to the current conversation so I let the thought float in space.

"Someone is lying," Detective Kanui said. He glanced pensively at the ocean as if expecting the surf to wash an answer up on the sand. When it did not, he said, "Mr. Ellis told us he once met Mrs. Humphries at a condo strata meeting and that he had never set eyes on her daughter."

"Well," I said, "I bet the prize for lying goes to Larry, not Leone."

"You've known him a long time."

"He's been my brother-in-law for almost eighteen years. Telling the truth was never his strong point."

"And Mrs. Humphries? Is she an honest woman?"

"As far as I know, but I only met her last week."

The detective smiled. "Mr. Ellis is not a clever liar. He must have known we could check up on him."

"Does that make Larry a suspect?"

"Yes, along with a few others."

The remark made me nervous. I hesitated to ask, but finally did: "He's a suspect, like me?"

Detective Kanui chuckled. "Ms. Nightingale, you certainly are a person of interest to the police, but you are not high on their list of suspects."

"Thank you for that."

"What about Tim's contact at the Tattoo Parlour?" Brent asked.

"We checked it out. The owner is a tattoo artist and his wife is a hair dresser. She keeps the phone numbers of both their clients. They are persons of interest, but not suspects."

Detective Kanui bowed politely and apologized again for taking up our time. We said goodbye and watched him disappear on the nearby beach access path. Trying to make sense of our individual thoughts, we said nothing.

Finally Brent spoke. "You know, solving a crime resembles solving an engineering problem. You check every detail until the cause is found."

"It's also like working on a jigsaw puzzle. You sift through other people's lives searching for motives and clues. When they fit together, the criminal is arraigned and convicted."

"Philomela, there's a big difference between jigsaw and murder. One involves a game and the other involves a death."

"That's why we should help the detectives find the murderer."

Looking pensive, he studied me a moment. Then he asked, "Would you like to become a professional detective?"

"Good grief, no."

"That's a relief. Living with a detective would be intimidating."

CHAPTER 28

The afternoon was as usual, sunny and warm. With the energy of two delighted dolphins Brent and I frolicked in the sea. We gazed at waves rolling on the surface and at sparkles lying on the sand below. Splashing each other we sent droplets of water high in the air and on their descent the droplets resembled fluffy snowflakes. They reminded me of how lucky we were to be here, even though our vacation was marred by murder.

It was to be hoped our morning chat with Detective Kanui had provided him with new leads, but at the moment it concerned us not one whit. All afternoon our puzzle-solving brains enjoyed a temporary rest. We relished swimming in cool salt water and breathing sun heated air. We kicked our feet in the sea and with the help of heavy black fins travelled a fair distance from shore. Besides sand and fish we sometimes observed other swimmers.

My skin had been covered with waterproof sunscreen, thereby removing worries of sunburn. Brent's flesh had already turned a beautiful shade of tawny brown so his worry about burning was nearly negligible. With no untoward effects from the dazzling sun or from unseen sea monsters, we finally walked out of the salt-chuck. With sighs of contentment we stretched on our backs side by side on the soft dry sand.

Brent closed his eyes. "I've had enough exertion for today. Wake me up in half an hour."

I smiled, not really believing he would fall asleep. His breathing grew slower and deeper and more regular, and lying on my side I watched him enter the land of nod. I rolled on my other side and gazed at the passing parade. Some walkers paused to search for treasures in the sand and others simply admired the sea and sky. I noted a few clouds gliding under the hot sun mainly because they turned the world a shade or two duller and a degree or two cooler.

Unlike Brent, sleep evaded me. Feeling wide awake, I decided to join the parade of treasure seekers. I left him asleep on the sand and walked in the opposite direction from the murder site. Moving toward *The Nest* where Larry, Glenn and Zelda currently resided, I wondered if I might run into someone I knew.

I had not asked the two intellectual gentlemen the name of their condominium building, nor had I heard it mentioned during casual conversation. That was no problem because I was not looking for them. Nor, for that matter, was I looking for anyone else. I was searching for treasures in the sand but really didn't expect to find any. A leisurely walk on the beach was enjoyment enough.

Afternoon beachcombers were not as friendly as early morning walkers, possibly because they were too intent on finding shells and other prizes washed up by the surf. Or maybe they felt uncomfortably warm; intense heat often made people irritable and reduced their desire to implement social skills. Afternoon walkers, unlike morning ones, seemed not to consider their promenades a form of healthy exercise or a time for pleasant social interaction.

Actually, I enjoyed the peaceful interlude and soon felt no compulsion to speak to or smile at anyone. My stroll resembled a silent, meditative retreat that occasionally included mundane treasure hunting. Who knew what valuable coral or interesting shell I might find? Once I was even tempted to filch a coconut that had fallen from a palm tree and rolled onto the beach. I refrained from doing so because I knew it would be heavy to carry and difficult to break open. My hunting was pleasurable and my gathering was negligible. Then a piece of paper fluttered toward me.

Like a lump of litter it landed in front of my right foot. I bent down, picked it up, and rued people who left bits and pieces of garbage to clutter the pristine beach. Whoever had dropped this piece of paper could have picked it up as easily as I did, and with a minimum of effort could have tossed it in a garbage container.

The paper was rectangular and small and inconsequential. I held it in my hand and paid it no attention. I walked farther on the sand then finally gave the paper closer scrutiny. It was a credit card receipt. As my fingers started to crumble it, the signature jumped out at me—Glenn Shaw.

Slowing my steps, I moved toward a spreading tree whose branches drooped over the beach. I stopped in the shade of the largest branch and its leaves encompassed me with dappled shadows. If I had been a spotted leopard or a brown bear no one would have given me a second glance. My hands smoothed the remaining wrinkles from the paper and I read the print more carefully. The receipt came from the Tattoo Parlour and was dated last Friday at 16:03 p.m.

Had Glenn gotten a tattoo at four in the afternoon, several hours after stalking me on the beach access path? I had no idea what a tattoo would cost, but this, if it were a tattoo, was priced at five hundred dollars. In my estimation such a tattoo must have been a considerable work of art, not just a small heart with I love Zelda etched inside it.

The piece of paper was of no value or meaning to anyone but Glenn. If perchance he suddenly appeared, I would give him a magnanimous smile and present him with the receipt. Of course, the chances of that happening were nil, so I decided to drop it in the garbage container at *Hale Sun and Surf.*

A noise startled me; it sounded like a sneeze in a snorkel. Wrapped in thoughts about the Visa receipt, I had paid no attention to voices drawing near on the lawn. Now I listened and to my surprise recognized one of them. It was an amazing revelation because the familiar voice was uncharacteristically soft. I stepped deeper in the shade of the tree and tried to hear the conversation.

"I won't tell anyone," Tim Jones said. He sneezed again and then continued speaking, "You'll have to help me get the stuff, even if you don't want to use it yourself."

"That can be worked out." The words were whispered and I didn't recognize the second voice.

"We have to be careful. We don't want to be investigated for murder."

I shivered and felt an urge to move from the shade of the tree and run away.

"You have no idea how shocked I was when I saw that dead body. All I could think of was talking with her the day before."

"She was a good piece of tail, eh."

"I wouldn't know. The sores on her mouth and face turned me off." The whisperer's words ended with a loud sigh.

It was the little boy sigh I recognized. I had heard it on our beach access path after Glenn failed to seduce me. Was it about seven hours later that he had considered paying for that particular act with Marlene? Had the sores made him change his mind? What of Zelda, young and beautiful and doubtless waiting and willing at *The Nest*?

"It's a good deal, don't you know." Tim's voice grew louder. "Your five hundred dollars is enough to pay for the stuff tonight. After it's sold, your investment will earn interest, high interest."

It sounded more like a business deal for drugs than for sex. My ears tingled and I tried to blend in with the tree trunk.

"That's good." Glenn spoke softly but no longer in a whisper. "When can I expect the money?"

"In a day or two. Be patient."

"I'll try."

"Be sure and steer clear of the police. You don't want them snooping around."

"I hope that stupid detective in the bright Hawaiian shirt doesn't question me again. His eyes are really weird. Up on the dune I felt as if he was looking right through me and reading my mind."

Glenn's description of Detective Kanui was apt, except for the stupid part. I concurred with the mind-reading part because the detective's eyes made me feel exactly the same way. I shivered. How could I possibly agree with Glenn's assessment of anything? The idea was chilling.

The whole scenario made me want to toss Glenn's credit card receipt to the four winds. I didn't want to touch anything he had touched. To think I had considered presenting him with the receipt if he appeared, and now he had appeared and I knew the receipt would not change hands. I had no intention of admitting to eavesdropping on his conversation with Tim Jones.

Feeling grimy and dirty, I stood still and waited until the two men sauntered back in the direction of the condominium. I watched them for a few minutes then took a step away from the tree trunk and tossed the vile paper away. Unintentionally I joined the rank of careless litterbugs. A slight breeze moved the tree branches then caught the paper and made it flutter a few metres along the beach. The breeze petered out and the paper shuddered and fell on damp sand at the water's edge.

Litterbug or not, I was happy to be free of that tidbit of information. More than ever I wanted no part of Glenn Shaw, not even his paper receipt.

My throat dried and triggered a cough reflex. I held both hands over my mouth to muffle the sound, but peering amongst the leaves I saw the two men turn around and stare in my direction. Did they see my motionless body? The dappled shadows must have accomplished its camouflage job for they both turned and continued to walk toward the condominium.

Their voices faded in the distance, their backs moved side by side as their feet strolled across the lawn. They both wore swim trunks, making Glenn's relatively slim, muscular waist and hips contrast sharply with Tim's flabby physique. It was apparent which of the two looked after his physical health. They reached the large building and I tried to see a name sign, but none was apparent. I suspected the structure was called *The Nest.*

Perhaps Tim was renting a unit in the same building as Glenn and Zelda and Larry. They lived in two different cities, but they could have obtained rentals through an internet advertisement.

The three men were not what I'd call upstanding citizens. None could be touted as a role-model for growing youths. Each of them seemed to be involved in shady business ventures in both Hawaii and Canada. The more I thought about them the more they reminded me of three rotten peas in a pod. The main difference between them was that Glenn was better looking than Larry or Tim. Was Tim the only one actively involved with drugs?

My curiosity to learn more failed to engulf me. Thankful they had not seen me I glided away from the overhanging branches and ran on the sand as fast as possible toward Brent. I kept glancing back, half suspecting to see them pursuing me, but the only people I saw were a few innocent beachcombers. By the time I reached Brent my lungs gasped for air and my heart thumped like a terrified bird's.

He was awake, sitting on the sand with his arms around his bent knees. "You're back," he said. "I thought I'd lost you."

"You almost did. I nearly committed murder."

He chuckled. "Do tell."

"You don't believe me."

"Philomela, circumstances would have to be dire indeed for you to commit murder."

"Well, the circumstances were dire." I sat down beside him and bubbling like a fountain run amok told him about finding the receipt on the sand. I related what I had heard on the other side of the tree and he listened with tolerance, patience, and interest. When he remembered that Glenn Shaw was the man to whom I had been engaged, his tolerance dissipated.

"The bastard. And to think I went out of my way to be nice to the guy. I might go over there right now and punch him in the nose."

My hands rested on his shoulders, mainly to keep him from getting up. "Don't do it, Brent. He's not worth a bruised knuckle."

"I suppose he's not."

"Besides, if I had married him I might never have met you."

He laughed. "Maybe I should bow to the east and give Glenn my thanks."

"That's hardly necessary." I removed my hands from his shoulders, placed them on my lap, and asked, "Could Glenn he involved with Tim Jones's criminal activities?"

"From what you just told me, it sounds like he could be stepping into a lucrative drug trade. Then again, he could be expecting a shipment of imported tea or coffee."

"Tim warned Glenn to be wary of the police. Glenn may not be the most ethical of men, but I hate the thought of having been engaged to a criminal."

"Let's look at the credit card receipt."

"It's long gone. I couldn't get rid of it fast enough. I threw it away."

"Too bad." Brent shook his head sadly, "Detective Kanui would have found that piece of paper not only interesting but informative."

"Good grief." My hands flew to each side of my face. "I really am stupider than dumb."

"Don't fret, Philomela. He obviously loaned money to buy something. But the important question remains...do you think he could be a murderer?"

I pondered the idea for a moment. "Glenn's a lot of things, many of them undesirable. But a murderer? I don't think so."

CHAPTER 29

We drove north on the highway to Lahaina. Thanks to my previous perusal of a guide book, I had assimilated tidbits of information about the town. Thinking Brent might like to know its illustrious history, I opened the book and quoted:
"*When King Kamehameha the Great united all the Hawaiian Islands, the town of Lahaina became the capital. It later gained international fame by evolving into the whaling capital of the world. Today it continues to gain world wide popularity as a holiday destination and currently is considered the tourist capital of the west.*"

My tour-guide spiel came to a halt and Brent murmured, "Very interesting."

With no more history to report, I leaned against the back of my seat and enjoyed the passing scenery. On our left, the ocean crashed against the shores of curving bays and rugged promontories, and every so often picnic tables sprouted from beaches of white sand. On our right, mountain peaks tried to pierce fluffy clouds. Directly above our positions on the highway no clouds defaced the clear sky..

For several seconds a tunnel encompassed us and blocked all views. The world turned dark and when we emerged my blinking eyes adjusted slowly to the return of color and light. A short while later the outskirts of Lahaina appeared.

We exited the highway, drove through a sprawling residential area and eventually reached the busy town centre. Cars were everywhere and finding a vacant parking spot was next to impossible. We finally found one and left the car in it, only to discover that walking was also next to impossible—the narrow streets were filled with moving masses of humanity.

The entire area was awash with shops selling T-shirts, coral, seashells, ornaments, jewellery, shoes, summer clothes, paintings, sculptures, and who knew what else. On Front Street we spotted the biggest Banyan Tree and strolled under and around it. A sign explained that in 1873 one shoot had been planted; it grew and dropped numerous air-roots into the ground and they in turn sprouted new tree trunks which then sent forth new air roots until eventually one basic tree covered over half an acre of land. It was hard to believe that a small forest could consist of only one tree.

Sun beat down on us and its heat inspired Brent to ask, "Was it Noel Coward who coined the phrase, *Mad dogs and Englishmen go out in the noonday sun?*"

"I think so. He could have been describing Lahaina."

"How so?"

"According to the guide book, the word *Lahaina* means *Cruel Sun*."

"Very fitting." He wiped his brow with the back of his arm. "Let's get out of the cruel sun and find a cool drink."

Several restaurants looked inviting, but they were packed with air-condition-seeking tourists. We continued weaving our sweaty way amidst throngs of people. Debating the pros and cons of eating lunch in town, we finally reached our rental car. We climbed inside and Brent turned on the air-conditioning. What a relief. Feeling cool and comfortable we headed north, hoping to find a restaurant on the outskirts of town. All we saw were high-rise condominiums towering around us and hiding views of the Pacific Ocean.

"This area is known as the Gold Coast," I informed Brent. "I wonder if the name originated from the color of sand."

"It probably describes the color of coins tourists spread around hotels, shops, restaurants, and golf courses."

I chuckled and Brent drove on. Gradually the tall buildings were replaced by lower ones.

"Turn left," I ordered. "There's a restaurant sign."

Brent pulled into a parking lot, eased the car into an empty space and turned off the ignition. We walked into the foyer of an attractive low-rise building and asked a clerk sitting at a desk about the restaurant. She pointed toward the ocean.

"Just follow the path," she said.

We walked outside. Each end of the building extended into an arm of townhouses stretching toward the water. We walked between them on the paved path, curved past a swimming pool and ended near the ocean at a larger swimming pool. A stone's throw from the second pool was a structure comprised of roof and pillars but no walls. It perched out on a small cliff overlooking the Pacific Ocean and was named *The Gazebo*. Savoury aromas wafted from it and entered our nostrils, enticing us to move closer.

Our timing was perfect; the hostess led us to the last empty table overlooking the water. We settled on white plastic chairs and our eyes naturally gazed out to sea. As we had already discovered, every seaside location offered a different view and a different ambience. Here the rocky cliff dropped steeply down to a small sandy beach that was being gently washed by the always moving sea.

My eyes feasted on the tumbling surf then shifted over to a haphazard row of chaises longue. They sat between the swimming pool and a stone wall that was high enough to prevent careless tourists from tumbling down the cliff, but not high enough to block the view. Standing with a few people near the pool was a man I recognized.

"Good grief," I exclaimed, and reached across the table and grabbed Brent's arm. "Look over there." With a less than lady-like gesture I pointed the index finger of my other hand..

His eyes followed the direction of my finger. "What are you looking at?"

"That man in the yellow flowered shirt."

"Where?"

"He's standing by the pool."

"I see him. Who is he?"

"Motor-Mouth. Tim Jones."

"Are you sure?" Brent sounded disbelieving, but he continued to stare at the man.

"I'm positive."

"What's he doing here?"

"You tell me and we'll both know."

"Maybe he booked into one of the townhouses."

I leaned across the table and whispered, "Probably he's delivering drugs or soliciting sex."

"Or maybe, like us, he simply enjoyed a picturesque drive and stopped for nourishment in *The Gazebo*."

Our conversation ceased as a waitress came up to our table. After taking our lunch orders she walked away and we again turned toward the swimming pool. Tim Jones glided from the group near the pool and slithered to a less populated area. He stopped beside two people relaxing on chaises longue and started a conversation. True to form he did most of the talking. He regaled his two listeners who were young and male and they responded with hearty laughter. Obviously encouraged, Tim sat down on an empty chaise longue and continued with his successful comedic act. I noticed his arms were partially covered by the sleeves of his colourful shirt and his hair was neatly tied behind his neck. He looked more civilized than the last few times I had seen him.

Nervously, I realized he held his new young acquaintances in the palm of his hand. I squeezed my eyes shut because the area around them seemed to turn a depressing grey. My abdominal muscles tightened but not with hunger. I was sure Tim was up to no good. His smooth talk was sucking the young lads into a vortex of evil. I opened my eyes and the colors of his shirt and nearby flowers and trees returned to normal.

An urge to do-good overpowered me. I wanted to save the world, well, not the world, just those two young men, boys really. Without expressing my intent to Brent, doubtless knowing he would try to stop me, I stood up, marched out of the gazebo, and strode with purpose toward the threesome. Reaching them, I stopped directly in front of Motor-Mouth.

"Hello Tim," I said. He looked up and I gave him the sweetest smile I could muster. "Nice to see you." Even to my own ears my voice sounded friendlier and pleasanter than I felt.

He stared at me and asked, "Hello. Should I know you?"

In my cheeriest tone of voice I countered his question by asking another, "Have you heard if the police have caught the person who murdered your girlfriend?"

My words were what might be called an icebreaker and I don't mean a form of crystal meth. The two young men stared at me and their mouths fell open as if trying to expel ice-cubes. They blinked, wide-eyed, and sat very still. They said nothing.

Tim glared at me. He had no words with which to answer my question or counter its implication. It was with satisfaction that I noted the two young fellows shift uneasily away from him. Their faces paled and their eyes grew as large as toonies.

"If you hear anything about Marlene's murderer, please let me know." I smiled sweetly, leaned toward him and added, "I'll probably see her mother tomorrow."

He nodded blankly and with apparent confusion muttered, "Say hello to her for me, eh."

"I'll do that. Needless to say, she's very distraught. It's not easy coping with the murder of a child, especially an only daughter."

Our eyes locked and his gaze became so venomous it was all I could do to keep from looking away. I also wanted to step backward, beyond the reach of his vile arms. Silence encompassed the four of us for what seemed an eternity and my eyes shifted for a peripheral peek at the boys. One had eased to the edge of his chaise longue. Both their mouths had closed but their faces remained pale.

I gazed directly at Tim, extended my right arm toward the gazebo and said, "Nice place isn't it."

"Very nice," he mumbled.

"Did you ever bring your dead girlfriend here?"

If looks could kill, I would no longer be prancing on planet earth. Ignoring his expression I made an idiotic offer: "My husband and I are going to have lunch in the restaurant. Would you dare to join us?" I emphasized the word, dare.

"I've eaten," he said. Seeming to regain a semblance of composure, he added, "I soon have to drive back south. I have a six o'clock dinner date at *The Wave*."

"With a new young girlfriend?"

He glared at me again and said nothing.

"You aren't wasting any time replacing your dead girlfriend, are you?"

"Not with a girl," he growled. "My dinner date is with two male friends, don't ya know. As if it's any of your business. I don't even know you."

"Quite right. You don't know me, but I know you." Glancing at the two young lads, I wondered how often they shaved. Twice a week, I guessed, if that. I gave them both what I hoped was a motherly smile. Then I leaned forward and patted the top of the head of the lad closest to me. As I stepped backward he rose from his chaise longue and his companion followed suit.

I gazed at them with maternal concern and asked, "Are you young boys enjoying your stay here?"

They nodded mutely. The one who had stood up first said, "We have to go and get ready for this evening. It's New Year's Eve."

"So it is. I have to confess it had slipped my mind. Must be the result of the traumatic murder. " I shook my head with genuine sadness. Then I managed a weak smile. "Since this is the last day of the year, a party for young people is certainly in order."

With obvious discomfort they nodded their heads. The spokesman glanced at Tim, cleared his throat and with a nervous croak said, "Well, we should be on our way." He took three steps back.

The other lad's eyes shifted uneasily from me to Tim and then he too stepped back.

The first lad politely said, "Goodbye. Enjoy your stay and have a Happy New Year." Then he turned toward the paved path.

"Happy New Year," I said.

His friend nodded at me then scurried after his friend along the gentle curves of the path. They disappeared from sight.

For the first time ever, I felt the rush do-gooders must feel when they do something good. My joy had no bounds. I swelled with pride. With a few simple words I had saved two young lads from becoming drug addicts. Those same few words had put a known drug-pusher and pimp and possible murderer in his place. It was the next best thing to convicting him in court.

I smiled sweetly at Tim and said, "See you around." Then I turned on my heel and marched away.

Entering the gazebo I snapped with vigour, virtue and valour. I stopped at our table and took control of the chair by firmly plunking my buttocks on the plastic seat. I placed my serviette on my lap, looked directly across the table at Brent and noted his expression of shock and awe. He stared at me, momentarily speechless.

With studied casualness I said, "That worked out well."

"What in the world did you say to them?"

I shrugged nonchalantly. "I simply asked Tim if the police found the person who had murdered his girlfriend."

Brent's face wreathed in a smile and his shoulders moved slowly up and down. Then, unable to contain his mirth any longer, laughter bubbled out between his lips.

I quietly remarked, "The two young lads seemed duly impressed by the question."

Brent got his laughter under control. Able to speak again, he agreed with my assessment: "I could tell they were impressed. In one felled swoop their appreciation of Tim's humour faltered and they looked like scared rabbits. They sidled away as if you and Tim were bearers of the plague. A moving virus couldn't have made them dash faster down the path. I'd wager that right now they're driving on the highway in excess of the speed limit."

"From now on they'll be inclined to associate illegal drugs with murder." Our lunches had been delivered during my absence so I picked up my fork and started to eat. Never had food tasted so delicious.

Brent cleaned his plate, leaned back in his chair and gazed over at the swimming pool. "Your friend Tim has gone."

"He mentioned having a six o'clock dinner date at *The Wave*."

"Well, I wonder who with."

"Two male friends, he said."

Brent gazed at the swimming pool. "The water in that pool looks inviting. We can have a dip when we get back to *Hale Sun and Surf.*"

"Was it just yesterday morning that we chatted with Detective Kanui on the beach?"

"It was."

"Time flies when you're having fun,"

Fun was an inappropriate word, but I couldn't think of a better one.

CHAPTER 30

*D*uring our drive south, I leaned against the back of the passenger seat and thought about our departure from the land of summer and our return to the land of winter. The holiday would recede in memory and Brent and I would become busy with the familiar routines of work and everyday life.

A few disturbing thoughts skirted the fringes of my brain. What if the police forbade us to leave? What if an unexpected occurrence made it necessary for us to remain on Maui? As much as I loved the climate and the beauty of this lovely island, would I want to remain here forever?

No. My answer surprised me until I realized it was based on the boredom of sameness. Variety is the spice of life and that was why I loved spring, summer, autumn, and winter. For me, a perennial summer lost hands down to the four changing seasons.

As Brent drove into the condo's parking lot, I turned and asked, "Do you realize we only have two more nights in paradise?"

"I do." He eased the car into an empty parking space, switched off the ignition and pronounced, "It is imperative we enjoy every minute."

I climbed out of the car, looked over the hood at Brent and said, "The drive and lunch were delightful. A super way to spend the last day of the year. Even my encounter with Tim Jones couldn't ruin it."

"If anything," Brent said, "your encounter with Tim added to it."

I grinned and glanced at my watch. "It's four-thirty. We made good time."

"And I didn't even exceed the speed limit."

"The police must love you."

While Brent unlocked the door of Number 309, I surreptitiously listened at the door of Number 308. All was quiet; the owner must not be home or else he was napping or reading. Brent entered our unit and suggested we go to the pool for a quick dip.

Several minutes later, wearing our swimsuits, we walked down the two flights of stairs.

"Do you think the police will let us go home as scheduled?" I asked.

"Why wouldn't they? They know how to contact us."

"I wonder if Detective Kanui gets tired of dealing with badness all day."

"Dealing with goodness might be less tiring, but it also might be more boring."

Thinking about Brent's assessment of goodness, I turned into the dimly lit passageway and almost crashed into a person. With a gasp, I muttered, "Good grief."

"Oh sorry," The voice belonged to Leone.

Trying to avoid a second near-collision, we both moved in the same direction at the same time and once again barely missed crashing into each other.

I giggled, gave her a queenly wave and said, "Hi Leone."

"Sorry," she again said.

I moved to my right and she moved to her left, and we experienced another near-miss. I giggled, louder this time. "Want to dance?" I asked.

The logic of my illogical question evaded her. In the dim light she looked at me as if I were a drunken sailor. My attempt at humour sank like a sailing ship with a hole in the hull. I tried a different tack.

"It's another sunny day in paradise."

The ridiculousness of this cliché in a consistently warm and sunny climate usually triggered a smile. Not this time. The remark failed to amuse Leone. As my eyes adjusted to the dim light, I noted the dullness of her eyes and the lack of an upward crescent on her lips. I had to admit my lack of comedic talent was not the only reason she failed to smile. Right now she had very little to smile about.

"Are you okay?" I asked no long attempting to be funny.

"As well as can be expected."

I nodded sympathetically. "Have you heard any new developments from the police?"

"No. Have you heard anything?"

I shook my head. "We were gone most of the day. We drove up the west coast this morning and ate lunch at a restaurant north of Lahaina." I hesitated, wondering if more details were appropriate and decided they were. "We had the misfortune to run into Tim Jones. He was talking with two young men. I suspected he was up to no good."

"I'm sure you suspected correctly."

"I spoke with him briefly. He said he had an early dinner date tonight at *The Wave*."

"Did he say who with?" She gazed down at her feet.

"Not specifically. I suppose the dinner will be an early start for a New Year's Eve celebration."

She said nothing, just continued to study her feet as if they would provide insight to all her problems. Finally she looked up at me. "He's probably going to dine with some teenage girl and solicit her to take Marlene's place."

"Leone, I accused him of that exact thing. But he said he wouldn't be dining with a girl, but with two male friends."

Pursing her lips she moved her head from side to side. The very thought of Tim Jones seemed to put her in a mood of disgust and despair. She glanced back at the laundry machines and let out a long, sad sigh. When she again turned to me her eyes were less dull and her facial expression was contemplative. Maybe my humour had helped after all.

"I hope," she said, "that he doesn't hook someone else on drugs."

Tim Jones did not make for happy conversation, so I thumbed through memory pages to find another topic and came up empty. Then I noticed her colourful bikini and how it accentuated the hills and valleys of her well-proportioned figure. I adeptly changed the subject. "Your swimsuit looks fabulous on you, Leone. Have you been out sun-tanning?"

She gazed at my face and smiled. "Yes, I was. Fred called down from his lanai and suggested I go up to his place for a drink. I'm going there now."

"That's good. He's a nice fellow."

She smiled rather wanly, but it was definitely a smile. "Yes, in most ways he is."

I didn't reply. After all, this was the same man who had availed himself with her daughter's sordid profession. With a bit of effort, I managed a cheery tone: "We're off for a swim in the pool. See you anon."

"Righto."

Not knowing what else to say, I gave her another queenly wave then followed Brent who was already waiting on the terrace at the other end of the corridor.

"Bye Brent," Leone called.

"Bye Leone."

The pool was empty of people so we eased into the water and swam a few short laps. After climbing out we lay on two chaises longue on the lawn. The western sun was low but warm enough to dry our wet swimsuits. I figured the late afternoon sun was too weak to burn my exposed skin so I ignored putting on sunscreen.

Less than an hour later, back in the condo, I was preparing a light meal when Brent said, "Philomela, come out to the lanai. The sun's starting to set."

The red orb began its daily descent below the horizon. The sky was clear and no clouds reflected the sun's vivid colour. The yellow orb was almost gone when our neighbour loudly blew his conch shell and other resident sun-watchers applauded.

"The green flash," I squealed.

"I see it too," Brent said.

The green flash lingered a nanosecond then disappeared below the curve of the planet. We gave each other a big grin, a high five, and flowed into each other's arms. We indulged in a lovely bear hug.

"We've seen the green flash three times," I said. "How lucky is that?"

"It's only fitting we should see it on the last night of the year."

"It's a good omen. The gods will be with us for the next fifty-two weeks."

"Are you making up a new old-wives-tale?"

"Maybe." I glanced down at the lawn and saw Andrew Strong walk toward the beach access path. Wearing a colourful shirt, white pants and shoes, he looked ready to party. His handsome physique and his graceful movements were a treat to behold, a picture that could entrance any young girl. Was there one waiting for him? Surely the death of his former girlfriend would not prevent him from enjoying the last evening of the year with someone else.

Over a light meal on the lanai, Brent and I discussed the day's pleasant drive and interesting lunch. As darkness deepened we spoke softly, and the entire ambience was peaceful and relaxing. Holiday mode was in effect.

A loud cacophony rent the air and made us both jump. Startled, we saw a series of bright shooting stars explode in the sky. Noisy crackles, lingering buzzes, loud bangs and strange screams bombarded our ears. Brilliant pinwheels, fiery waterfalls, and more shooting stars dazzled our eyes. We stood up and stared over the lanai railing toward the ocean and with each eruption we "oohed" and "aahed". The zinging and screaming continued and repeated themselves as did the brilliant flashes of sparkling light. It was too much to ignore. Every so often a loud bang resembling gunshots occurred and each time I shuddered. Was someone else being murdered?

The noises and the sparkling designs were caused by firework displays rising one after another all along the beach. We watched colourful sprays shoot up from different areas and light the sky then fizzle back down to earth. We listened to the loud noises and wished we had earplugs.

On the beach shadowy figures danced enthusiastically around sparkling caldrons. Every so often the sparkling lights faded, leaving only the gibbous moon in the sky and its reflection on the water. Wispy clouds occasionally obliterated the orb and its reflection which made the blackness blacker. Finally the noise and brightness dissipated completely.

"It's finished," Brent said.

And then the entire procedure began again.

"Enough," I said. "I'm going to clean up the kitchen." Brent offered to help and I gave him an out: "The dishes are few and the kitchen is small."

"Maybe I'll go down to the beach and get a closer look at what's going on. Where are the earplugs?"

I laughed.

After he departed I cleared the table, pulled the gliding door shut and almost but not quite obliterated the noisy sounds. In the kitchen I washed dishes, stacked them in cupboards, wiped counters clean, and swept the floor. I glanced at my wristwatch. Seven twenty. Would Motor-Mouth still be at *The Wave* with his friends?

In the bathroom I acknowledged New Year's Eve by applying lipstick to my lips and running a comb through my unruly hair. I decided the firework folks must be interesting because Brent seemed a long time coming home. I went to the living room, closed the drapes and turned on the TV. I was lounging on the sofa enjoying a choir's version of Christmas carols when Brent returned.

"A lot of crazy celebrants down there," he said. "The world has gone mad." He looked at the closed drapes. "I see you've shut out the awful noise and the bright lights. It's a relief."

Our pleasant little cocoon surrounded us and like an old married couple we sat side by side and tuned into a 1939 classic movie. The sizzling noises outside were not loud enough to disrupt our focus on Charlie Chaplin in *The Great Dictator*.

An hour later our relaxed concentration was interrupted by a knock on the door. Brent got up, walked down the hall and answered it. I heard him talk with a man who I hoped was not Detective Kanui.

Wondering about the identity of our unexpected guest, I tried to recognize the voice. Unable to see the person at our door, I craned my neck but the visitor remained out of sight. Recognition occurred when I saw Leone and Fred walk down the hall toward me. Their swim suits were replaced with smart casual outfits, Leone in skirt and matching top and Fred in white pants and golf shirt. They entered the sitting room and I muted Herr Hingle and Herr Garbage and stood up.

"Happy New Year's Eve," I said.

Fred returned the greeting and fussed with the top button on his shirt. He seemed ill at ease. "I hope we aren't interrupting anything important," he said.

"Just an old classic movie," I replied. "We saw it years ago. Please sit down and make yourselves comfortable."

They ignored my suggestion and continued to stand.

"Would you like some decaf coffee?" I asked, trying to make them feel welcome. They failed to respond and I wondered if they heard me.

Brent said, "How about a drink of something stronger."

Fred came to life. "That sounds good." Seeming a bit embarrassed at his forwardness, he explained, "It's New Year's Eve."

Brent grinned. "So it is. And being no longer young, we should toast it at Calgary time. Three hours early."

Fred chuckled. "Good idea." He placed his hand under Leone's elbow and guided her to the sofa. They sat down beside each other.

Half way to the kitchen, Brent paused and turned to Fred. "What's your poison? I only have gin and wine."

His use of the word poison struck me as inappropriate until I recalled Fred using the same terminology on Leone's lanai. Leone apparently disagreed with my initial reaction to the word for she smiled.

"Poison it is," she said. "I'll try your gin and tonic."

"I'll have the same," Fred said.

"Have you had dinner?" I asked, hoping they had eaten.

"I'm full," Fred replied. "We've been nibbling for the last three hours."

"That's just as well," I said. "Our larder is almost bare."

Fred explained their lack of hunger pains by saying, "We ate heavy hors d'oeuvres earlier at my place. I've had enough food to last 'til next year. I don't know about Leone, though."

I looked her a query and she responded with a shake of the head. "I couldn't eat another bite. I sipped and nibbled at Fred's place then around seven he went for a walk and I went to my condo for a nap. A short while later at his place we started to eat again. "

"Did you watch the fireworks?"

"A bit. We've seen them before. Many times."

"A little goes a long way." Brent spoke from the kitchen. "I understand setting off fireworks is how Hawaiians traditionally celebrate New Year's Eve."

Fred nodded. "It is. But don't ask me why."

Brent brought two tall glasses of gin and tonic into the room and handed them to our guests. Then he turned to me. "Philomela? Gin or wine?"

He knew an alcoholic drink would not be my choice. A cocktail before dinner and wine during dinner were fine, but drinks after dinner ensured I would suffer a hangover the next morning. He usually refrained from drinking alcohol after dinner, too. Our guests seemed unaware of our preferences. "Decaf," I said. "I'll make it."

Realizing they were going to stay awhile, I flicked off the TV, sauntered to the kitchen and put the kettle on the stove. I waited for it to boil and listened to the casual chatter in the sitting room. After the water boiled I poured it over instant decaffeinated granules and carried two steaming mugs into the living room.

Brent, who sat on an arm chair, took a mug from me and turned to Fred. "You don't have much holiday time left, do you?"

"Four days." Fred took a small sip. "This gin and tonic tastes good. I may start drinking it from now on." He returned to Brent's question and said, "I believe you two leave before I do."

"Day after tomorrow," Brent said. "Provided the police allow us to depart. Have they suggested that you stay longer than planned?"

"No," Fred replied, "they haven't. Not yet, anyway. Their prime concern was having a record of Leone's and my whereabouts after we leave. They want to be able to contact us if necessary."

"Us too," Brent said.

"When are you leaving, Leone?" I moved a chair from the dining area close to the coffee table and sat down.

"I don't know what I'm going to do. My condo hasn't been rented until the first of February, so I may stay until the end of January."

"That's good then...."

"Righto. I guess it is. Marlene has been cremated." Her eyes blinked and she cleared her throat. "I'll have lots of time to think about a memorial service."

The shadow of her daughter's death hovered over us like a black cloud. Leone had broached the subject herself, so there was no point in ignoring the deep shadows.

"I wish the police would find the murderer," I said.

"I do, too." Fred raised his glass to his lips and took a hefty sip. "Convicting the murderer won't bring Marlene back, but it might stop someone else from being killed."

"Or becoming addicted," Leone said.

"Yes, that's a good point." I nodded at her with sympathy.

She sat beside Fred and clutched her glass so tightly that her knuckles were white. She turned from me and stared at the liquid in the glass as if hoping to find answers to life's many problems.

My heart went out to her but my words seemed useless and mundane: "Would you like a cracker, nuts, or something else, Leone?"

She looked up at me. "Nothing, thanks. This drink is just what I needed." She turned to Brent and she actually smiled. "I'm surprised at how refreshing your gin and tonic is."

It was at that moment we heard another blast of noises. The first one was so loud I jumped with alarm. "Is that a gunshot?" I asked.

Brent chuckled. "Fireworks. Again. Do Hawaiians celebrate New Year's Eve after midnight?"

"Yes they do," Fred said. He stood up and moved to the gliding doors. He pushed aside the drapes, opened the door and went out on the lanai. "Look at these. They're good ones."

We all went outside and watched a spectacular display of colourful stars rising from the beach to form brilliant umbrellas in the sky. When the display finally fizzled out another started farther away. One after another they went off.

"It lasts until they run out of fireworks," Fred said.

A few minutes later, tired of watching the displays, we closed the door and drapes and sat down again in the sitting room. We sipped our drinks and looked at each other.

"Leone," I asked, "do you have much contact with Andrew Strong?"

"Just when he's working on the grounds. He's a nice young man. But we have no reason to keep in touch."

"You said he almost became your son-in-law."

She nodded. "He and Marlene made a stunning couple. Unfortunately, Andrew learned about her fling with Larry. He was young and idealistic, so he naturally blew his top. She responded in like manner and flew off to Calgary where she got a job. That was where she met Tim Jones. He enticed her to experiment with drugs, just for kicks, and before she knew it she was hooked." Leone took a lengthy sip of her drink and said, "If only she had not taken off to Calgary, I think she and Andrew could have worked things out."

"How sad."

"Yes, it was." Leone turned to Fred and changed the subject. "Do you have any plans for tomorrow?"

"Nothing. Maybe we could go to the aquarium or take a drive up island like Brent and Philomela did?"

"Let's sleep on it and then decide."

"Okay."

The conversation continued in a pedestrian manner. Nothing of great interest was imparted, our repartee lacked wit and wisdom, our pauses were un-philosophical, and our stories contained little excitement. There were many lapses of silence and they were uncomfortable ones. At times we all seemed to rack our brains to find a cheery subject worthy of discussion. Marlene's violent death was always present.

Gleaning the bottom of the conversational barrel, I asked, "Have you happened to run into Larry Ellis?"

Leone gave her head a negative shake.

"I've been watching for him," Fred said, "but so far he hasn't appeared. When did he arrive on the island?"

"According to Detective Kanui a few days before Christmas."

Leone sighed. "That means he was here when Marlene died."

Why had I thought Larry would be a neutral and safe topic of conversation? He too, of course, had known Marlene.

Finally Fred said, "Leone, it's time we let these good people go to bed. Have you discussed your important items?" He looked at her with concern.

"I think so."

"Good. So let's be off."

"Righto." She got up from the sofa.

After they left, I wondered what Leone considered important. As far as I could discern, the only important item discussed during the entire evening had been Marlene. Had Leone and Fred merely come to our place for companionship? I could think of no other reason. Nothing had been said that was remotely worth remembering. The entire conversation had been prosaic and rather boring. The most exciting part of the evening had been the fireworks and as time went on they turned into noisy aggravations.

Oh well, the colourful celebrations and our companionship may have provided Leone and Fred with needed diversions. And Leone certainly needed brief respites from her current sorrow.

"You know," I said to Brent. "Leone's lucky to have Fred. He seems to truly care about her. He treats her with concern and thoughtfulness. I think he's a very kind man."

"He certainly gives that impression."

"You don't sound convinced."

"It's just that appearances can be deceiving."

"Are you implying he could be the killer, that his kindness might be hiding guilt?"

"Philomela, I wasn't implying anything. I just made an innocent observation."

"Well, right now Leone needs all the kindness she can get."

"I won't argue that."

CHAPTER 31

It was our second last morning of summer. Brent and I welcomed it with our routine walk on the beach. We strode briskly to the end of the bay, retraced our steps, and while passing the dismal dune experienced no trepidation. Back in the condo we sat on the lanai and ate bacon, eggs, papaya and toast. Our conversation focused on last night's fireworks.

"Some of the bright displays were amazing," I said. "But It went on far too long. I bet it was after two in the morning when the noise finally quit."

"Fred warned us it would last until their supplies ran out."

We finished breakfast and were sipping coffee when a loud knock sounded on the door. "I bet it's Detective Kanui," I said and leaped up from my chair. With nervous anticipation I hurried to the main entrance and opened the door. Sure enough, there stood the man with mindreading eyes. He's here to tell us we can't go home on Sunday, I thought, but managed to smile and say, "Good morning, Detective."

He nodded politely. "Happy New Year, Philomela."

First name again. A good sign. "And happy New Year to you."

"Are you well this morning?"

"Very well indeed. And you?"

"The same. Obviously neither of us misbehaved last night. Am I disturbing you?"

"Not at all. Brent and I just finished eating breakfast. Would you like to join us for coffee on the lanai?"

"I would like that very much." He sounded pleased, as if expecting the invitation.

So far so good. Receiving no vibrations of being a murder suspect, I led him out to the lanai. I left the two men sitting at the green plastic table and went to the kitchen where I filled a mug with freshly brewed coffee. Ignoring cream and sugar because the detective had previously taken his coffee black, I carried the mug outside. Deep in conversation, they hardly noticed me.

I set the coffee mug on the table in front of Detective Kanui and both men looked up, surprised to see me. Here it comes, I thought, we won't be allowed to go home.

"Philomela," Brent said. "Detective Kanui just told me some bad news."

Waiting for the travel hammer to drop, I lifted my still warm coffee from the table and looked over at him.

"Tim Jones is dead."

"What?" The mug almost dropped from my hand. This was not the hammer I expected. I stared first at Brent and then at Detective Kanui. Comprehension evaded me; for several seconds I failed to grasp what Brent had said. He repeated the news and this time his words registered. "Tim Jones is dead? We saw him yesterday and he seemed fine. Are you telling me that my number one murder suspect has followed his victim beyond the beyond?"

Detective Kanui placed his hands in a prayer position under his chin. Looking sad, he slowly nodded his head. "We think he may have ingested a type of poison."

"A drug overdose?" I asked.

"Possibly."

Suddenly I felt sorry for the way I had behaved with Tim yesterday. Had my unkind words triggered a depression that caused him to end it all? Feeling puzzled and guilty, I gazed into the detective's eyes. "Was it a bad drug or did he purposely overdose?"

"It might have been an unintentional overdose, but we think someone assisted him."

"Someone assisted him?" A cobwebby film cluttered my mind and obstructed clear thinking. I shook my head, trying to clear my thoughts. The movement helped. "Who would do such a thing?" Without hesitation I answered the question myself. "Probably dozens of people wanted to finish him off."

"It's quite possible." Detective Kanui's eyes continued to focus on mine. "I was wondering if this development might prompt new thinking on your part."

New thinking on my part? Was he kidding? Tim was dead. Feeling the detective's mesmerizing eyes probe my mind, I thought, "Oh-oh, I'm still a suspect." Did he think Brent and I murdered Marlene then seven days later committed the second dastardly deed? I lowered my eyes and slowly said, "I'm surprised...stunned...shocked. I thought he was the murderer." My throat dried up so I swallowed, trying to moisten it. It didn't work so I sipped some coffee. Then I asked, "Where and when was he was poisoned?"

"His death occurred early last evening. We're not sure of the exact location. He was found on the sidewalk in front of the Shoe Store."

"Near *The Wave* restaurant?" I asked.

"That's correct." He leaned toward me and his eyes brightened expectantly. "He was found five shops away from the restaurant."

I gazed at him and thought: Here we go again—I know more about this murder than an innocent person should. I again cleared my throat and swallowed. "Tim told me yesterday that he had an early dinner date at *The Wave*."

"Very interesting. Where did he tell you that?"

I explained how we had run into Tim at the resort north of Lahaina. My voice was weak because I still had trouble believing Motor-Mouth would no longer be able to verbally blast the air around us. How did our prime murder suspect become a murder victim? What an ironic twist of fate. I managed to describe the two young lads with whom Tim had struck up a conversation and reluctantly admitted to intentionally saying words that would encourage them to depart.

"I wanted them to leave," I conceded. "But I shouldn't have mentioned the murder of Tim's girlfriend in such a rude manner."

With a soft chuckle, Inspector Kanui lowered his hands and picked up his coffee mug. "That was exactly the right thing to say, Ms. Nightingale. Maybe in later years those two young fellows will mentally thank you for interrupting a transaction that might have ended in dangerous experimentation."

"I hope so. The alternative is to be remembered as a brash interloper." Suddenly realizing his words had given me a verbal pat on the back, I sat up straighter and felt better about my last contact with Tim. Then my thoughts shifted from Detective Kanui's opinion of me to the death of Marlene's pimp. "Was Tim seen with anyone in particular at *The Wave*?"

"The police are questioning people at the mall as we speak. I hope clerks in the nearby stores and staff at the restaurant will come up with some good leads."

"I hope so, too," Brent said. "I'd like to see these killings wrapped up before we leave Maui."

Detective Kanui nodded thoughtfully. He lifted his mug, sipped some coffee and then set the mug carefully back on the table. "So would I," he said.

"You know, I accused Tim of planning to dine with a young girl to replace Marlene. He said he was meeting two male friends for dinner."

"Did he mention their names?"

"No, he didn't." I shook my head then said, "I thought Tim had murdered Marlene. I guess his death changes that scenario."

"Possibly, but not necessarily."

"Two murderers running on the loose is really intimidating," I said. "One was bad enough."

"One is *more* than enough." Detective Kanui gazed pensively off to space and when his moment of meditation was over he slowly raised the mug to his lips. He took a sip and in slow motion set the mug back on the table. "This is very good coffee, Ms Nightingale."

"Thank you. It's Kona coffee, so it should be good."

He smiled and again activated the art of silence.

After a long sixty seconds I broke the silence. "Going back to Tim's demise, I must say Leone Humphries won't be heartbroken. He was not her favourite person."

"She had reason, I think, for not liking him. I haven't visited her this morning, but I'll go to her condo after I leave here. What about her friend, Fred Pederson?"

"He lives next door. Do you want me to get him and bring him here?"

"Thank you, no. If he's home, I'll see him on my way out."

"I know you can't tell us anything definite," Brent said, "but do you have any leads that point to a particular killer, or killers?"

"Leads, yes. Definite ones, no."

"I've never been involved with a murder before," I said and gazed respectfully at our guest. "It's disconcerting. It's dreadful. And of course it's sad. Yet at the same time the idea of finding the murderer creates a strange sense of anticipation, even excitement. It's a conundrum."

"Yes, murder is a puzzle for those trying to solve it." The detective's eyes looked pensive, not mesmerising. "It's hard to think like a murderer. Most of us can't comprehend a motive for such a horrific act. Solving the puzzle often relies on hope. Hope is an important ingredient for creating energy and desire to succeed in anything, including finding a murderer. I and my colleagues hope to find enough clues to bring the violent brute to justice. Hope is what keeps many policemen going."

As if having revealed too much of himself, he drained his mug and stood up. "Thank you, Ms. Nightingale. The coffee was delicious. In the long run, your conversation with Tim yesterday may prove very helpful. And thank you, Mr. Lark." He shook hands with both of us. "I promise to keep you informed of any new developments." He turned and walked from the lanai to the sitting room.

I saw him out of our condo and before closing our door heard him knock on the adjacent door. I stood under our open bedroom window and heard Fred's door open. The conversation between the two men floated clearly through the open window.

"Detective Kanui," Fred said. "Hello."

"Good morning and Happy New Year, Mr. Pederson. Could I take a minute of your time?"

"Certainly. Will you come inside?"

"That won't be necessary. I just want to inform you that Tim Jones died last night. It looks like it might be murder. "

"Tim? Dead?" Fred's voice trembled. "Another murder? That's terrible, though I confess to knowing a few people who will disagree with that assessment. I must say he was not the nicest banana in the cluster. Two murders within a week. That's a bit much."

"Yes, it is. And at the moment we have no definite suspects. I was wondering if you have any ideas that could aid our search for a killer."

"I don't know what to say. I can't think of anyone who might have done it. As you probably already know, Tim hung out with a sleazy crowd. Could it be one of them?"

Listening under the window, I cringed. Ezekiel and Daniel did not fit my definition of sleazy.

"It could be." The detective's reply seemed overly smooth. Or was it just my imagination? Then he said, "Did you know anything about the deceased?"

"Only what Leone told me. I've seen him on a few occasions. The last time was in the Japanese restaurant. I've never spoken to the man."

"Your friend Leone disliked him."

"She blamed him for getting her daughter on drugs and then forcing her into prostitution to pay for her habit. It was a dismal picture for both mother and daughter."

"Yes, the horror of drug addiction rests not only on the addict, but on family and friends as well."

They were silent a moment. I waited unabashedly under our bedroom window.

Finally Detective Kanui said, "Here's my card, Mr. Pederson. Please phone me if anything comes to mind. Something minor and seemingly unimportant often helps solve a case."

"I'll give it more thought. Have you talked with Leone Humphries?"

"I'm going to see her now."

I envisioned their hands touching in gentlemanly fashion then heard the detective's footsteps move toward the stairs. The door in the next condo closed with a loud click and all was quiet.

Back on the lanai, I sat down, picked up my coffee mug and took a sip of the cold brew. Looking at Brent I said, "Detective Kanui spoke with Fred."

"What did he say?"

"He told him about Tim's probable murder and asked him to phone if he thinks of anything...."

A grin spread across Brent's face.

"Good grief. You think you're so smart."

"Philomela, with no effort on my part you just admitted to being an eavesdropper." His grin turned into a chuckle.

"I wasn't eavesdropping," I said rather indignantly. "I was listening for clues that might help solve the murder."

"Did you collect any?"

"Well...."

"Do you think Fred killed Marlene?"

"No."

"What are you basing your assumptions on?"

"Woman's intuition."

Brent did not bother to reply.

CHAPTER 32

$\mathcal{D}$etective Kanui was a good detective; that was obvious. Of his many skills, five stood out as being most important. All five were subgenres of three general categories: intuition, art, and science.

A good detective needs intuition to help decide what investigative route to follow; he needs art to understand what he observes and hears; he requires science for calculating and deducing everything. These five skills are well developed in all clever detectives. And Detective Kanui was certainly clever.

Though I could not claim cleverness such as his, I did have three of the skills even before Marlene's murder loomed to the fore. During most of my life I had been intuitive, a keen observer, and a good listener.

The intuitive part was genetic and the observer part became well developed while producing T*he Integrator.* The listener part started early in my marriage when I learned that interrupting Brent's monologues was counterproductive. During the past week I developed another skill: eavesdropping—to obtain information of course. This achievement did not make me particularly proud. .

Scientific skills were my weakest point. My efforts at calculation and deduction needed more practice. Not that I wanted to become a professional detective—good grief, no. Nor did I want to become an amateur detective. These goals were beyond my talent and desire. To attain the heights of either would take years of intense training and numerous life experiences. I wanted only to help solve the two ghastly deaths, one from assault and the other from poison.

The wound on Marlene Rathbone's head had been inflicted by a hunk of white coral; that was pretty much a given. My observational skills had resulted in the discoveries of both her body and the murder weapon, two feats of which I was justly proud. Naturally I tried to suppress the egotistical feeling because the Greek myths had taught me that hubris goes before a fall.

The second death did exactly that—it knocked down my pride. No matter how strong my desire to solve both crimes, I was now bereft of clues or ideas. The type of poison used in Tim's murder would not be known until the coroner and the lab technicians completed their examinations. An announcement would be withheld until the police deemed the timing to be appropriate, so at the moment there was no point in speculating on the poison or its method of administration or who did it.

I had always considered myself intuitively astute. However, my recent loss of pride felled my intuitive reasoning and dropped it into a deep dungeon of doubt.

The killing of Marlene Rathbone by Tim Jones initially had been as clear as a colourful picture. Tim's surprising death painted another scene on top of the original one. Though the two dead bodies remained vividly clear, the identity of the killers grew murkier by the minute. The confusing canvas needed new brush strokes

I pondered the situation, hoping to regain my intuition and pride by finding the perpetrators.

Maybe Tim Jones fatally assaulted Marlene Rathbone. Maybe the deed was done by an addict who, like Brent surmised, simply wanted to steal money from her purse, if she carried a purse. Maybe a John like Fred Pederson killed her because of a secret penchant for violent sex that he didn't want anyone to know about. Maybe Andrew Strong did the dastardly deed because his love had turned to hate. Maybe Larry Ellis lied to Detective Kanui about his arrival on Maui because he was mixed up with the tragic happening. And why did Glenn Shaw deny previously meeting Marlene? Ezekiel Hoffman and Daniel Epstein knew Marlene and didn't hide the fact, yet they offered no rational explanation regarding her death.

Tim's demise made it necessary to find a new perpetrator, or maybe two perpetrators. Did someone kill Tim for his supply of drugs and his wad of money? Was he poisoned by an unhappy John? Did Andrew commit the murder to avenge the pimp's part in ruining Marlene's life? Or did one of Tim's unhappy business partners provide his final solution?

The biggest question remained: did the same person kill both victims?

It was a dastardly dilemma. It haunted my thoughts so they dwelled on little else. What a stupid way to spend my last full day on beautiful Maui. What a stupid way to celebrate the first day of the new year. I hoped this was not indicative of how the rest of the year would play out.

My detecting process was proving sad, disconcerting and slow. Searching for murder clues and finding no answers was frustrating and depressing. Perhaps I should forget the entire process, be content with my mundane life, and leave murder solving to the professionals.

The fact remained that I wanted justice to be served. In order to achieve that end the murderer or murderers must be apprehended. Detective Kanui had complimented me on being helpful and his praise had wetted my appetite for doing more. But time was running out—-only a matter of hours remained in which to solve two fatal crimes.

"Brent," I said. "Who in your estimation might have the most information regarding Tim's murder?"

"Detective Kanui."

"Other than the detective. Someone with knowledge of both victims."

He gazed over the top of his book and without hesitation said, "You."

"Me?"

He chuckled at my amazed response then lowered his eyes to the printed word. Though concerned with the murders, he was not consumed by them. He wanted to relax and enjoy his last full day of vacation. How better to do that than by lazing around reading an adventure story, something he seldom did at home?

For no good reason his book reminded me of the one he had given me and the one I had bought at the *Outer Fringe* shop. With so many busy diversions, I had not cracked either of them. Normally I couldn't wait to slip between the covers of a book and launch myself into a foreign world of interest and excitement. But not this past week. During the last seven days I had experienced an overabundance of interest and excitement. And all of it was real.

I briefly wondered if Ezekiel's sister would like the gift he had purchased for her. The thought made my little grey cells start to churn.

"Ezekiel and Daniel knew both victims," I said. "They should have some insight to the murders."

Brent lowered his book. "Do you suspect them?"

"Of what?"

"Of being the murderers."

"Of course not." I shuddered. "At least I hope not."

"I wonder if Detective Kanui has eliminated them."

Those two gentlemen, for reasons beyond my comprehension, had frequently associated with Tim and at least once had talked with Marlene. They would understand things unknown to the detectives and unknown to me. Had they told the police everything?

In my estimation Brent's implication was unfounded, but it deserved analysis. I mulled over his suggestion that the two gentlemen were murderers and concluded it was preposterous. I felt sure they were incapable of such crimes. This deduction was based on a bit of objective observation and on a great deal of subjective intuition.

They were staying in a condominium complex farther down the beach, this I knew. But where were they staying? Was it *The Nest*? I didn't think so. Searching them out might prove difficult but it was worth a try. I avoided mentioning the idea to Brent because for safety reasons he would advise against it. I knew, however, he would not try to stop me.

"Do you want to go for a walk?" I asked.

He shook his head. "I'm in an exciting part of my book. I hope to finish it before we leave Mau."

"Well, I think I'll take a stroll. I need some exercise."

"Don't be too long," he said. "Let's go out for a Farewell to Paradise lunch. It could also be a Happy New Year lunch."

"It could also be a No-Food-In-The-Kitchen lunch." I giggled. A few minutes later I opened the main door of the condo and called, "See you shortly." The door clicked shut behind me.

Walking on the beach, I closely examined every building I passed. They were easy to see because no sand dunes blocked the view. The first few structures looked more like private homes than condominium complexes.

Recognizing the tree with branches spreading over the beach, I walked over to it and ducked under the branches. I stepped on the coarse grass that Glenn and Tim had recently walked on and stared at a big, three story structure with a wide terrace and a large swimming pool. It was probably *The Nest*. I walked toward it, wondering if I might encounter Glen, Zelda, or Larry.

On one side of the big building stretched a public park and on the other a one story house, long and low and large enough to contain two or three rental units. I walked boldly across the grass and studied the larger building and its pool in which no one swam and its long terrace on which no one sat.

I turned around and went back to the beach. Next I entered the yard of a set of twin duplexes and tip-toed cautiously like the trespasser I was. There was no sign of Daniel or Ezekiel or of anyone else. I retraced my steps then did the same tip-toe routine at two large buildings that looked like a thousand other big box condominiums. I saw no indication in either location of the two gentlemen so I tip-toed back to the beach.

I retraced my steps to the tree with spreading branches, again ducked under the foliage and again angled across the lawn. This time I ignored the large building and walked over to the long, low house that could easily contain two or three rental units. I saw no one in the small pool or on the terrace, but for no good reason I walked closer. I used all my observing and listening skills and came up empty. Resigned to failure, I turned and started to walk toward the ocean.

"Philomela." The voice came from behind me.

I whirled around and looked at the house. There in front of an open gliding door stood one of the very people I was hoping to meet. His white hair was neatly combed, his glasses perched above his nose, and he wore blue swim trunks and carried a blue towel. He stood and stared at me.

"Ezekiel," I exclaimed. "You're the very person I've been looking for." I walked boldly toward him.

"Really? Should I be flattered?"

"Yes and no."

He moved in my direction and we stopped face to face on the terrace. "Happy New Year," he said.

"And Happy New Year to you. Do you have a moment?"

"Being on holidays, I have several moments."

"If you don't mind, I'd like to discuss murder with you."

"Marlene's?"

"Yes. And someone else's."

"Someone else was murdered?" He looked me a query then said, "Perhaps we should sit down over at that small table."

I followed him to a tiny metal table near the gliding door and he indicated one of two chairs. I sat down on one and he sat on the other.

"If you're concerned enough to search me out, the reason must be serious."

"It is serious," I said.

"Are you looking for a suspect?"

"Yes."

"You suspect me?"

"No. I just want your help."

"In what way?"

"Have you heard what happened to Tim Jones?"

He leaned slightly forward and with a puzzled frown studied my face. "No. What happened to him?" If he knew about Tim's demise he was an excellent actor.

"The police didn't contact you earlier this morning?"

"They might have come by when Daniel and I were out for breakfast and a walk. What's going on?"

"Tim Jones is dead."

He stared at me in disbelief. He repeated my statement as a question: "Tim Jones is dead?"

"He died last night."

Ezekiel seemed more shocked and shaken than I would have expected. "Are you sure?" he asked.

"Yes. Detective Kanui told Brent and me this morning."

"How can that be? Tim rents the duplex next to us. Daniel and I had an early New Year's Eve dinner with him last night at *The Wave*."

"So you two were his dinner date." I felt reassured—my intuition was swinging par for the course. My search for the two gentlemen was already proving worth the effort. Not only had they seen the victim last evening, they had eaten dinner with him. "Neither of you got sick?"

He shook his head.

"Did you eat the same things?"

"The three of us ate Mahi Mahi, and it tasted delicious. Daniel and I are fine. Could Tim's fish have been bad?"

"No," I replied. "The police don't suspect bad food."

"What do they suspect? A drug overdose?"

"Perhaps. They also think he might have been poisoned."

"Poisoned?" Ezekiel's eyes widened until they seemed to take up most of his face.

"They think he was murdered."

His chest heaved and his head dropped dejectedly. "Just when Daniel and I were making headway with him."

I felt a twinge of nervousness. Was he talking about an illegal business deal?

"We were encouraging him to enter a detox clinic. He knew his life was a mess and he knew the only solution was to get off drugs. All he lacked was someone to give him a good shove and a whole lot of support...financial, moral, and physical. We were providing the shove and part of the support. We even planned to take him under our wings in Victoria after his detoxification was complete. He would live and work with us on our acreage until he lost the heavy craving. When he gained new self-esteem and courage we hoped to help him get re-established."

I listened in amazement. Recalling the man on the fixed wing plane volcano tour, I concluded he had been right...Ezekiel was involved with the sleazy side of life, but not in the way the man had implied, nor for that matter in the way I had surmised. I stared at him. His white hair and sad expression reminded me of Mother Teresa—except he was male and lived not in the smarmy slums of India but in the lap of luxury on two beautiful islands: Maui and Vancouver.

"You're a do-gooder," I murmured, thinking of my effort to save the two lads at *The Gazebo* restaurant. "A *real* do-gooder." I gazed at him with awe and admiration.

"No, I don't think so." Sounding more forlorn than humorous, he chuckled. "Most do-gooders want other people to plan the intricate details and do the hard work for their projects. They also want donators and taxpayers to provide the necessary cash. Daniel and I don't work that way. Our plans are specialized to fit each person's needs. We pay from our own pockets for the costs of treatment and the initial physical rehabilitation. The only repayment we expect is that they in turn will help someone else."

I shook my head in wonder. "You wanted to help Tim get off drugs. And I wanted to put him in jail for murder."

"You think he killed Marlene?"

"I did. And I'm not the only one who thought that."

"An understandable assumption. Under the right circumstances he could have been guilty of murder, as could all of us. But such an act for Tim was unlikely because he still had the remnants of conscience and empathy. He lacked that certain touch of evil needed to purposely snuff out another person's life."

"He pushed drugs," I said. "Isn't that a form of murder?"

"Indirectly, yes. But Tim was not a murderer at heart and he heard no voices giving him such directives."

"You mean he lacked a murder gene and he was not afflicted with hallucinations?"

He nodded his head then said, "He also lacked the training provided by an early environment of horror. He lived an average childhood. His upbringing was not the happiest but it was not the worst. He came from a poor working class family. His parents were religious and strict, but not abusive. He got into drugs like so many young people, innocent experimentation that led to addiction."

"No wonder you wanted to help him." I sat and continued to stare at him in amazement. For a fleeting second I peripherally glimpsed a pale blue and gold aura pulsate around his head and shoulders. I looked directly at it and it wasn't there. It briefly reminded me of the green flash at sunset. Logic returned and I asked, "How did you first meet him?"

"In a restaurant here on Maui exactly a year ago. We sat at adjacent tables one evening at dinner and started talking. Daniel and I drove him up the Haleakala volcano to see the extinct crater and we later enjoyed several meals together. He even came to our condo for drinks a few times. Early on, he offered us cocaine so we knew of his addiction. We refused

his offer, but we kept in touch with him, cards at Christmas and Easter and an occasional phone call. Then this year we met again."
"During breakfast at *The Wave*."
He nodded. "And you sat at the table adjacent to ours."
"Yes."
"Since last year he's deteriorated considerably. It's sad to see. During that morning at *The Wave*, Daniel and I knew we had to do our utmost to help get him off those debilitating drugs, or it would be too late. We had drinks with him here a few times and discussed various treatment plans. He was open about his problems. He knew his health issues resulted from malnutrition, dirty needles, and unsafe sex."
"Do you think he was serious about going to a detox clinic?"
"Definitely. And he knew he couldn't do it alone."
"What about Marlene?"
"She grasped the theory of staying off drugs, one day at a time, like an alcoholic. At first she seemed willing to join Crystal Meth Anonymous and follow their twelve steps to induce spiritual awakening. The idea of prayer and meditation guiding her to a more honest way of living was no problem to her. The problem, whatever it was, arose when I mentioned sharing her experiences with others. She was paranoid about that."
"She didn't want to admit the things she had done while under the drug's influence?"
"That may have been part of her reluctance. But something else seemed to trouble her. I offered her the same deal we offered Tim."
"You offered to take her into your home?"
"Yes, we have a small farm that has two houses, a barn and a machine shed. Our manager kicked the drug habit with our help three years ago. Right now he and two fellows fresh from the detox centre live in one house and help on the farm, especially with the animals. Daniel and I live in the other house, except during our holiday in Maui. The other eleven months we work in the orchard and garden and cook and serve meals to everyone staying with us. I was a civil engineer and Daniel was a professional chef."
Speechless, I listened to him elaborate: "I was never an addict, but Daniel was. I met him just as he was getting involved with PNP...." He saw my puzzled frown so explained, "PNP is short for 'party and play' which in turn means 'sex and drugs'. Crystal meth, known as 'tina', is a favourite. It's cheap and increases energy. It also causes a loss of sexual inhibitions resulting in casual sex that precludes the use of condoms."
"Daniel is completely cured?"
"He's free of drugs each day and has been for four years."

"Like members of AA."

"Exactly. Fortunately, he hadn't contacted Aids or Hepatitis. He was lucky. Our manager and Daniel are our best role models. There are others who are working at various jobs away from our place, and we keep in touch with them. There have been a few failures, but hopefully the failures will try again. You know—if at first you don't succeed, try, try again."

I placed my elbows on the table and leaned into my hands. "Now that I understand your relationship with Tim Jones, I'm sorry he was killed. Have you any idea who did it?"

"None whatsoever."

"A drug customer? A drug supplier? A psychotic john? A thief?"

Ezekiel shrugged. "Are you sure Tim didn't die of a simple overdose?"

"Detective Kanui said he suspected a combination of drugs and poison. The test results were not back so he didn't know for sure."

"I see."

"Ezekiel, have you met a couple who are renting a unit at *The Nest*? Their names are Glenn and Zelda Shaw."

"Yes, I've met them twice. Glenn's gregarious, outgoing and friendly, incredibly so. We first met him on the beach two days before Christmas. He was with Tim. I invited them here for drinks. The two men had been involved with a couple of real estate deals in Calgary."

"Would Tim try and entice Glenn to buy drugs?"

"Possibly, but Glenn is wise about the consequences of drugs. He's also far too conscious of his body beautiful to cause it any serious harm." Ezekiel noticed my smile and asked, "Do you know him?"

"I was engaged to him. Eons ago."

"Oh dear. How small the world is."

"You've dissected and analyzed Glenn's character with tremendous accuracy." I nodded my approval.

He placed his right hand over his heart and bent his torso in a humble bow. Sitting us straight, he asked, "Did you learn anything else about Tim's death?"

"Detective Kanui didn't know much, and he was telling less. Tim was found dead on the sidewalk at the mall near the *Shoe Store*. That's five shops from *The Wave*"

"He was in fine form when Daniel and I left him."

"Did anyone else join him?"

"Not while we were there."

"How could the poison have been administered? Who could have done it?"

Ezekiel put his hand under his chin and sat for a moment in the classic thinker pose. Finally he lowered his hand. "I have absolutely no idea."

CHAPTER 33

𝓔zekiel had been informative regarding his and Daniel's association with Tim and Marlene. He had offered no clue to help solve the two murders, so my detecting efforts remained waylaid in a dead end with no detour in sight. Actually, that was not quite true; he had more or less exonerated my prime suspect for Marlene's death.

Leaning back in his chair, he gazed at the table and then looked across it at me. His eyes met mine and they were gentle and kind, not penetrating and mesmerizing like Detective Kanui's.

"I'm trying to recall who else was in the restaurant," he said. "The waitresses, of course, and several people Daniel and I did not know. Tim didn't seem to know any of them either."

"I don't suppose your waitress could have put something in his food."

"I doubt it. She seemed a pretty sensible girl." He seemed miles away as he slowly said, "This is probably totally irrelevant...."

I leaned forward, waiting for him to continue. I refrained from mentioning that Detective Kanui often stressed the importance of trivial recollections.

"Well," he continued," as Daniel and I were leaving the mall and heading for home we saw someone who resembled your friend, Mrs. Humphries. It was dark, difficult to identify anyone. Whoever the person was, she was walking from the general direction of your condo building. I don't know where she was going. Probably just taking an innocent evening stroll."

I leaned closer to him. "Leone was out walking last night?"

"It could have been someone her size with fair hair."

"Leone was at our place last night. I don't recall her saying anything about going for a walk." I explained that Fred and Leone had visited us during the height of the firework displays, and then I raised and lowered my shoulders and shifted uncomfortably on my chair. "What time did you see this person?" I asked.

"Let me think. The sun went down around six, shortly before our Mahi Mahi was served. None of us had dessert. But we did have decaf coffee. Daniel and I left the restaurant, let's see, it must have been shortly after seven. Several minutes later we saw the person who resembled your friend. As I said, I can't be sure of her identity. The street was dark. There were a couple of lone gentlemen out walking, too. It was dark, but both men seemed to have blond or white hair."

After a quick mental calculation I said, "Leone and Fred came to our place shortly after eight." To avoid jumping to conclusions, I chose not to elaborate on how Leone had stressed taking a nap before returning to Fred's condo and then subsequently coming to ours. I also didn't mention how she and Fred had discussed an important item she wanted to tell me. I never did learn what the item was. Aloud I asked, "Do you know anything about Fred Pederson?"

"I think I met him briefly last year and that was all."

"You didn't see him last night?"

"One of the men out walking could have been him, but I don't know."

"I wondered because he apparently went for a walk on the beach around seven."

"We didn't go to the beach at all, just came straight home from the restaurant. As if in explanation, he added, "We've seen and listened to fireworks in previous years so felt no need to do it again." He smiled and added, "Did you watch them?"

"We did. And like you, we've now been there, done that, and bought the video."

He smiled and made a remark about the fireworks that escaped me. I was too busy visualizing Leone and Fred taking different routes to *The Wave* and then play-acting an unexpected meeting there. Had Leone diverted Tim's attention while Fred dropped poison in his coffee?

I returned to the present and looked into his eyes. They glistened with moisture. Tim was his failure, an addict who broke his own drug habit with tragic finality. I asked, "Do you think Fred and Leone are capable of committing murder?"

"I don't know either of them well enough to pass judgment. However, for their sakes I hope not."

We sat in silence again, and it was a comfortable silence. Ezekiel's mere presence was soothing. I could see how his kind, non-aggressive manner would benefit people trying to free themselves of an addiction. Recalling Fred's suggestion that Tim might be a front man for Ezekiel and

Daniel was in retrospect exceedingly stupid. How could I have considered believing it?

Suddenly I remembered someone else who had taken a walk during that time frame. My husband. I quickly shoved that thought away. Our silence was broken by the squeak of an opening gliding door. I looked over and saw Daniel step out on the terrace.

"Ezekiel," he said and then saw me. "Hi Philomela. I didn't know you had come by." I smiled and he turned his gaze back to Ezekiel, "The detective is here. Shall I bring him out?"

"Yes, Daniel, by all means."

"Maybe I should go," I suggested.

"No," Ezekiel said. "Stay a bit longer. Let's go and sit at that bigger table. There are more chairs there."

We left the tiny metal table, walked to the larger plastic one and stood waiting for Daniel and Detective Kanui to join us. After a few general pleasantries all four of us sat down. Ezekiel informed the newcomers that thanks to me he already knew of Tim's suspicious death.

"It's no longer suspicious," Detective Kanui said. "Apparently he swallowed Coumadin, an anticoagulant that's normally prescribed to thin the blood, especially for heart and stroke victims. It's an ingredient in the rat poison called Warfarin which can be bought in any hardware store. Crystal meth and alcohol were also in his stomach. The killer might have obtained illegal crystal meth and administered a massive dose to Tim, or Tim might have taken too much himself. The meth alone might have done the job, but the Coumadin provided the final touch."

"How could he be enticed to take a potent poison?" I asked. "Wouldn't it taste awful?"

"Warfarin is odourless and colourless. Sugar and flavouring would help camouflage the taste. Tim's taste buds may have already been destroyed by his unhealthy life style. He also had alcohol in his stomach and who knows what he had sniffed or injected?"

"He snorted meth at the table," Daniel said, "while we were eating our fish."

"Ice," I announced, unintentionally showing off my new knowledge.

Ezekiel and Daniel exchanged glances, frowned, and looked me a query.

"I first heard the expression from Marlene," I explained. "Detective Kanui told me ice is a well known term for the form of crystal meth that's inhaled."

"Have you ever tried it?" Daniel asked.

"No." I looked over at Detective Kanui who in turn studied each of us. I gazed at the individual faces of the two do-gooders and determined their expressions bore no guilt, only expressions of sadness and resignation.

Daniel said, "During dinner, we ordered a bottle of white wine and Ezekiel and I each had one glass. Then we ordered another and Tim drank it while Ezekiel and I had a cup of decaf coffee. The only sign of drugs I noticed was the one time he sniffed some meth. However, it's hard to know what he had taken earlier." He stared at Detective Kanui and added, "Ezekiel and I did not purchase any rat poison."

The detective smiled at him. "I'm not accusing you. The waitress who served you is out whale watching, but she'll be back later this afternoon. This morning we received interesting information from one of the other waitresses, not the one who served you. She said someone else joined Tim after you two left."

"Only one person joined Tim?" I asked, hoping against hope it wasn't Brent.

Detective Kanui gave me a quizzical glance then nodded. "This particular waitress didn't pay much attention to the twosome, but she did notice their waitress carry two bowls of chocolate mousse to the table."

"So Tim ate dessert after we left," Ezekiel said.

Detective Kanui nodded, leaned back in his chair and placed his hands comfortably on his lap. "The meth in his system would have made him hyper, at least for a short while. Then, as you said, he also drank a lot of wine and sniffed meth at dinner. The amount of Warfarin he consumed would have made him weak, caused a headache and perhaps started some bleeding in his skin and stomach. The combination could have killed a healthy man, and Tim was not healthy. His years of drug abuse and raucous living had damaged his body, leaving little resistance to fight off a virus or anything else. Even if he had been in good health he probably wouldn't have survived."

"But he was able to walk from the restaurant to the Shoe Store," I said. "Did someone help him?" I again thought of Brent's absence after dinner.

Detective Kanui nodded. "Nobody, so far as we know, noticed Tim or his friend leave the restaurant. The drugs must have taken complete effect after he went outside. He passed out and fell down on the sidewalk. He hit his head on the cement, but apparently not hard enough to kill him. The drugs, alcohol and poison, of course, had already ravaged his system."

"Did anyone see him fall?" Ezekiel asked.

"If anyone did, they've not reported it. A young couple found him lying on the cement sidewalk. They called an ambulance."

"Was he dead when the paramedics arrived?" I asked.

"Yes. They tried to revive him but it was no use. He was pronounced dead on arrival at the hospital."

"So," Ezekiel said, "no one knows for sure who joined Tim for dessert."

"Not yet," Detective Kanui replied. "But we'll find out when the waitress returns from her whale watching. However, the clerk in the hardware store gave us a clear description of a customer who bought rat poison late yesterday afternoon."

As he described the customer, the expression on his face appeared rather forlorn. When he glanced over at me, his expression was one of sympathy.

My stomach muscles contracted sharply.

CHAPTER 34

My eyes shifted uneasily from Detective Kanui's face down to my wristwatch. One-fifteen. Time was flying, and I wasn't having fun. I suspected Daniel and Ezekiel were not having fun either.

Under half-mast eyelids, I peeked across the plastic table at Detective Kanui. He sat with his knuckles bent and his index fingers in steeple position under his chin. His eyes seemed softer and less penetrating than usual, yet they still managed to surreptitiously shift and study each of us in turn. Ezekiel's suggestion that we move to the larger, round table had been a good one: all four of us sat in un-crowded comfort. Conversation, mostly led by the detective, had been informative, interesting, and subdued—until his revelation of the hardware saleslady.

Her description of the purchaser of Warafin put me on edge.

My stomach growled and disconcerting thoughts of Brent danced amongst my little grey cells. Lunch hour had come and gone. I cleared my throat and asked, "Detective Kanui, will you need me for anything?"

"I don't think so, Philomela."

He called me by my first name: a good omen. With increased confidence I said, "I'd like to go back to our condo. Brent and I plan to honour the New Year and our last day in Paradise with a celebratory lunch."

"Paradise?" Vertical lines formed between his eyebrows.

"Compared to the ice and snow at home, the warm air here is paradise."

The vertical lines between his eyebrows disappeared. "You've been a great help, Philomela. I have no reason to detain you any longer. Go before your husband suffers from starvation." He smiled warmly and I felt like his brilliant buddy. Then his smile faded and his demeanour changed from friendly to professional. "We have all the information we need from you. Our search now focuses on people who dined at *The Wave* last evening. With luck, we'll find someone who actually saw the poison being administered. When the waitress who served the chocolate mousse returns from whale watching, she'll doubtless give us a good description of the person who joined Tim."

I nodded, rose from my chair and slowly moved from the table. Combined with my onset of hypoglycaemia the description of the purchaser of Warafin made my stomach flutter, not with intuitive insight but with feelings of unsteadiness and faint nausea. I swallowed and cleared my throat. Though wanting to see the investigation finalized, I did not want the culprit to be anyone I knew.

Daniel and Ezekiel's report of their last supper with Tim bounced inside my skull, as did the reports that witnesses had already given Detective Kanui. The hardware clerk's description of the person buying Warfarin worried me more than anything else.

Pushing aside a disturbing suspicion, I smiled at the three men and said, "Cheerybye for now. I hope our paths cross again."

"Enjoy your lunch," Ezekiel said. "And I wish you bon voyage."

The other two reiterated his wish and I thanked them.

I walked on the coarse grass, ducked under the tree branches draping the sand, and moved along the beach. My mind mulled over the recently gleaned information. There was still a chance the murderer could be someone unknown to me, a drug addict, a john, or a common thief. But other suspects remained.

Glenn Shaw had not been one of Detective Kanui's prime suspects. The tattoo artist had Tim's phone number but that was all. Larry Ellis might have been involved with the killings for he had lied about being on Maui at the time of the first murder and he certainly had known both Marlene and Tim.

Andrew Strong was still in the running. He had known Marlene longer than any of the other suspects and he had the motives of hurt, anger, and revenge, but somehow I doubted he was capable of behaving with such malicious finality.

Fred Pederson remained an unlikely suspect, though like Larry and Andrew his fair hair vaguely fit the description given by the hardware clerk. Greying hair, like Brent's white hair, also looked fair in certain lights. Of course, the person who purchased the poison could have been wearing a wig.

Tim's death might be just—he had been instrumental in ruining many young lives and many older ones, too. But creepy as he had been, thanks to Daniel and Ezekiel my sympathies were leaning in his direction.

With those two kindly men, Tim might have had one last chance at living a real life instead of a drug induced daze.

Life is so enigmatic. On the surface it seldom seems fair: some people are burdened with unending problems, not always of their own making; other people sail through life trouble free; and some people behave cruelly and appear to escape punishment. It was impossible for someone like me to analyze from afar. Having no desire to walk in Marlene's or Tim's shoes, I was unprepared to judge either of them.

Could people who get a short stick in this life be paying for bad deeds in a former one? Conversely, could mean and cruel people who get off Scot-free in this life pay for bad deeds in a future life? Reincarnation might exist, but it could neither be proved nor disproved.

Approaching *Hale Sun and Surf*, I glanced back at my footprints in the sand. The next high tide would erase them forever.

I turned at the beach access path and paused at the warning sign. Water hazards had proved less dangerous than other happenings. I moved on and noted the manicuring job that had occurred in my absence. Andrew had cut the grass and weeded and deadheaded the flowerbeds. Glancing up at our lanai, I saw no sign of Brent. Doubtless he was inside the condo still reading, or maybe sleeping, or maybe he had gone out for a celebratory lunch without me.

Slowly I cleaned my feet under the foot-tap. With nervous reluctance I moved toward the condo building, strolled across the putting green and approached the ground floor lanai of Unit Number 10. I planned to bid my new best friend a fond farewell.

Through the open gliding door I could see her sitting on the sofa in the living room flipping the pages of a glossy fashion magazine. Her blond hair had been washed and styled and her shorts and shirt were cheery shades of yellow.

I knocked on the door frame and called, "Aloha."

She looked up and smiled warmly. "Hi Philomela. Come on in." I entered the room and she asked, "Have you started to pack?"

"No, but it won't take long. I didn't bring much."

"Righto. In this weather we need only a swimsuit, a sundress and a pair of shorts."

"That's true." I stood hesitantly beside the open gliding door, not knowing what else to do or what else to say. After a brief, uncomfortable silence, I dropped my intended, fond farewell speech and said, "Tim Jones is dead."

"Detective Kanui told me earlier. He didn't know any details."

"I just saw the detective. Tim took an overdose of crystal meth and also swallowed rat poison."

Other than a slight pursing of her lips, she showed no outward form of expression. "Does that mean Tim committed suicide?"

"They don't think so."

"Would taking rat poison be a worse way to die than taking a drug overdose?"

"I don't know."

She looked directly at me and her face glowed with an expression of benevolence. She seemed at peace with herself and with the world.

My words laboured on. "It happened after Tim ate fish and chocolate mousse at *The Wave*. He was found dead on the sidewalk near the Shoe Store."

She turned away from me and looked down at her magazine.

Did I imagine seeing a smile hover around her lips? Had all the recent happenings brought her to the edge of madness? "Leone," I said, "do you think Tim killed Marlene?"

"In a manner of speaking, he did." She shrugged and added, "I know he got Marlene on drugs and into prostitution, destroying any hope of her living a healthy normal life. Whether Tim inflicted the fatal wound or not is immaterial. He definitely caused the downfall that resulted in her death. I feel no sympathy for him."

"I'm sure you don't," and my voice sounded harsher than intended.

She turned in her chair and faced me squarely. "What are you implying?"

"Nothing, Leone. But a few facts are worrisome." I moved closer to her. "The police are waiting for last night's waitress at *The Wave* to return from whale watching. She'll give them a description of a person who ate dessert with Tim after Ezekiel and Daniel left him."

With sophisticated splendour she sat upright and nodded her head.

I continued, "The clerk in the hardware store described a person who bought rat poison yesterday afternoon." My heart thumped loudly against my ribs and my hands grew clammy. I stared at her and said nothing more.

Her shoulders dropped slightly; her posture appeared less sophisticated; her facial expression no longer glowed with peacefulness. She gazed at the magazine and remained silent. I sat down on the sofa beside her.

"Last evening at our place, you stressed that you had left Fred's condo and gone home and taken a nap. You didn't mention going out for a walk.

Ezekiel and Daniel, after leaving the restaurant, saw someone who looked like you walking toward the mall."

She sighed. My heart beat faster and louder and I silently waited. She looked up and turned to me.

"Philomela, it just got to be too much. When you told me about Tim talking with those young boys north of Lahaina, I envisioned two more young lives ruined. I felt an urgent need to stop Tim from doing any more harm. The police had no grounds to convict him for Marlene's death, so how could they stop his carnage? There was only one solution. And it was up to me to supply it."

"Oh Leone." Moisture filled my eyes. "You know you shouldn't have taken the law in your own hands."

She shrugged.

"Maybe you won't be charged with first degree murder. But you'll certainly be charged with something."

"Righto." She looked directly at my face. My eyes were moist, but hers remained dry. "It doesn't matter anymore," she said.

"Of course it matters. Fred will help you. And so will Brent and I. Because you were distraught coping with your daughter's death, a good defence lawyer could get you off completely. Maybe you could plead temporary insanity."

She stared at me blankly, as if not understanding my words. But she understood them. In an ominously gentle voice she said, "I was not insane, Philomela, temporarily or otherwise. I knew exactly what I was doing when I bought the Warfarin at the hardware store and took the powdered crystal meth from Marlene's purse. I also knew what I was doing when I put them in Tim's chocolate mousse."

The hair on the back of my neck rose and my stomach muscles contracted. The missing clue. Had Brent been right? Had Marlene's purse contained drugs as well as money? I shuddered perceptibly.

"I appreciate your concern, Philomela. Truly I do. But everything will come out sooner or later. It might as well be sooner. In plain words, I'm like your namesake. I'm a murderer."

"No you're not." I couldn't accept such a verdict. "Extenuating circumstances prompted you to act the way you did. You thought Tim had killed your daughter."

"I blame him for getting Marlene into drugs and into a horrid lifestyle, but he didn't strike the fatal blow on Christmas Eve."

"How can you know that for sure? Even the police suspect him of murdering Marlene."

"I know," and her pause was pregnant with passivity, "because I killed my daughter."

Her words took my breath away.

She smiled and it was wistful, not mirthful, and not vengeful. As the smile faded the expression on her face grew haunted. "You want to think I was temporarily insane or seriously sick. But Marlene was the one who was temporarily insane and seriously sick. She was not only full of debilitating drugs and suffering from malnutrition, she also suffered from Aids. She said it was a virulent form that was progressing quickly. Although Marlene had often encouraged her johns to use condoms, she had not informed any of them of her illness. Who knows how many men she infected? Tim's illegal drugs had already started her on a downward path and the Aids virus speeded up her lethal trip. I don't know if it was a man or a dirty needle that gave her the disease, but I'm afraid she gave it to others."

"Leone, how do you know all this?"

"She told me as we walked the beach together late Christmas Eve. She explained that she had seen two doctors before coming to Maui and both had confirmed the virus. She was lucid and almost seemed like her old self until I suggested she come home with me and be treated. That made her angry. She yelled that it was too late, doctors couldn't help her, and I should mind my own business. She lunged at me and knocked me flying. As I lay on the sand, stunned, she pounced on me and started to strike my head and shoulders with her fists. Her strength seemed superhuman. To be honest, I feared for my life. A large hunk of white coral lay beside me and I grabbed it and struck her on the side of the head. She fell off me and I thought she was unconscious. I got on my knees, expecting her to come around. When she didn't, I felt for a pulse and there was none. Nor was she breathing. I didn't want to contact the authorities because what could they do for her? And I didn't want to leave her on the beach to be discovered by early morning walkers, so I carried her to the bottom of the dune. She was light, having lost so much weight, and my adrenaline must have given me added strength because I somehow carried her to the top of the dune. I laid her out on the groundcover and closed her eyes. She still looked pretty, except for the sores on her face. I straightened her legs and smoothed down her dress then climbed down to the beach. I picked up her purse and the hunk of bloody coral. I threw the coral in the ocean, but a big wave washed it back up on the beach. I carried it up the dune and hid it under some groundcover leaves. Fingerprints didn't enter my mind, and never did I dream you would be the one to find her. I brought the purse home."

On the sofa I sagged like a rag doll.

Leone raised her shoulders, sat upright again and continued speaking: "I don't know if she gave the virus to Fred or not. If she did, then he has unwittingly given it to me. Maybe it's fate, a form of heavenly justice." A haunted chuckle bubbled from her throat.

Fate or not, the entire situation was worse than a Greek tragedy. "How can you cope with it?" I asked.

"Philomela, killing Marlene was an accident. Killing Tim was planned and I don't regret doing it."

"The first death resulted from self preservation and the second from malice aforethought."

"Righto. Marlene already suffered from exhaustion, abdominal cramps, nausea, and muscle spasms. She needed more and more illegal drugs to alleviate pain and keep going. There was no hope of her ever getting off them and no hope of her ever recovering from her illness. Tim had threatened to dump her because her poor performance and fading beauty were distracting Johns. She refused to come home with me because she knew doctors would only prolong her misery. Her days were numbered. I unintentionally shortened those numbers."

Wanting to help Leone, I thrust my shoulders back and cleared my throat. "Striking her on the head with a hunk of coral was a matter of survival. Self defence. I know for a fact Marlene was paranoid and sometimes violent. One morning on the beach I witnessed it. She accused me of following her and she tried to strike my head, Fortunately, I shifted position so her fist struck my shoulder instead."

Leone's eyes widened. "I didn't know that," she said. "But it doesn't surprise me. Her paranoia has been in effect for some time, but until Christmas Eve I was unaware she was capable of such physical violence. Just before flying at me on the beach, she laughed hysterically about sharing her disease. The drugs were talking, not my daughter. 'Misery likes company,' she told me, 'so I'm generously giving Aids to others, even to your boyfriend.' Her eyes blazed with the fire of hell and her body seemed taken over by the devil."

"Does Fred know any of this?"

"He knows the Aids part. He said he used a condom so maybe he'll be lucky. It's not a sure protection, but it's better than nothing. I didn't tell him about my part in all this."

Someone coughed and I turned toward the open gliding door. Detective Kanui stood outside quietly observing us. I knew he had heard every word Leone had spoken.

She looked up and saw him, too. The expression on her face registered resignation. "Well," she said, "the gig is up. I can't complain, I've had a lot of good years. I just wish Marlene could have said the same." She reached over to me as if seeking support.

Through my tears I gazed at her and then I put my arms around her. She felt frail and fragile and forsaken. "Oh Leone, I'm so sorry things have turned out this way."

"Don't be." She patted my shoulder as if I was the one who needed reassurance and support. "The last two years made this day a foregone conclusion. Marlene is at peace and no longer in pain. Tim can no longer entice youngsters to a life of addiction. And I will pay the consequences for my part in solving those two problems."

No one invited Detective Kanui to come inside, so he took the initiative and stepped through the open doorway. He moved to the sofa and stopped in front of us. Leone and I shifted away from each other and stood up. With a tear stained smile she held out her hands to have handcuffs put on her wrists.

"That won't be necessary, Mrs. Humphries." Detective Kanui's voice sounded surprisingly soft and his eyes looked at her with uncharacteristic kindness. "Perhaps you would like to gather a few personal things such as tooth brush and comb to take with you."

"Righto." She actually smiled and then disappeared in the bedroom. A few minutes later she reappeared with a purse and a small overnight bag. "I assume I'll have to wear prison garb," she said. "I hope the colour doesn't clash with my hair."

I grinned, admiring her spirit. With all the sham and broken dreams in her life, she still managed an air of optimistic cheerfulness.

"If you give us a key, Detective Sanders will lock up your condominium."

Detective Sanders leaned against the wall near the open door. Leone took a key from her purse and handed it to him. I followed Leone and Detective Kanui through the dim passageway and in the brilliant sunshine on the other side stopped and watched Detective Kanui open the door of the police car.

"I'll tell Fred what has happened," I said.

"Righto. Remind him to see a doctor and get tested."

"I will."

"Philomela, maybe I'll turn into a bird like your namesake." She smiled flirtatiously as Detective Kanui helped her climb in the back seat.

Detective Sanders appeared and climbed in beside her. Detective Kanui got behind the steering wheel and the vehicle glided away and disappeared around a corner.

When I knocked on Fred's door, he answered promptly.

"I have bad news," I said, wasting no time on pleasantries. He gestured for me to enter and I walked inside. With forthrightness I told him everything that had just happened.

"She's gone through so much hell with Marlene," he said.

"Fred, you must see a doctor and be tested for Aids. With luck you won't have it."

He nodded his head and accepted the advice calmly. He was not a stupid man; he knew that dallying with the charms of a lady of the evening, even in the daytime, could be a dangerous game.

"Will you keep in touch with Leone?" I asked.

He nodded. "I'll contact a good lawyer for her."

"Be sure to tell the lawyer that I'll act as a witness for a plea of self defence." I told him of my experience with Marlene's paranoia and violent behaviour. "Andrew Strong could also verify her violence. There's not much else we can do, except write to her once in a while."

At the table in his dining area he wrote my email address and phone number in a little address book and I wrote his on a scrap of paper.

"I'll let you know where she ends up," he said.

"I'd appreciate that."

The more I learned of life, the more it puzzled me. Who could possibly explain the past, present, future, and hereafter? Did we leave this planet like a snowflake in the air or a footprint in the sand? Would we attain wondrous wisdom in the great hereafter? Marlene and Tim already knew those answers. Curious as I was about that knowledge, I was in no hurry to gain it.

In Number 309, Brent greeted me with the enthusiasm of a town crier. "Good news," he proclaimed, "Procne just phoned. Her lawyer said Larry had attempted to pull a fast one, but it failed. I think Detective Kanui had something to do with it. That means Procne will come out of the marriage financially secure."

"Great. I have news, too. The father of her two children will not be charged with murder."

"Was he a genuine suspect?"

"Briefly." I flopped gracelessly on the sofa and told Brent of my discovery of Ezekiel and Daniel's condo, our conversation with Detective Kanui, and my chat with Leone that was overheard by the detectives. I also told him about exchanging email addresses with Fred Pederson.

During my commentary Brent looked appropriately astounded, shocked, sympathetic, and sad.

He also was annoyed. "Gawd. Two murder mysteries and I missed the denouement of both."

I hate to admit it, but I laughed. It was a wonderful emotional release.

A minute later my eyes filled with tears, and they were copious. They appeared again the next day before and after we boarded the plane for the Great White North.

"Too bad our holiday wasn't perfectly perfect," I said, eating a surprisingly good airline dinner.

"We still managed to have fun. You gained an article for *The Integrator* and I gained...." He pushed up his sleeve.

"A tattoo?"

"No. An excellent suntan."

I giggled.

In the Calgary arrival area we retrieved our small bags from the carousel and walked outside. Snowflakes floated from the sky and landed softly on our heads and shoulders.

"I'm glad to be home," I said.

"Me too."

Inside our bedroom, Brent bent down and placed his sandals on the bottom shelf of his shoe rack. "I won't need these for a while." He stood up straight, gazed at me and murmured, "Almost single handed you solved two murders."

With justifiable pride I nodded my head.

"Will that encourage you to become a professional detective?" His brows furrowed, his lips pursed, and he looked terribly serious.

"Good grief, Brent, I couldn't stand the stress."

"That's a relief." And he smiled.

The End

CPSIA information can be obtained at www.ICGtesting.com
Printed in the USA
LVOW040327170312

273454LV00001B/5/P